UGLIER THAN HOMEMADE SIN

LEE ANN SONTHEIMER MURPHY

This is a work of fiction. Names, characters, places, and incidents are products of the author's imagination or are used fictitiously and are not to be construed as real. Any resemblance to actual events, locations, organizations, or persons, living or dead, is entirely coincidental.

World Castle Publishing, LLC
Pensacola, Florida
Copyright © 2025 Lee Ann Sontheimer Murphy
Hardback ISBN: 9798282411119
Paperback ISBN: 9798891263970
eBook ISBN: 9798891263987
First Edition World Castle Publishing, LLC, May 26, 2025
http://www.worldcastlepublishing.com

Licensing Notes

Cover: Cover Designs by Karen
Editor: Karen Fuller

CHAPTER ONE

He'd been told many times he was an ugly man. Angus Beaton owned a lean, thin face and a tight, square jaw. He seldom smiled, and after decades of riding rodeo, his eyes had permanently narrowed from squinting against the sun or bright arena lights. At forty, crow's feet flanked both eyes, worry lines etched the center of his forehead, vertical lines cut deep near his mouth, and a scar divided his left cheek. He might be hard-featured and homely, but Angus didn't care about his appearance. When he rode bulls, he preferred jeans clinging to his legs like a second skin. His bright-colored Western-style shirts boasted pearl snaps. Angus wore dark brown felt cowboy hats with a flat brim and rounded crown. He might skimp on some things but not tack and never boots. He kept his feet shod in the finest leather footgear available.

Angus competed in close to a hundred rodeos every year, so he lived on the road. When he wasn't traveling, he had a small house not far from Rusk in East Texas, southeast of Dallas/Fort Worth and southwest of Shreveport. His place sat in the Piney Woods, beneath the tall evergreens giving the region its name. His property boasted a house, barn, fenced pasture, and a corral. When he was home, he trained horses. His grandfather built the place in the early 1970s, and Angus came to live there when he was in junior high. Pop finished raising him after his parents died in a late-night collision with a moving freight train. When the old man died, he left the place to Angus.

Angus owned a vintage, compact camper, one which fit into the bed of his truck. It provided all the comforts he needed. He had a bunk, a three-burner stove, a small fridge, a sink, a table which folded into a couch, a chemical commode, and a tiny stall shower. He spent more nights there than at the house. Angus ticked off his life by miles on the road more than counting years. Steel-belted radial sang his personal ballad

, but he preferred the soft rush of wind through the pine trees at home. When he got too old and crippled to ride bulls, Angus would retire there. He'd raise rough stock or train horses full-time.

The life Angus had built wasn't a particularly good one, but it wasn't bad, either. If he wasn't happy, his status made no difference. Happiness was elusive. Give him a wild bull to best, a medium rare steak to savor, a bottle of cold ginger ale, a cane pole when the fish were biting, or a chocolate bar, and he came close enough.

Sometimes, he experienced loneliness in his solitary life and wished for a woman. If he had one, he would cherish her. Angus could take his pick of buckle bunnies if he wanted, but he didn't. Nothing about the women in their tiny shorts or brief mini-skirts appealed. He didn't care for heavy makeup or bleached, teased blonde hair or lips in a full, crimson pout. Angus didn't do one-night stands or casual relationships.

What he craved was an old-fashioned woman, one who combined smart with pretty. He wanted a gal who could bake biscuits, offer sympathy for his aches and hurts, and laugh at his lame jokes. If a lady meeting his criteria existed, Angus hadn't met her yet, and at forty, he doubted he would. His best buddy, Bart Birdwell, never quit trying to find him a woman.

"Mindy's got a cousin down in Beaumont, just got divorced." Bart crossed his legs, showing off his new boots, as he sat on Angus' worn-out couch. "She's about your age."

"Kids?" Angus didn't want to raise another man's babies.

"Three, but they're in high school. They'll be grown and gone before you know it. Want me to give you her number?"

Angus shook his head. "No, thanks. Too old and too far away. I ain't commuting to court any gal."

"Mindy could probably talk her into driving up to watch us ride in Fort Worth next week." Bart gave Angus a sly grin. Mindy acted as dedicated as her husband to finding Angus a mate. "Want to see a picture of her? I've got one on my phone."

"It'd be a waste of time. Chili's ready if you're staying for supper." Angus took three steps to the kitchen and stirred the pot. A savory aroma wafted through the house.

"I am, bro. Mindy's at the boys' soccer game." Bart rose and sniffed. "I hope you got crackers to go with that."

"Saltines, corn chips, shredded cheese, hot sauce, and I chopped up an onion. We're set." Angus got out the pair of the flat rimmed soup bowls he used to serve chili. Like most of his dishes, he had two. He owned an odd assortment of kitchen essentials. Some dated to his grandfather's time, and others he'd added over the years. His beverage cups included a collection with logos emblazoned on the side. "You want tea or soda pop?"

"Pop's fine. You got any sour cream?" Birdwell took a seat at the kitchen table.

"Naw, it goes bad before I can use it up." Angus handed his pal a spoon and bowed his head to ask a blessing.

Bart waited and dug in as soon as the prayer ended. "You got a good scald on this, Angus."

"Thanks." Angus tasted his chili and nodded. "I've tweaked Grandpa's recipe more than once. Is Mindy bringing the kids to watch us compete in Fort Worth?"

"Yeah, and Kathleen plans to drive down, too."

"How old is she now?" Angus paused after swallowing a spoonful of chili. "Did she start college yet?"

Bart guffawed. "Reality check, buddy. Kathleen graduated from college in May."

"Surely not. How old is she?" Angus swallowed a bite of

chili and followed it with a corn chip.

"Twenty-three. When's the last time you saw Sis?"

"Lord only knows." Angus digested the information. He remembered Kathleen as a little girl with tandem braids or pigtails toting around a rag doll. Vague memories of a pretty young woman at a few of the rodeos surfaced. "It's been a minute. I guess she's all grown up.

Bart hooted. "You bet she did. She'll be in Fort Worth. Figured we'd go out for steak after the rodeo. You're invited."

"Maybe." Angus hitched one shoulder in a shrug. "It sounds more like family time."

"You're like my brother. Close enough. Promise you'll come. You're competing, aren't you?"

"Yeah, you know I am. Are you riding bulls or busting broncs?"

"Broncs," Bart stated. "I'm done with bull riding. I'm almost as old as you are, and I'd rather not die in the arena."

"Broncs ain't safer, buddy. Remember the kid who died…"

Bart interrupted. "I don't want to, Angus. Besides, Mindy swears she doesn't want to be a widow. Don't you ever worry about breaking a bone or getting seriously hurt?"

Angus laughed. "I've already been hurt about every way I can be. I'll likely give rodeo up before long. I guess I'm just looking for a reason."

Bart rose and refilled his bowl with chili. He added cheese, onion, and a few corn chips. "Don't wait till you're in a wheelchair or something to decide."

He imagined himself in one and shuddered. *Granny called it a goose walking over your grave. Felt like a gaggle of geese tromped over mine.* "Bite your tongue, Bart. I sure don't want to end up crippled."

"Neither do I," Bart told him. "Or dead. I wouldn't want to bury you, my friend, or leave Mindy to plan my funeral."

Angus didn't like the direction their conversation had taken. It quelled his appetite, and once he finished his bowl, he shoved it away. "I don't look my best in black."

Bart hooted. "You do take all, buddy. Sometimes, I think you're as mean as you are ugly, probably meaner."

The casual insult stung. Angus believed he had a good heart tucked deep in his chest. He didn't mistreat anyone and wasn't unkind. "What do you know? You can't tell a skunk from a housecat."

"Maybe not." Bart wolfed down the rest of his chili, then belched. "Dang, the chili's spicy."

"It's the hot sauce you added, not what I put in it." Angus grinned. "Don't complain about a free meal."

"I wasn't," Bart told him. "I'm heading home. Call me tomorrow and we'll figure out the details on Fort Worth." Bart lived in Jacksonville, a fifteen-to-twenty-minute drive from Angus's place. "I'm looking forward to seeing Kathleen. I haven't seen Sis since her graduation."

As Angus put away the leftover chili and then washed the pot and dishes, he thought about Bart's little sister. Hard to believe she had graduated from college. He tried to recall when he'd last seen her but couldn't. She must have been no more than thirteen, maybe fourteen. Kathleen had resembled a rag doll, although her braids weren't made of red yarn, and her brown eyes weren't buttons. She'd always been a cutie, and he imagined a grown-up version of the doll. Then Angus put all thoughts of her out of his mind and focused on the upcoming rodeo.

On Saturday morning, Angus rose early. He decided not to put his camper on the truck but to stay in a hotel near the stockyards. Burt recommended the upscale chain, but when he arrived, the multi-storied place daunted him. Angus entered the ornate lobby, then paused. A fountain sparkled in the center of the vast space. Tall, green plants thrived, growing toward the skylights in rock planters in several places. Couches and easy chairs grouped around coffee tables fashioned from marble. Old-fashioned street lights provided additional illumination. A busy carpet swirled royal blue, forest green, sunshine yellow, and brown into geometric shapes around the edges. Pristine tile floors made pathways to a bar in one corner, and a small café in another, to the check-in desk, and to a bank of elevators. He squelched an urge to go back outside and wipe his feet to avoid tracking dirt or manure into the fancy lodging.

He didn't, though. Angus gathered his courage and marched across the floor as if he were a Texas rich oil man instead of a rodeo bull rider. He might not wear an expensive suit, a dress shirt, or a tie, but he had the bucks to pay for his stay, so he walked without shame.

The desk clerk didn't blink as she registered him and handed him a card to unlock his room on the sixth floor. She thanked him as 'Mr. Beaton,' a name he wasn't used to hearing. In and out of the arena, he was Angus.

His room boasted a king-sized bed with three thick pillows propped against the headboard, a nightstand on either side of the bed, a desk with a rolling chair, a leather recliner, and a huge flat-screen television. Angus dropped his duffle bag near a counter with a coffee pot, microwave, and mini-fridge. He sighed as he ambled to the window to gaze out at Fort Worth. As best he could figure, he was five minutes away from the stockyard district. *Big room for one lonely cowboy.*

It wasn't quite two in the afternoon, so hours loomed until Angus would head for the arena. He hadn't eaten since a quick breakfast at home, so he ambled his way to the lobby and the adjacent small café. Angus wouldn't eat again until late after the rodeo ended, so he chose a double cheeseburger with a side of onion rings. He indulged in a slice of chocolate pie for dessert, idling as he watched people come and go in the lobby. Far as he knew, Bart had arrived earlier and napped in his room. Angus thought he might spot other rodeo pals on arrival.

A woman strolled through, rolling an oversized suitcase. Her straight, auburn hair trailed free across her shoulders. She glanced up, and her brown eyes sparkled. When she waved, he lifted his hand to acknowledge the gesture, but he didn't know her. *Must be friendly. She's pretty, too.* If she didn't look so young, he might have tried to strike up a conversation. Angus liked redheads, and he wished he could get acquainted. He dismissed the notion, however. She didn't have the loose-limbed gait of a rodeo gal and probably wouldn't give him the time of day.

Angus watched her until she passed out of sight and sighed. Maybe he would never have one, but he surely wanted a woman, one a lot like her. A text from Bart jolted him out of his reverie. Angus read it, sent a reply, and headed upstairs to his room. He had time to rest before heading out to ride.

At the indoor arena, Angus caught up with Bart. They hung out before separating to ride. Angus rubbed rosin into his ropes, a concoction of his making he'd perfected over the years. Every bull rider used a slightly different formula, but the goal was the same — to make the rope sticky and easier to hang onto when the bull went wild.

Once the event got underway, a crowd packed the place. By luck of the draw, bull riders competed first, and Angus completed his ride long before Bart's turn. Angus scored a solid 90 and stayed on the raging, snorting bull for the full eight seconds. Since he'd finished for the night, he hung around the chutes to watch Bart take on a saddle bronc named Looney Tunes. The mount had a reputation for being difficult, and once Bart hit the arena, Angus saw the horse had earned it.

Five seconds into the ride, Looney Tunes bucked Bart, but his hand became caught in the rigging. The horse drug Bart around the arena before the wranglers could stop it. The out-of-control animal stomped Bart several times. Once he got free, Bart crumpled to the ground. Angus moved in to assist and caught the edge of a flailing hoof. Pain exploded, and bright stars danced around the edges of his consciousness, but Angus didn't pass out.

Bart had. He lay unmoving on the gurney as medics loaded him for an ambulance ride to the nearest medical center. Angus followed, dashing for his truck, searching for Bart's wife, Mindy, but never caught a glimpse. If she, sister Kathleen, or Bart's teenage sons were at the arena, they would head for the hospital.

Angus ended up in a cubicle at the emergency department. If the hoof had struck with full force, he would be unconscious, seriously injured, or dead. Instead, a four-inch-long gash above his left eye bled profusely, and the doctor decided Angus didn't have a concussion. "Keep the wound dry and take pain meds," the physician advised. "I'll write you a script and give you a few to take with you. Get some rest, and don't compete for a couple weeks."

"I gotta see about my buddy. He's hurt worse than me." Angus struggled to snap his Western shirt, then picked up his hat. "Anybody know where Bart Birdwell is?"

The doctor hesitated, then shared. "ICU. I imagine you'll find his people in the adjacent waiting area."

Hat in one hand, Angus roamed the medical center until he found the waiting room. He pushed the door open and halted. A large room featured groupings of couches scattered throughout. Each provided some measure of privacy, and he spotted Mindy in a far corner.

"Hey." Angus squatted on his heels in front of her. "How's Bart?"

His guts clenched tight as he waited for her reply.

"He's hurt bad." Mindy twisted a tissue between her hands. "He broke his right hip and pelvis. He's had some internal bleeding and injuries, a damaged artery, spinal bruising, and he can't feel anything in some of his muscles, mostly in his back and legs. He has a skull fracture, too." She hesitated, then cried, "The doc said he might not make it."

Angus' guts twisted into a knot. "Aw, don't listen. Bart's too tough to let a bronc take him out. Was he conscious?

Mindy shrugged. "No, not that I know. He's in surgery now, but he'll be brought here afterward. I thought you'd gone to the hotel. Someone said you were injured, too."

Angus touched his left temple and grimaced. "Caught a hoof to the head, nothing too terrible, or I wouldn't be standing. Glanced off my forehead. Some doc checked me out in emergency. No concussion, just a knot on my head and a bad headache."

"You look awful." Mindy blotted tears from her face. "Go get some rest."

"I always look like I got whupped with an ugly stick." Angus meant to joke, but his words fell flat. "I reckon I'll stay awhile, see how Bart's doing."

She nodded. "I can use the company. Kathleen took the boys back to the hotel. They were upset. I'll be here until I know he'll be all right."

Lord, please don't take my buddy. Let Bart recover and heal. Angus didn't want to think about what happened if he didn't.

Despite a pounding headache, Bart sat with Mindy. Every hour, she could spend ten minutes with her husband. Twice, Angus accompanied her. A nurse had to buzz them into the inner ward, and they couldn't go any farther until they scrubbed their hands with antibacterial soap. Seeing his buddy in critical condition sobered Angus. He wasn't sure Bart would walk away from this injury after he'd observed him. *Don't seem right. He's the one with a wife and family, but he's broken in pieces, and I'm upright.*

Bart's wife departed around four a.m. "I'll be at the hotel," she told Angus. "Call me if you hear anything or if Bart needs me."

"I will." Angus walked her to Bart's extended cab pickup in the lot. "Take care."

Mindy kissed his cheek. "I will. You really ought to get some sleep. Why don't you come back to the room for a few hours?"

Although his head still hurt and his body ached, Angus shook his head. "Nah, I'm all right to stay here. I might stretch out on one of those couches."

He did, although it proved uncomfortable. His legs were longer than the furniture, and he lacked a pillow or blanket. Angus tossed his denim jacket over his body instead. He shifted into a snug spot and dozed. When he woke, sunlight streamed through the east-facing windows into his face. He blinked and sat up with a groan.

"Good morning, Angus."

The sweet feminine voice startled him, and he squinted to find the source. The woman he'd seen in the hotel lobby sat across from him in an oversized chair, feet tucked beneath her. Angus stared, confused, and scrubbed his face with his hands. "Howdy."

"I brought you a cold pop." She pointed to the bottle on the table. "I figure you're hungry, too, and I thought while we're waiting to see Bart, we could grab a bite downstairs."

Angus scratched his cheek and downed a swig of ginger ale. "I could maybe eat."

His headache lingered along with a sense of confusion about her identity. Angus considered the clues. She knew him by name and referred to Bart in a familiar fashion. He took another gander at the auburn hair, brown eyes, and upturned snub nose. If he added tandem braids, a child's gap-toothed smile, he recognized her. "Kathleen!"

She met his gaze. "What?"

Reluctant to admit he had failed to recognize her, Angus grinned. "You grew up pretty."

Kathleen blushed. "I don't know if that's true, but thank you."

I must be an idiot not to know it was her. Bart sighed and touched his bandaged forehead. He winced.

"Does your head still hurt?" she asked, digging into her hobo bag.

"Yeah. It could be worse." His wound must look terrible.

Kathleen held up two different over-the-counter pain relievers. "Which one do you want?"

"Ibuprofen, thanks." Angus washed down four tablets with a swig of soda.

A nurse approached. "I'm sorry, but everyone has to leave during shift change. You can return at eight-thirty."

He and Kathleen were the sole people who remained in the waiting room. "Yes, ma'am." Angus rose and stretched.

"Let's eat." Kathleen picked up her purse. "At least have a cup of coffee."

At the mention of food, his hollow stomach rumbled. If he could hear it, so could Kathleen. "I missed out on a steak dinner last night, and I'm hungry."

In the corridor, she hesitated. "Do you know how to find the cafeteria?"

"No." Angus put on his hat. "I can follow signs, though, and the smell of food. I'm blessed with a good sense of direction."

She laughed. "Then lead on, please."

He forged ahead and, after a couple wrong turns, found the way. They exited an elevator near the cafeteria and joined those seeking sustenance. Many were employees wearing rumpled scrubs after a night's work. The pickings were slim, but Angus ended up with biscuits and gravy with a side of sausage. Paired with coffee strong enough to suit his tastes, the meal sated his hunger.

Kathleen joined him at a tiny corner table, distant from most of the din, and when she bowed her head to pray, Angus followed suit.

They ate in silence, both wondering about the extent of Bart Birdwell's injuries. Neither mentioned the possibility he might not live, but the chance he could die lay heavy on their hearts.

CHAPTER TWO

Angus stood a few feet away while Kathleen took a position at Bart's bedside. She gripped her brother's right hand and crooned to him as if he could hear. Angus had a sinking suspicion his buddy wouldn't regain consciousness. He was far from a medical professional, but this wasn't the first time he'd visited someone in the hospital. He'd sat with his grandfather through the last days of his life in a similar cubicle. Angus had been a patient more times than he wanted to count. His injuries had ranged from minor concussions to broken bones, and the worst time, internal injuries. Watching the vital signs monitor, Angus noted Bart's condition wasn't stable. His erratic heart fluctuated from one hundred twenty beats a minute up to one sixty, even one-eighty. Birdwell's blood pressure continued to drop, although his temperature remained steady and normal.

"His hands are so cold," Kathleen remarked as she cradled Bart's limp left hand between both of hers. "I think we should ask the nurse to bring something to cover him."

"We can do that." Angus stepped into the corridor to find someone. He couldn't bear gazing at Bart much longer. *I don't think he's gonna make it.* Tears burned in the corners of his eyes, but he blinked before Kathleen noticed.

After a nursing assistant tucked a warm blanket around Bart, the doctor entered. "Are you family?" His brusque tone matched his salt-and-pepper hair and immaculate white coat. "I'm Dr. Kevin Watling."

Kathleen lifted her face with a wad of tissues balled up in her right hand. "I'm his sister. Bart's wife is at the hotel with the boys. She should hear whatever you have to say, not me."

Dr. Watling twisted his lips together. "This can't wait. I'll be frank. His prognosis isn't good. Mr. Birdwell's in critical condition, as well as in a coma. I repaired the damaged aorta, but his other internal injuries are severe. I also removed the spleen. If he survives, the skull fracture might heal, but he's weak, and his body is damaged. I urge you to contact his wife and any other family members. I wouldn't estimate he will last more than twenty-four hours. Two people at a time can be here, no limits, not in this situation."

Kathleen's expression crumpled. "He's dying?"

Angus' heart hurt for her sake, as well as his own. Although he had suspected his buddy would pass away, hearing it hit hard.

"I'm sorry." Dr. Watling spread his hands wide. "I wish I could give you a better outlook. No one will be happier than me if I'm wrong. I advise you to gather his near and dear. I'll be back this afternoon and will update Mr. Birdwell's condition."

As soon as he departed, Kathleen sank into a chair and buried her face between her hands. She sobbed hard, her body shaking with the effort.

Angus moved behind her and placed his hands on her shoulders. "Honey, I hate this. It doesn't seem possible." He knew, though, it was. A few nights ago, he and Bart had talked about the way they flirted with death. Angus hadn't believed it could happen, not this soon, and never to Bart. "It ought to have been me."

She tossed back her head, hair flying in a cloud around her face. "Don't say that. Don't you ever say it again, Angus."

A nurse arrived before he could reply. "You'll need to step out for a few minutes. It won't be long, I promise. Dr. Watling informed me of the situation, and you can spend as much time with Bart as you'd like. The exception is when staff needs to turn him or perform other tasks."

Kathleen rose and dashed from the room. Angus followed.

He caught her in the waiting room. She stood at the far end of the space, staring through the window, still crying. "Hey." He touched her left arm. She turned toward him and threw her arms around him. "All I meant is that he's got a family, and I don't. I might be missed by a few, but Bart will be mourned hard. It's gonna be rough for Mindy, the boys, and you."

"And Mom." Kathleen rested her head against his chest. "I don't know how to tell her. She should be here, but…"

Angus tightened his arms around her. "I'll call if you want." He didn't relish the thought, but he could do the task. "I'll even go fetch her if you think she'll come."

The Birdwell's mother, a feisty sixty-year-old, still lived between Rusk and Palestine on the family spread. Marisol doted on her son, the only boy and the oldest. Two other sisters were between Bart and Kathleen. "It's close to three hours from here and three hours back." Kathleen lifted her head. "I don't know."

"It needs to be her choice, honey. Mindy and the kids need to hear first, though." Angus stared through the window without seeing what lay beyond the pane. "I figured I'd go over to the hotel and fetch her. Do you want to go or stay here?"

Kathleen sighed. "I don't want to leave Bart alone, just in case anything happens."

"All right." Angus picked up his hat, which he'd left on one of the couches. "I'll head over, then. Is there anything you want me to bring?"

"Just get Mindy, Austin, and Travis." She sat in an oversized chair and put her purse on her lap.

His head hurt, with a sharp pain center in his left temple. Angus touched a tentative finger to the bandage. "Got any more pain relievers in your bag? I could use a couple." He needed sleep, too, but rest had to wait. *I didn't get but about four hours' worth.*

She scrabbled through the handbag. "Sure. Are you okay?"

He wasn't, but he nodded. "I'll do." Angus took the pills and washed them down with tepid ginger ale in the bottle he'd had earlier. "I'll be back as soon as I can. If anything changes, call me. Here's my number."

Angus rattled it off as Kathleen entered it into her phone. As soon as he knew she had it, he left. On the way to the hotel, he tried to find the words to inform Mindy she was about to become a widow. Tim McGraw's hit song, *Live Like You Were Dying,* came over the radio. The words hit hard. Bart would never have the chance to do any of the things mentioned, and Angus wept. Tears tracked along his cheeks as he navigated Fort Worth's Saturday morning traffic. At the hotel, he parked, dried his face on the fast-food napkins he kept in the glove box, and drew a harsh breath. If he could wait, he would, but there wasn't time.

He walked through the lobby with slow steps, the kind a man on his way to the gallows would take. Mindy might be upstairs in their room or elsewhere. As Angus debated whether he should call or take the elevator, he heard his name.

"Angus, we're over here." Travis, Bart's oldest at seven, shouted. "How's our dad?"

Mindy and her sons shared a table at the café where he'd eaten a burger the day before. Her haggard expression and red eyes indicated she hadn't rested well, if at all. She held a half-full coffee cup between her hands. A few scraps of waffle, end pieces of bacon, and a scant amount of eggs remained on the boys' plates.

"Do you want coffee, Angus?" She tried to smile but failed. "Take a seat."

He doffed his hat, hesitated, then sat. "Thanks, but not right now. Mindy, I wish I brought better news, but I can't." He paused and answered the youth's question. "Travis, your dad's dying. I hate saying it, but the doc didn't give him much of a chance. Fact is, he said y'all should be at the hospital."

Mindy stilled the way a deer might once a hunter had it in his sights. The color drained from her face until even her lips were pale. "I was afraid of this. We'd best get around and go."

"Do you want to ride with me?" Angus wasn't sure she should drive after the dire news.

"No." She shook her head. "Why don't you take the boys with you? I'll be there as soon as I change into clean clothes."

Angus didn't argue. Fitting three others into the cab of his pick-up would be tight anyway. "I will. Let's hit the road."

"Is Aunt Kathleen with Dad?" Austin, mature for almost thirteen, asked.

"Yeah, she didn't want to leave." Angus put his hat on and led the way to the truck. Silence reigned on the trip to the medical center. He guided them to the ICU waiting area, then excused himself to visit the men's room. His breakfast churned in his gut,

and he bent over the toilet, vomiting. Angus rinsed his mouth and washed his face before he joined Kathleen. Her nephews flanked her on the couch, and she had her arms around both boys. Austin and Travis were crying, and his heart broke for them. He'd lost both his parents in junior high, and he'd never lost the grief. For a long time, he carried anger, but thanks to his grandfather, Angus let it go years ago.

"Hey." He found a place across from them. "We can go back, two at a time, whenever you're ready."

Kathleen stood. "Travis, do you want to visit first?"

"I'd like Angus to go with me." The kid's lip jutted out in a pout.

"If that's what you want, okay." Kathleen tightened her lips and sighed. "I'll be here with Austin."

Angus demonstrated the protocols required in the unit. After they scrubbed their hands, he brought Travis to Bart's cubicle. "Your dad looks rough," he explained. "He's not responsive, but you can talk to him if you want."

"Stay with me." Travis' rough whisper was very low. "I mean, like right next to me. I don't know if I can do this."

"You can." A scrap of something he had once read floated through his head. "When it's time to be a man, you will be. It's now, Trav."

Travis swallowed. "Yeah, I get it." At his first sight of Bart, the youth gulped. He exchanged a glance with Angus, then approached the bed. "Hey, Dad, it's Travis. Man, you got busted up this time, for sure. I'm here, so's Austin, and Mom's on the way. Aunt Kathleen's in the waiting room, and Angus is with me. We're pulling for you, so hang on." His words jumbled together as he spoke, but he didn't cry or shed a tear. "I'll be praying, hard."

Angus draped his left arm across Travis' shoulders. Although the kid managed an even tone, he trembled as he spoke. "Bart, we're gonna let Kathleen and Austin visit. Soon as Mindy's here, she'll be with you."

For a split second, he thought Bart gave a nod. If so, it happened fast. Angus didn't mention the possibility since he might be wrong. Mindy hunkered beside Kathleen in the waiting room. She'd brought a bag of sausage biscuits, several cups of coffee with lids, and a ginger ale. "Mine?" he asked as he grabbed the bottle.

"Yes." Mindy twisted her loose hair into a ponytail. "I figured you might need a drink."

"Thanks." He sipped the sweet beverage, hoping it might settle his stomach. "Y'all can see Bart anytime. Dr. Watling said we don't have to wait anymore." As he had promised, he phoned Marisol, Bart, and Kathleen's mother with the tragic news. "If you want to come, I'll make the drive so you can."

"I thank you, son, but I won't put you out like that. Claudia and Susan would want to come, too. I reckon it's simpler if we stay here. If you want to drive me to Jacksonville for the funeral, I'll accept your offer. You're near as much a son to me as Bart." Marisol's voice broke. She had always called Angus 'son' since he arrived in Rusk. It mattered and touched his heart all the more now.

For the next two days, they visited Bart two at a time, in shifts. The waiting room became base camp for the Birdwell clan, and Angus. Although sometimes one or two made the trip to the cafeteria, most of the time, they nibbled snacks or tried to eat food carried into the hospital. Angus discovered a chapel down the hall from the ICU and made it his refuge. He retreated there to pray or for a quiet respite. Kathleen usually went with him. Twice, Angus hauled the boys to a nearby green space for some fresh air and a break. On another trip, he took Kathleen. The terrible circumstances erased any distance from the years since he last saw her, and Angus liked the woman she had become. Sometimes, he caught glimpses of the little girl he recalled, but his feelings were far from brotherly. Angus had a strong attraction to Kathleen, and beyond that, he admired her. She possessed the qualities he wanted in a woman, and the sole flaw was their age difference. He told himself they couldn't have a relationship. She was barely older than Travis and Austin, although Kathleen carried herself with the maturity and quiet dignity they lacked.

"How's your head?" she asked, as they shared a bench overlooking a manmade pond. "I noticed you took the bandage off."

"It doesn't hurt as much." Angus had a headache now, but he chalked it up to stress and fatigue. "Looks terrible, though." He sported a nasty bruise on his temple. The multi-colored contusion had streaks of green, yellow, and black.

Kathleen touched it, her fingers light and tender as she did. "If you need more medicine, ask. I have plenty."

"Thanks, will do." Angus wished he could stretch out on

the bench with his head in her lap. He imagined her hand gently stroking his hair, careful not to touch the sore spot. *Dream on. She probably considers me an old man. She's nice because I'm a family friend and she's known me almost forever.* "We'd better go back. I thought we'd stop and pick up some fried chicken on the way. The boys will like something fresh and different. I wouldn't mind a biscuit or two, but I prefer homemade."

"I've been told I can make a good biscuit." Kathleen slipped her arm into his as they rose. "After I'm settled in Rusk, I'll invite you over."

Angus shook his head to clear the cobwebs. "Are you moving back to Rusk?"

She frowned. "I thought you knew. I'll be teaching first grade when school starts."

"If Bart told me, I forgot after this mess happened. I know you graduated from college in May." Angus counted the months in his head. "School starts in less than two months, in early August."

"That's correct." Kathleen smiled. "I have to be there for training and staff stuff by the end of July. I already have a place rented."

"House or apartment?" Angus might accept her invitation, although he shouldn't. If he ate a meal at her place, it would fuel his dreams that they could be a couple.

"Apartment." Kathleen named the complex, and he nodded. "I'll fix you the best biscuits and gravy you've tasted."

Despite his self-imposed reservations, Angus grinned. "I'll look forward to it, honey." He savored the moment, all the more once they returned to find Bart's condition had deteriorated.

"The doctor said he'll probably pass away in the next twenty-four hours." Mindy dabbed her eyes with a tissue. She stood near the windows. "I'm not ready to be a widow, but I guess I'll have to adapt."

"I am so sorry," Angus offered a hug. He couldn't get the last conversation he had with Bart out of his mind. "I'm here to help however I can." With a desire for God's word in his heart, Angus attended a brief church service in the hospital chapel. He lingered afterward and read the Bible for another half-hour. Kathleen did the same.

Death became imminent. On Sunday evening, the staff turned off the monitors, and once the family, including Angus, gathered in Bart's cubicle, they pulled the curtains to the hallway for privacy. With five people, the tiny space became tight. Mindy, Travis, and Austin stood on Bart's left. Kathleen, her hand linked in Angus', was on the right. Her small hand fit into his. The nurse on duty suggested they might share a farewell message with Bart before she withdrew.

"Bart, we've been best buds since I came to Rusk to live with Grandpa." Angus cleared his throat. "We made it through junior and senior high school, prom, football games, and rodeo. We've both been busted up before. I never had a brother, but if I had, I'd have wanted him to be you. I'll be here, looking out for your family as best I can, but I'll miss you, buddy." He had to quit talking. His chest ached, and his heart hurt.

Kathleen squeezed his hand. She stretched and kissed his bruised forehead. Her lips were a light brush, but the slight touch sent chills down his spine. "Bart, you're the best big brother a girl could have. I'm the youngest, and Daddy died too soon, so you got to be both for me. Claudia and Susan swear I talk you into anything. I wouldn't be who I am without you, and I would have never made it through college if you hadn't paid the bills when my grant wouldn't stretch. Good night, Bart. I'll always love you, and someday, we'll meet again on the bright and golden shore. It'll be a short wait for you and a long one for me."

She bent and kissed Bart's cheek, wiping tears away with her free hand. "Let's go, Angus. Let Mindy and the boys have their moment."

Although he'd meant to stay until the end, Angus nodded. It made sense. Bart's family should spend the last few minutes of his life. "We'll be in the waiting area," he told Mindy.

They emerged to find the room was now occupied by cowboys he and Bart had ridden with for years. He halted at the sight. "What's going on?" Maybe someone else got injured.

Sammy Dickens, a grizzled bull rider and one of the oldest on the circuit at almost fifty, stood. "We're here for Bart. Heard he ain't gonna make it, so a bunch of us figured we ought to come."

Angus sucked in a harsh breath. A knot of tears choked his throat. Their appearance moved him more than he had words to say. "Ain't nothing you can do, but he'd appreciate the effort. Mindy will, too. She and the boys are with him now. He won't last much longer."

"We'll do anything we can to help." Zachariah, always called Zach, Cooper, rose too. "Figured some of us will provide a cowboy escort for the hearse when he's driven back home. There's enough of us to give rides to anyone who needs it, too. I'd be happy to haul Bart's gear if necessary."

Answered prayer. Angus had worried about the logistics of returning to East Texas. Mindy had driven her small compact car. Austin and Travis had ridden with Bart. Kathleen had driven her small-size pickup, and he'd driven his truck. He wasn't sure either Kathleen or Mindy would be mentally ready for the three-hour drive. "I'm glad to hear it. I think that solves a big problem none of us talked about yet."

Kathleen sank into a chair. "I wondered about getting back, especially with Mindy's car and Bart's truck. Thank y'all for coming."

Aidan O'Neill, a young bronc buster, nodded. "Ma'am, I'd be proud to carry you home if need be unless you're with ol' Angus. Are you his niece or something?"

Angus twisted his lips. His recent attraction to Kathleen had many potential problems. The age difference was one of several.

"Not hardly," Kathleen spoke. She reached for Angus' left hand, grasped it, and tugged until he took a seat beside her. "He's a good friend, and I'm Bart's youngest sister."

Aidan's eyebrows lifted to his hairline. "Pleased to meet you. You must be Kathleen. I don't think we've met. I would have remembered."

Jealousy flashed through Angus. Aidan had to be within a few years of Kathleen's age, not to mention handsome. He resisted an urge to punch the kid square in the nose. "Did any of you ride this afternoon?"

"I did." Sammy stretched. "I won and brought home a fair-sized prize. I thought I'd donate it to Bart's family. Deacon Levant said we ought to start a fund or something."

"Good idea." Angus wondered if Bart had passed away yet. He figured they'd know when Mindy exited the ICU. The other three cowboys didn't speak. Yancey Cartwright, Jones Brown, and Davy Dupree, the one they all called 'Frenchy,' stared at the floor.

"Angus." Kathleen nudged him. "Would you walk me down to get a cold drink? I'm thirsty, and I'm not feeling very well."

"Sure, honey." He came to his feet. "Let's go. Boys, I'm sure Mindy will be here when—it's over. Her bag is here. If she asks, tell her we'll be right back."

They walked down the long, quiet corridor. "What's wrong, Kathleen? Are you sick?"

"I've got an upset tummy. I thought a soda would settle it. Besides, I had to get out of there. I know those men mean well, but I needed some space." She still held his left hand in her right. "I want it to be over. Is it wrong of me?"

"Nah, honey, it's not. I feel the same way. If Bart's dying, he needs to make the journey for him and for us." He didn't want to go as far as the cafeteria in case Mindy needed his support. "The other day, one of the nurses told me they could give us a pop if we wanted. Let's see what they have."

Once Kathleen held a miniature can, Angus took her to one of the courtyards he had noticed. He savored the slight breeze and fresh air. She sipped her soft drink as she sat beside Angus on a bench. "Thank you. This is what I needed."

"Feeling better?" he asked. He brushed her hair back from her face. Her ponytail had come undone during the long day.

"Much. I know we have to go back inside soon, but I'm glad we could take this moment."

Angus ignored an urge to kiss her. It wasn't the right time or place. He shouldn't anyway, no matter how much he liked the idea. "Me, too."

Ten minutes after they returned to the waiting room, Mindy emerged. Her arms were around her sons, and all three were weeping. "He's gone."

Although he wasn't family, Angus shared the necessary information with the hospital staff. He provided the name of the funeral home in Rusk. Although Bart lived in Jacksonville, he knew his buddy would be buried in his hometown. Kathleen remained at his side, offering additional details when needed. Angus suggested they spend one more night at the hotel, then head home in the morning, but Mindy refused.

"I can't stay in this town another minute." She blotted her eyes with tissues. "Let's go pack and head home. It's just three hours."

"True," Angus replied. "Let's get some of the guys to drive. You're in no shape, and the boys aren't old enough."

Mindy argued, then conceded. "All right, then. Whatever gets me home. In the morning, will you help me at the funeral home? I've never made last arrangements before."

"I will. I'll come up to your place around nine if it's not too early." Angus factored in some rest time. He needed to sleep if he could. "I'll bring Marisol and Kathleen with me."

"I'm riding with you tonight," Kathleen stated. "I have to call Mom unless you will, Angus."

He nodded. "Let's go and get packed. I'll call her from the hotel."

Angus stared through the window at the nightscape as he phoned Marisol Birdwell. Although she expected the call, she began crying the moment she heard his voice. "Marisol, Bart's gone. He never woke up and passed easily. Mindy, Travis, and Austin were with him. There's a time for everything, and it was Bart's time to go. I don't understand why, but the Lord does.

"Son, he fought the good fight and kept the faith." Marisol referenced the fourth chapter of Second Timothy. "Where's Kathleen?"

"With me. I'll bring her home." Angus scratched his chin.

"I'll have breakfast ready. If you would, maybe you'll drive me to the funeral parlor. Claudia and Susan will be here by then."

He could have told her he would have Kathleen there sooner, in the wee hours of the morning, but he didn't. "I'd be happy to, Marisol. Make sure the coffee's hot and strong. I'll need plenty."

A little after midnight, Zach Cooper loaded Mindy, Travis, and Austin into his club cab pickup. Sammy drove Bart's vehicle, Aiden took the wheel on Mindy's subcompact, and Yancey drove Kathleen's small truck. Angus led the way with Kathleen riding shotgun. Little traffic clogged the roadways at the late hour. If they got separated, they did, but Angus had faith everyone could find their way to Rusk or Jacksonville. The drivers would ride home with Zach after the funeral. Jones and Frenchy joined the caravan.

Head aching, heartsick with grief, Angus drove through the night. Kathleen cuddled close, and he liked it. The radio played a steady stream of country gold hits. Some hit home and brought a few tears. Tomorrow, once they finished with the funeral arrangements, Angus would sleep, but until then, he would remain on duty, ready to serve.

He wasn't sure if he filled the shoes of a brotherly friend for Kathleen or if something different and deeper brewed between them. Despite his grief, he was smitten, but for now, he held his peace. If he ever shared his feelings, it would be much later, but he might not. After all, Angus was an old man of forty and ugly, and Kathleen was not far past twenty as well as beautiful.

All he could do for now was dream.

CHAPTER THREE

He needed sleep, and at three o'clock in the morning, Angus figured home would be the best place to find rest. He wouldn't rouse Marisol at this hour. Kathleeen dozed in the seat beside him, her head against his shoulder. Maybe he should have shifted her but he liked her close. When he glanced at Kathleen, Angus didn't think about the little girl he remembered but the woman she had become. In the few short days since he'd seen her again, they had bonded as friends. For whatever reason, she demonstrated a familiarity which surprised him.

"Wake up, Katy-did." The old nickname he hadn't used in years slipped from his lips. "We're here."

She roused and blinked. "It's your grandpa's place. I remember it. He had a fat little pony you and Bart used to let me ride when I was little."

"Festus." Angus remembered the Welsh Mountain pony his grandfather kept. As a small boy, he'd ridden the animal, too. "Named for the character on *Gunsmoke*."

"What happened to him?" Kathleen uncurled from his side and reached for her handbag.

"Grandpa or the pony?" Angus climbed out of the truck and offered her his hand.

"Both."

"Grandpa passed away ten years ago, and I sold the pony to a family over near Many, Louisiana, for their kids. I knew I'd be gone rodeoing and couldn't take care of him." Angus shook his head to clear it. "Let's go in the house. I thought we'd try to get a little rest before going to your mom's for breakfast."

"All right." Kathleen trailed him as he headed to unlock

the front door. "I went to John's funeral. He was a good old guy, closest thing to a grandfather I ever had."

Angus didn't recall she'd been there. Of course, he hadn't been paying much attention. His focus had been on the service and burying his last close relative. "I didn't know you knew him very well." He led her into the living room and tossed down his keys on the table.

"Mom used to bring me out once in a while to visit, even after I outgrew Festus." Kathleen flopped onto one end of the couch. "I used to help your grandfather around the house sometimes. Mom used to bring him meals once or twice a week."

Angus sank onto the sofa. "I didn't know. He never said."

Kathleen shrugged. "You were gone most of the time on the circuit."

He did some mental math. She would have been thirteen when his grandpa died. "Yeah. I always made it back, though, sooner or later."

She slipped out of her shoes. "John always kept me updated on where you competed and how you ranked. Then Bart did, but after he married Mindy, not so much."

Angus considered what she stated. "Bart's been married eight years. Travis just turned seven."

"I know." Kathleen offered a small smile. "Don't you remember? I was a bridesmaid at the wedding."

Was she? I don't remember. He tried to recall, and when he did, Angus slapped his thigh. "You wore a sage-colored fancy dress. Your hair was pulled back with a humongous matching green bow. That was you?"

"Yes. I guess you didn't recognize me, which explains why you didn't say more than a few words to me." She undid her ponytail and shook her hair free.

"I thought you were a friend of Mindy's. How old were you?" He fingered the bruise on his temple as a headache brewed.

"Almost sixteen." Kathleen shook her head. "I bet you didn't know me at the rodeos either."

"Guess not. I feel like the worst kind of fool." Angus remembered the pretty bridesmaid. He'd wanted to get acquainted but didn't. He'd been tied up with his best man responsibilities. Besides that, he figured she wasn't from the immediate area and hadn't expected to see her again. "You still came to the rodeos?"

"I did while I was still in high school. After I started college in Tyler, I didn't show up as often. I always had a job somewhere. When I did, I usually came with friends." Kathleen laughed as she rose. She stretched. "If you're going to sleep, you'd better do it. You look tired, Angus."

"I'm beat. I'm heading upstairs. I sleep in Grandpa's room now, but my old bed has clean sheets if you want to stretch out." He removed his boots with a sigh.

"I'll hang out on the couch. I slept most of the way here." She rose when he stood. "Take some aspirin or something for your head. I'll see you in the morning." She planted a kiss on his right cheek. "Good night."

"Night, Kathleen." Despite being weary, Angus didn't fall asleep right away. He hadn't meant to snub Kathleen, but he hadn't recognized her at the wedding. She would still have been far too young to date, but he wished he had known who she was. He racked his brain, replaying every rodeo he'd ridden in the last five or six years, but couldn't conjure up any images of Kathleen in the stands. His focus had been on bucking broncs and wild bulls.

Angus woke to daylight and bolted from bed. He glanced at the alarm clock with a sigh. He'd slept past seven, which was rare for him. He took a quick shower and dressed in clean clothes. On his way downstairs, he caught the wafting aroma of coffee. *Bless Kathleen, I need some caffeine.* She sat at the kitchen table with a mug cradled between her hands. Like him, she'd changed.

Kathleen now wore a simple denim dress. She had piled her hair on top of her head and secured it. "Good morning. I appreciate the java."

"I thought you might need the boost. Do you feel better?" She took a sip and smiled.

"Yeah, headache's gone, but I'm still tired. I meant to get up sooner." Angus wasn't used to anyone showing any concern over his health, but he liked it. "Soon as I drink this, we'd better hit the road. Marisol is probably looking out for us now."

"I called her earlier. We don't have to be at the funeral home until ten, but she's got biscuits and gravy, coffee cake, and scrambled eggs ready. My sisters made it in last night, and all the rodeo guys are already there."

He laughed. "Figures. They ain't about to miss a good feed."

At Marisol's simple cement block house near Maydelle, the yard brimmed full of cars and trucks. Angus pulled behind Kathleen's small vehicle. Marisol met them at the door. She hugged Kathleen, then pulled Angus close for a hug. "I'm glad you're here, son. Come eat while there's still food. We'll head over to Rusk in a bit."

Although Angus had little appetite, he downed some biscuits and gravy with a slab of coffee cake. "Where's Mindy and the kids?"

"She'll meet us there." Marisol hovered with the coffeepot, ready to pour refills. "She'll bring some clothing for Bart. Claudia and Susan spent the night in a motel in town but they'll join us to make the arrangements."

Yancey cleared his throat. "We're all heading out before long, Angus. Let us know when the funeral will be, and we'll be back to attend. I don't mind if I miss competing this week, but next week is Cowboy Christmas. I got a bunch of places to ride. So does everybody else."

The Fourth of July week always had so many rodeos no one could make them all, but they tried. The nickname 'Cowboy Christmas' came from the many fat purses and prizes waiting to be won. "I'm gonna lay out for a while." Angus would keep his promise to Mindy to help however he could. He planned to support Kathleen and Marisol as well. "I'll give you a buzz and let you know the funeral time. Ride safe, you hear?"

"Will do." Yancey clapped Angus across the back.

At ten, Angus pulled up outside the funeral parlor. Kathleen's sisters, Claudia and Susan, stood near the door, purses tucked under their arms. He helped Marisol and Kathleen down from the truck. Mindy and her sons arrived. Angus offered Mindy his arm, and she accepted. Once inside the funeral home, a funeral director ushered them into a quiet room. The family, including Angus, who wasn't related, sat at a large round table.

"First, I want to say how sorry I am for your loss. I'm Matthew Etchison, and I'll assist your family with the arrangements for your loved one. Do you know what kind of service you'd like for Mr. Birdwell?"

"Simple," Mindy spoke in a quiet voice. "I'd like it to be at the church, if possible."

"Certainly." Etchison knew his role and performed it well. He used a series of questions to determine the family's preference.

Mindy named their pastor, asked for the passage from Ecclesiastes about time to be included in the service, and delivered Bart's final outfit. The Western-cut black suit and dark blue shirt had been a favorite, along with a string tie. Like any cowboy worth his salt, Bart would be buried with his best boots on his feet. Choosing the hymns proved more difficult, and selection became a group effort. A local singer had already told Mindy he would play his guitar and sing at the service.

The hymns would be "Just A Closer Walk With Thee," "On The Wings of A Dove," "Victory In Jesus," and "I'll Fly Away."

Angus suggested the last. He loved the old hymn and thought it would provide a good send-off for his buddy.

Mindy balked at choosing the casket. "I can't," she said and buried her face in her hands.

"I will," Kathleen stated. "Who wants to help?"

"Not me," Marisol cried. "I think it's the hardest part."

Neither Susan nor Claudia wanted to make the selection, so Angus and Kathleen did.

He hated the large display room filled with caskets. The place reminded him of a car lot with makes and models ranging from flashy to sedate. Angus noted he could buy a vehicle for what some styles cost but said nothing. Kathleen grasped his hand as she walked from one to another. Angus sighed with relief when she rejected a gold style. When she reached several wooden caskets, she paused. "I like these."

So did Angus. Etchison explained they were fashioned from cedar and, in one case, from barn wood. "I think Bart would like the simplicity." Choosing a coffin for his best friend seemed surreal. Less than a week ago, they'd been eating chili, joking, and joshing, and now he had been tasked to pick a box to put his buddy in the ground. Angus wanted to weep, but he also possessed a desire to lash out in anger.

"He would." Kathleen ran a hand over the smooth wood. "I choose this one."

At the funeral director's urging, she also chose a vault. When every detail had been planned, Kathleen asked if Angus could take her to a local florist to choose the flowers. "Sure, honey."

Inside the small shop, Angus felt like a raging bull in a quiet garden. The sweet scent of flowers filled his nose, and he tried not to bump into any of the displays. They browsed through photos of casket sprays, but when he saw a Western-style, he pointed to it on the page. "This." The arrangement included red roses, bright yellow sunflowers, orange daisies, wheat, and greenery. A cowboy hat rested on top with a ribbon reading, "Last Ride."

Kathleen gasped. "It's perfect. I'll get one of Bart's hats from Mindy."

The service time was set for ten a.m. on Wednesday at the church where Bart and Mindy were married. Bart would be laid to rest in the same local cemetery where Angus's folks and grandfather were. A dinner at church would follow. "I'll make the calls to the guys so they know when," Angus told Mindy. "What else do you need me to do today?"

She shrugged. "We're heading to Marisol's now, I guess. I'd like you to come, too. It's just starting to set in that Bart's really gone."

Angus spent a long day with the family. He took the boys outside, reminisced with Marisol, Claudia, Susan, and Kathleen, and answered the door to a steady stream of visitors. People delivered cakes and casseroles. Someone brought a large meat-and-cheese-deli-tray. An old woman Angus knew by sight but not by name showed up with two loaves of homemade bread. Neighbors arrived to offer condolences, and distant cousins camped in the living room. By late afternoon, Angus dragged. Fatigue dogged him, and he fought another headache. He thought he could sneak out without being noticed, but Kathleen caught him on the porch.

"Don't leave." She took his arm in a fierce grip.

"Aw, nobody but you will know I'm gone." He liked her touch, but he ached to go home. "I'm worn out. I need some sleep, and I can't eat another bite."

"You can lie down in my room. It's stacked with my stuff from college plus moving boxes. Mom's gonna want you to stay. I think Mindy wants to ask if you'll talk about Bart at the funeral, too."

Angus sighed. "All right. Show me where it's at."

She led him to the smallest bedroom near the back of the house. As described, the room was a mess, but the single bed was clear. Angus removed his boots so he wouldn't soil the pretty floral comforter and stopped. Two framed photos of him hung on the wall. One had been taken at a rodeo as he tried to best a bull. The second featured him in the stands, one hand over his heart with his hat in the other. "Why do you have pictures of my ugly mug?"

Kathleen blushed. "I had the awfullest crush on you, Angus. I idolized you when I was a teenager. I still do, although it's more admiration now."

His heart skipped a beat. He hadn't even been aware Kathleen attended some of the rodeos and had failed to recognize her at Bart's wedding, but she'd been lovesick over his sorry carcass. *I wish I'd known, but I would have been way too old. That seventeen-year difference mattered a lot, then.* "Oh, honey." His new feelings for her surged through him. Maybe, despite the age gap, there could be something between them. "You can do better than this old bull rider."

"I don't know about that." She stood near the open doorway with her arms crossed over her chest. "Get some rest. I'll wake you before it gets too late."

"Thanks, girl." Angus longed to say more, to explore this old crush or new admiration, but didn't.

He woke after dark and became momentarily confused. For a brief moment, Angus wondered if he'd ended up in a motel somewhere. He sat and groped for a lamp. The illumination revealed Kathleen's room, and he remembered. As he reached for his boots, Kathleen poked her head through the door.

"Almost everyone's gone if you want to come eat a bite. Pastor Johnson brought some fried chicken and a peanut butter pie."

"Okay. Mindy still here?"

Kathleen nodded. "Her parents came and picked up the kids, though. My sisters went home hours ago. Right now, it's Mom, Mindy, my best friend Tawny, and a couple cousins."

Angus ate some chicken, let Marisol coax him into a piece of pie, and drank a cold ginger ale. He let Mindy talk him into giving a short eulogy at the funeral, although he'd rather not. Public speaking wasn't his forte. He lingered for a few more hours, then excused himself to head home. By then, Mindy had gone. Angus hugged Marisol. "I'll see you tomorrow night at the visitation. If you need me for anything before, call, okay?"

"I will." Marisol planted a kiss on his forehead.

"I'll walk you to your truck." Kathleen flipped on the yard light. "Watch for snakes."

Angus kept an eye on the ground but saw no serpents. At this truck, he leaned against the cab. "I guess I'll see you tomorrow, too."

"Are you upset with me?" Kathleen pursed her lips into a pout.

"Why would I be?"

"Because I told you I had a crush on you." Her voice grew husky and low.

"I ain't mad, sweetheart. I might be a bit confused." Angus inhaled the sweet fragrance of honeysuckle on the wind. He ached to kiss her, to explain his feelings, and to start a new era with Kathleen.

"I don't understand." Kathleen frowned.

"It's the part where you kinda said you still do." He met her brown gaze without blinking. "Do you?"

"It's not a crush. I'm not a teenager anymore, Angus." She moved a step closer.

"I'm very aware."

"And you don't like the idea?" Kathleen asked.

Angus caught a whiff of her perfume and swayed. "I do,

that's the thing. I'm smitten, Kathleen, and I don't know what to think."

"Don't over analyze, Angus."

He could blame it on the moonlight or the summer night. Right now, he didn't feel forty. Angus shivered as a rush of youthful passion swept him. He quit pondering and acted. He moved forward and took Kathleen into his arms. She stood shorter than he was, and he didn't have to bend much to kiss her. His lips touched hers, and he lost any restraint. Angus kissed her with a slow, gentle mouth. Kathleen yielded, and when he broke contact, she leaned against his chest.

"I probably ought not have done that." He spoke words with uncertainty. "It's not the best time."

"It's fine." She brushed his cheek with her right hand. "Don't get knotted up over it."

Angus covered her hand with his. "I'll try not. Good night, Katydid."

"Sleep well, Angus."

As he backed out and followed the driveway to the road, he glanced back. Kathleen stood on the porch, her fingers stroking the lips he'd just kissed. She didn't go inside until he reached the blacktop. His tires hummed against the pavement as he piloted the truck the few short miles home. For once, he didn't turn on the radio. His thoughts echoed loudly within his head. *What would Bart think?* His friend made such an effort to find Angus a woman, but he'd never suggested his baby sister. Like Angus, he would have thought the age difference too great.

Angus half expected he wouldn't sleep well after his nap. He did, however, and dreamed about Bart. When he woke, he failed to recall the details, but he thought Kathleen had been part of the focus. He pushed thoughts of the lovely young woman aside to work on his eulogy for his friend. Angus scribbled out several versions on the kitchen table before he warmed up some of the leftover chili. He finished it before he completed what he planned to say and almost immediately decided it'd been a mistake.

There was little else in his cupboards or fridge, so he'd eaten it, but it didn't agree with his guts. Angus suffered through an unpleasant bout of indigestion. It passed by the time he got ready for the visitation. Tonight, he wore dark slacks with a Western shirt. Tomorrow, Angus would wear his one suit.

Bart's visitation took place in the funeral home chapel. Early tomorrow, the staff would move the casket to the church. A huge number of people turned out to pay their respects. Angus, with Kathleen at his side, shook hands, accepted condolences, and made small talk. Most remarked how well Bart looked, but Angus didn't agree. His friend resembled a wax figure. He looked dead. Bart had never been one to be still, so his prone position, with his eyes closed, disturbed Angus. Flowers and plants surrounded the casket, and their perfume became overwhelming. Despite air conditioning, the crowds made the room overheated. "I gotta get some air," he whispered to Kathleen. "Want to go outside?"

"Oh, yeah." She linked her arm through his as they slipped away. "I couldn't stand much more."

"Tomorrow will be worse." Angus hated to think about the funeral, the graveside service, and the dinner. "I got my eulogy written, though."

"Read it to me." Kathleen walked a few feet to stand beneath a sweet gum tree. The spiky balls from the branches littered the sidewalk.

"Nah, you can hear it tomorrow." Angus joined her and put his left arm around her waist.

"Hold me, please." Kathleen turned toward him.

He didn't kiss her but cuddled her close.

At the church, Mindy insisted he sit in the family pew, so Angus did. He struggled not to weep as the songs were played and the eulogy given. Bart's closed coffin rested in front of the raised platform. Angus mounted the steps and pulled his handwritten pages from inside his jacket. He cleared his throat and tried not to be nervous.

"I hadn't lived in Rusk very long when I met a kid at the junior high. He was a smart-mouthed guy and nosey. Asked all about me, who I was, where I was from, why I lived here now. I didn't want to share anything. My parents had passed away, and I'd moved in with my grandfather, John Beaton. A lot of you likely remember him. I had sulled up like a opossum and wanted to be a loner, but Bart wouldn't let me. He shared his locker, ate lunch with me, and before long, we began a friendship that lasted until last week. He talked me into playing baseball, and by high school, he got me to rodeo. We've ridden some wild broncs and bad bulls over the years. A long time ago, we did some team roping. I never expected him to die, at least not until we were old coots. But he did, and it tore a hole in my heart. It did the same for his wife, Mindy, his two boys, his mom, and his sisters. A lot of other rodeo folks are here today. Everyone thought well of Bart Birdwell. He would always lend a hand, offer an ear to listen. He's gonna be missed. I sure don't understand why God called him home, but Scripture says it better than me." He paused and paraphrased Ecclesiastes. The preacher had also referenced the chapter. "There's a time for everything and a time to die. Bart's came sooner than expected."

Angus read some of the lines and others he spoke from memory. He directed his words to Kathleen. When he pretended he talked only to her, it eased his nerves. When he finished, she brushed tears from her cheeks and offered Angus a small thumbs-up. The rest of the day passed in a blur. As one of the pallbearers, Angus did his part in carrying Bart's body to the waiting hearse. At the cemetery, he provided his last service to his best friend.

At the dinner, he ate little of the baked ham, turkey and

dressing, salads, side dishes, and desserts the ladies of the church provided. Angus tasted little of what he did. When the day ended, he went home and stared at the walls. Grief cut through his heart like a knife, and he wept without restraint for the first time since Bart's death.

On Friday, he and Kathleen traveled to Jacksonville. She helped Mindy pack away Bart's clothing and possessions. What Mindy didn't keep; Angus loaded into his truck to donate to charity. "Are you sure?" he asked the new widow. "It seems awful soon."

"Yes. I've put away some things for the boys for when they're older. I have some keepsakes I will treasure, but I can't bear to keep the rest. I can't stay here. Before school starts, I want to sell the house and move to Gladewater, where my parents still live. We'll move in with them. Most of the insurance will pay for Bart's funeral."

Angus bowed his head. "I can understand. Let me know what help you need, and I'll be here."

"Won't you be back on the circuit?" Mindy's eyes widened with shock.

"Not right now." Watching his buddy get fatally injured by a bronc destroyed much of his enthusiasm for the sport. Taking a hoof to his temple removed the rest. Angus wasn't sure what he wanted in life, but he was sure it wasn't to die in the arena. At forty, he could retire and not lose any face or respect. "Gladewater's not far. I think it's around an hour. My offer's still good, there or here."

"You're a good man, Angus, and you've been the finest friend anyone could have." Mindy hugged him. "I'll call if I need you."

Kathleen had ridden with him. After they dropped off Bart's belongings, she spoke for the first time since leaving Mindy. "I don't think she will."

"Won't what?" Angus didn't follow.

"You remind her of Bart, so she won't call you after this. She'll run away to Gladewater and try to forget."

"That might be," Angus agreed. "I'm here, though, for you and Marisol."

"I know, and we won't turn you away." Kathleen scooted across the seat. "It's not much more than a month till I start teaching. I have to get moved into my new place. I'll need you for that."

"I'm available. Why don't you live with your mom, though? It's not very far."

Kathleen shook her head. "I'm a grown woman. I love my mama, but I can't live with her. She'll be fine, and will I."

Angus took her left hand and cradled it. "You will, honey. Want to grab a bite to eat before I take you home?"

"Definitely. Can we get catfish?"

"You bet. I know a place."

They dined on crisp fillets with pinto beans, fries, and cornbread muffins. Angus savored the food, but he enjoyed the company even more. Afterward, he delivered Kathleen home and headed for the house. The place had never seemed lonelier as he entered, and for a short time, he allowed himself to dream about what might be.

Reality kicked in, however, and by evening, Angus moped. Kathleen was too young and lovely to want to spend her life with him. *I'm an old man compared to her, and I'm ugly to boot.* Her teen crush hadn't stood the test of time, and he feared her new emotions were no more than a backlash response to her brother's death. If he pursued a relationship and she realized it was no more than a fleeting infatuation, Angus couldn't stand the heartbreak.

It might be better to remain her friend and never reveal his emotions.

Because Angus now realized he loved her in every way a man could love a woman.

CHAPTER FOUR

Angus retreated into his small house and stayed there. As much as he longed to be with Kathleen, he kept his distance. When she or Marisol asked for his help, he gave it. Once the task or chore was finished, he went home. He wasn't hateful or unkind, but he remained reserved out of a desire for self-protection. In mid-July, Kathleen phoned Angus.

"My apartment's ready, and I can start moving in. Are you free to help?"

He sat in a kitchen chair tilted back on two legs against the house. "Sure, honey."

"Do you want to start now or in the morning?" Her voice over the phone rang clear. "Or are you busy?"

Angus laughed for the first time in days. "Nah, I'm sitting outside sweating and doing some thinking. I can come get a load now. What time is it?"

"Not quite two. If you hurry, we can probably take two truckloads before we stop for supper. I'll buy yours if you want."

He lowered the chair to all four legs. Angus hadn't eaten much besides bologna sandwiches and canned hot tamales lately. A frozen pizza had been a splurge. "I appreciate the offer, but you know what I'd like even more?"

"What's that?"

"A home-cooked dinner." He craved her company, and although he still feared heartbreak, Angus would risk it to spend some time with Kathleen. "I'd love a good meatloaf supper or maybe a decent pork chop."

"I don't know." Her tone turned hesitant. "My kitchen stuff is all in boxes. I'd have to unpack to make a meal."

Angus heaved a sigh. "Never mind, then. You can buy me a burger or something."

"Hey! I've got an idea. How about I cook at your place when we're finished? That would work."

Kathleen here, in his house, bustling around his kitchen, appealed. "*Mi casa, su casa.*"

"Then hurry over. Let's get done so I can. I've missed you, Angus."

Her simple words moved him. "Same, Katydid."

At Marisol's, he toted boxes and plastic totes to his truck. He unloaded it at the apartment complex not far from downtown. Kathleen carried a few, but he refused to let her lift the heavier ones.

"Show me what to put where," he told her once they reached her new place. He huffed a little after carrying a load up the exterior stairs.

"Put those down, and I'll show you around." Kathleen's eyes sparkled. "This is the living room, and that's the kitchen."

"I figured that out, darlin'." The front room opened to a galley-style kitchen with a table for two tucked in the rear. Across from it, the bathroom held the usual fixtures. A walk-in closet filled the space between it and the single bedroom. "It's nice. Laminated floors throughout appeared to be wood but weren't. The open floor plan seemed spacious for the small apartment. All the kitchen appliances were black.

"I like it. I bought the table and two chairs up in Jacksonville. I don't have much furniture. Mom said she can give me a few things, but I thought maybe you could take me over to Palestine to shop. I'd go myself, but I don't have a truck." She leaned against the tall bar that divided the kitchen from the living room.

His resolve to back off faded. "Of course. Do you want to go tomorrow?"

"That or Friday, unless you're gonna rodeo somewhere."

"I haven't, but I might. If I do, you wanna go with me?" Angus flashed a grin and stuck his hands in his jeans pocket so he wouldn't put his arms around her.

"You bet! I haven't seen you in weeks. Have you been busy?" She crossed the floor to stand beside him.

He shrugged. "Not really. Just trying to figure out what I want to do if I give up rodeo."

"I know—you'll train horses or raise rough stock. You mentioned it." Kathleen threw her arms around him and hugged him. "I've really missed you, Angus."

His resolve melted like butter in a hot skillet. "I've been pining for you, too, honey. Let's go grab one more load, then we'll stop at the market to pick up something to cook. I've meant to go to the store but haven't." Angus hadn't been hungry, either, but now his stomach rumbled. The idea of home cooking whetted his appetite, and he wanted Kathleen in his home. His emotions surged, and he moved forward, craving a kiss. He tried to resist until she touched his forehead. Her caress filled a need within, and he savored it.

"Your bruise is almost gone. I worried you'd been having headaches or else didn't like me." Kathleen's fingers brushed his skin, lighter than a breeze, but he still shivered.

"Honey, I like you fine. I always have." Angus placed his larger hand over hers. "I been trying to hold back and keep a distance."

"Why?"

He sucked in a harsh breath and gave her as much gut-level honesty as he dared. "We're both still raw from losing Bart. Besides, I'm nearabout too old for you, Kathleen. I shouldn't be trifling with you. You'll probably meet some guy about your age, one that's not a broken-down old cowboy."

Kathleen shifted her touch to his cheek and outlined his scar. Then she put a single finger across his lips. "Hush. Most of the dudes my age are stupid. They don't know the first thing about real life, but you do."

Her words flattered him, but Angus found himself afraid to hope. "I reckon that's true, but a crush doesn't last in the long run."

"Then it's a good thing I don't have a crush on you." Kathleen met his gaze. "I *used* to, that's true, but now it's different. I know my own mind and my heart. I'm…"

Angus stopped her with a kiss. Her lips tasted sweet, but the sensation proved delicious. Kissing Kathleen soothed something within his lonely soul, the way a glass of ice water quenched his thirst on a triple-digit day in Texas.

She returned the kiss and then rested her head against his chest. "I was about to say I'm a woman, and you're a man. Our age doesn't matter."

Maybe it did. He had yet to determine how much. "I'm seventeen years older than you are. It's a big difference," he told her. He inhaled her soft lavender fragrance.

"It might have when I was twelve, and you were twenty-nine." Kathleen lifted her head and nuzzled his neck. "It doesn't now."

I hope you're right. I really do. "Have you ever known any couple with such a big age gap?"

Her brown eyes narrowed. "My grandparents. Granny Kathy was twenty years younger than Gramps, but they were married for thirty years. You should know that, Angus, you were around them."

"They were a matched set." He chuckled, remembering. "If I knew about their ages, I'd forgotten."

"Let's go get one more load, then I'll make supper." Kathleen picked up her purse and headed for the door.

An hour later, Angus sat at his kitchen table with a glass of iced tea. After dropping off another load of boxes and totes at her place, they visited the supermarket. Kathleen offered to make meatloaf or to fix a pot of chicken and dumplings. He opted for meatloaf and now watched as she blended together ground beef with bread crumbs, onions, and seasonings.

"Do you happen to have a loaf pan?" she asked, lifting her hands from the meat mixture.

"Like to bake bread?" Angus asked. "I doubt it unless there's an old one of Granny's tucked away. Are you making bread, too?"

She swiped at her cheek with an elbow. "Not today, but I'd use it for the meatloaf. I can just shape it instead."

His stomach growled. He hadn't eaten since he had a stale donut with his morning coffee. "How long will it be until supper?"

"About an hour once I start cooking this." Kathleen formed the mixture into something resembling a loaf. She washed her hands and then slid the baking dish into the preheated oven. "I thought I'd make mashed potatoes with brown gravy, fried okra, corn on the cob, and maybe biscuits. How does that sound?"

"Awesome, but leave the biscuits for another time." Angus thought he might drool just thinking about the meal. "Are you gonna use those mushrooms in the gravy?"

"Of course." Kathleen dried her hands and sat across from him. "I made the peach crisp before I started the meatloaf."

At the local grocery store, they'd bought the fixings for the feast. He had insisted on vanilla ice cream to top the cobbler made with fresh peaches and paid the bill. He refused to let Kathleen pay, although she argued it was supposed to be her treat. "You're cooking it," he'd told her.

The delightful aroma of brown sugar, peaches, oats, butter, and vanilla wafted through the kitchen. He rubbed his belly. "Smells good already. I'm likely to get a bellyache, but it'll be worth it."

"I don't want to make you sick," she said and laughed.

"I won't be sick, but my guts will gripe me. You can nurse me through it if it's too bad." Fresh peaches never agreed well with his inner workings, but he loved the taste. "Fair enough?"

"I guess. You need to be feeling fine if we're furniture shopping tomorrow." Kathleen reached into her jeans pocket. "I made a list."

Angus plucked it from her fingers, read it, and groaned. "I hope the store delivers, or we'll be making twelve trips back and forth from Palestine."

"They do." She grabbed the list back. "It's not that much – bedroom furniture, a couch and chair, maybe a coffee table, and a bookshelf. I have a small television in my room at Mom's, plus my stereo, so I may want an entertainment center, too. I think it could fit in one pickup load if necessary."

"If they deliver, it won't matter." He hoped they would. Angus would rather not tote all that up the steps to Kathleen's apartment. "Easier on my back, too."

The moment he mentioned his back, he wished he hadn't. Talking about aching backs, bellyaches, and such might make him sound all the more like an old man. He decided not to mention anything more about his aches and pains. Like any long-term rodeo rider, he had plenty. *I don't want to scare her off before we even see if this will work with us.*

Thunder rumbled in the distance before they shared the meal. Angus devoured the delicious meatloaf. He ate his portion of 'taters and gravy, but he took refills of okra until no more remained. He savored two ears of corn but left room for a hefty portion of peach crisp topped with two scoops of ice cream. Kathleen ate about half of what he did, but she cleaned her plate.

"Everything tasted delicious," he told her as he blotted his lips with a napkin. "Looks like there's enough left for a couple meatloaf sandwiches. I'll have those for supper tomorrow. Thank you, Kathleen. You're a good cook."

She lifted both hands in the air. "You earned it, Angus. I like cooking. Mom let me take over the kitchen whenever I wanted by the time I was fourteen or so. Any time she didn't want to make a meal, I did. I'll probably have a hard time cooking for one once I get moved." Kathleen stacked their dishes. "I'll have to invite you over sometimes."

Angus placed his silverware on his plate. "I'll be there, honey. I can do these dishes later if you want to go home before the storm hits."

Rain pounded against the roof with force. "I think it's here," she replied. "No hurry, Angus. I cooked, so I'll clean up. That's the way Mom taught me. You can keep me company while I do."

"I'll do better than that—I'll dry."

He enjoyed every moment of the domestic chore. On his own, he might let dishes soak in the sink for two or three days before he washed them. Angus often left them in the drainer to dry, but now, he wiped each piece with an old kitchen towel. They chattered as they worked. Once every item had been returned to the proper place and each surface shone clean, Angus sighed. "I suppose you want me to run you home now."

Kathleen shook her head. "Angus, it's still pouring. I'm in no hurry, so unless you're eager to get rid of me, I thought I'd stay a while."

Angus hadn't been paying attention to the weather, but he realized now that thunder continued to roll. Lighting flashes were visible through the windows, and before he could answer, he heard the unmistakable rattle of hail. "Fine with me. Maybe we'd better turn on the TV and see what the weather says."

In the long, wide living room, Angus parked on the couch resting against the side of the stairs. His television had been mounted on the opposite wall. Beneath it, shelves held a variety of movies, books, and some hunting magazines. To the left of the front door, bricks lined the corner to accommodate a vintage black cast iron wood stove. On the opposite side, pegs hung on the wall to hold outerwear, and beneath it, assorted boots, gloves, and gear sat on the floor. Angus had a recliner midway between the TV and the stove, with an old-fashioned floor lamp beside it.

He picked up the remote from the end table and flicked on the television. One of the Tyler stations displayed a weather map in the lower corner, but Angus couldn't quite make out what the colors meant. He squinted harder. "Looks like we're under a severe thunderstorm warning until eight, then a severe thunderstorm watch until midnight."

"And a tornado watch until one a.m." Kathleen slouched into the corner of the couch. "A flash flood is also in effect. I'd better stay here for a bit. Do you have a basement just in case we need to shelter?"

"Root cellar is out back, although I don't reckon it'll be necessary." He chuckled because he doubted she would like the place if they hunkered down there. Although he didn't keep anything much there, a few dusty jars of his late grandmother's jelly remained on the shelves, along with dozens of big spiders. Once in a great while, a snake took refuge in the cool, dark space. "Why don't we watch a movie?"

It took forty minutes sorting through his collection before they agreed on a film. Like many of those in his collection, it was a Western. *3:10 To Yuma,* a remake of an older 1950s movie. This version starred Russell Crowe, and by the end, the storm had moved eastward. Angus had one arm around Kathleen and realized his stomach didn't hurt. For once, fresh peaches didn't do a number on his stomach. He hadn't given it another fault and felt fine.

After Angus dropped her at Marisol's house, he drove down to the Neches River. After the thunderstorm, the river ran bank full, but the air had cleared. He inhaled the fresh aroma of water and mud with pleasure. He should take time to visit by daylight and bring a fishing rod. Maybe he could talk Kathleen into coming along. He caught himself and shook his head. Whatever this wild, wonderful thing might be with Bart's baby sister, he feared it wouldn't last. *I should back off now and save the heartache.* He should, but he couldn't.

In Palestine, Kathleen chose furniture with quick deliberation and dropped money with abandon. She chose a leather sofa in a quiet gray with a matching recliner. The salesman talked her into a pair of end tables and a matching coffee table. She chose a tall, four-shelf bookcase and an entertainment center.

Angus lounged on the edge of a couch in the showroom and watched with awe. Kathleen haggled and bargained to get a price break before moving on to bedroom furniture. She eyed every set offered before choosing the one Angus liked best of all. The rustic hickory bed came in both queen and king-size. Kathleen opted for the larger option, along with the matching dresser, a chest of drawers, and a nightstand. She chose a decent mattress without going top-of-the-line. When she checked the price tag on some lamps, she frowned.

"You know, you'd do better to get the lamps at a discount store. You could find a nice comforter, too, plus pillows, sheets, and blanket for a lot less." Angus sidled close and whispered in her ear. "You must have spent a couple of thousand dollars so far."

"I'll pay it on time." Kathleen folded her arms across her chest. "Once my teaching salary starts, I'll make extra payments. But, okay, you made a good point."

The furniture would have never fit in his truck. Kathleen signed for the goods, flashed her credit card, and arranged for delivery in a week. "That's gonna cut it close," she told Angus as they left the store. "It works, though."

"When's the first day of school, anyway?"

"I have to report on the first of August. Classes start on the second week of the month." Kathleen climbed into his truck. "Do you want to head to the discount store here or back in Rusk?"

Angus shook his head. "Gets earlier every year. I thought I'd buy you some lunch, sugar. Mexican, Asian, or a burger?"

"A thick ol' burger is fine with me, Angus. I can shop for the other stuff in Rusk or Jacksonville."

Over cheeseburgers and curly fries, Angus enjoyed the meal until the waitress made a comment which he didn't like.

"It's so nice to see a father take his daughter out to eat," she said as she laid the check on the table. "Pay me whenever you're ready."

His jolly mood faded like fog as the sun rose. "I'll take care of it now." Angus pulled out his wallet and handed the server cash.

"Excuse me." Kathleen took the bills. "You're out of line. Angus isn't my father. He's my date. If I were you, I wouldn't judge your customers. You just did yourself out of a tip. Give the change to Angus when you come back."

The waitress flushed. "Uh, I'm sorry. I just assumed…"

"Don't." Kathleen tapped her fingers on the table. As soon as the woman vanished in the direction of the cash register, she faced Angus across the booth. "I'm sorry about that. She had no business."

Angus sighed. "She just called it like she sees it, darling. I suppose I'm old enough to be your dad if I'd started young. I don't figure she'll be the first one to think the same or the last." He scooted out of the booth. "Let's go. Let her keep the change. It wasn't going to be much anyhow."

As they headed back toward Rusk, Kathleen sat close to him. "Angus, don't let it bother you. One, you're not old, and two, it's nobody's business."

It did concern him, but he said nothing. He forced a grin and tried to recapture the delight he'd experienced earlier. Angus couldn't quite manage it, but he kept up his end of the conversation until they reached her mom's.

"I thought we'd go to the apartment," Kathleen cried. "I need to start putting stuff away. I hoped you might help or at least keep me company."

Angus shook his head. "I would have, but I got a few things to take care of at home. If I'm going to ride in the rodeo over in Louisiana this weekend, I need to make some calls."

Kathleen nodded, but she wasn't smiling. "Sure. What time will we leave? You asked me if I'd like to go."

He had, but now Angus wasn't sure. "I wasn't sure if you still wanted to come."

"I do. Angus, you're not going to brood about what the stupid waitress said, are you?"

"Naw." He would, though, as well as do some deep thinking once he got home. "All right. I'll pick you up around noon if you want to watch me bust broncs."

"Sure. I'll be ready." Kathleen kissed him, her lips lingering on his. "Call me if you get lonely, Angus."

He made no promise. "I'll see you tomorrow. Take care."

Once home, he resisted an urge to punch something. Instead, he settled into his recliner with a book, but he couldn't keep his mind on the story. The doubts he'd laid to rest about pursuing a relationship with Kathleen surged. The waitress's careless remark bothered him, and he chewed on it all evening. After he ate a cold meatloaf sandwich, he wandered restlessly through the house. Unwilling to remain unsettled, he sank down on his knees in front of the couch and prayed.

Dear Lord, guide me. I love Kathleen. I never thought I'd finally find a woman or realized when I did, I'd be forty years old. I want to cherish her, to care for her, and provide for her. I'd even like a couple of little kids before I'm any older. If it's wrong, if it's not the best thing for her, then show me. Lead me where I should go, Lord. I'll try to follow.

Angus's mood improved, but he didn't phone Kathleen. In the morning, however, he rose with purpose. He got his gear together, then took a shower and scrubbed. He put on his best rodeo jeans and added one of his favorite Western shirts. He pulled his boots out to ride for the first time since Bart died and sang along with the radio on the way to pick up his lady.

On the way over to the Pelican State, Angus stopped for lunch at a small café he'd known for years. They feasted on fried catfish with hush puppies, brown beans, and fried potatoes. "I won't eat again until after I ride." Angus blotted his lips with a paper napkin. "Figured I'd best eat now."

"It was delicious." Kathleen touched up her lipstick. "Is this a big rodeo?"

"Nah, it's small at a county fair." It would technically be a parish fair, but he didn't care about being exact. "It's more of a way for me to get back into rodeo than anything else." Angus didn't confide the rest, but he wanted to decide how much longer he'd keep competing. Maybe it was time to settle down, train horses, and get married.

"I'm glad you invited me." Kathleen touched his hand across the table. "I don't want to let what happened to Bart keep me away from rodeos. I love the sport and always will."

Like Angus, she wore boots. Horses decorated her dark green, short-sleeved Western shirt.

"I'm happy you came with me." Angus stroked her hand. He ached to say more, but they had miles to go before they reached their destination. Once there, he paid his entry fees and led Kathleen to the stands.

"I'll sit with you as long as I can, sugar. Soon as I ride, I'll come back. We can stay or leave, whatever you want. If I score well, I'll ride tomorrow, and we'll come back."

The bleachers filled long before the rodeo began. Several cowboys tipped their hats to Angus and offered Kathleen condolences. Aidan O'Neill, one of the cowboys who came to the hospital when Bart was dying, would also ride. The young man swaggered up to their seats. "Howdy, Angus, Hi-de-do, Kathleen. Are you riding tonight?"

"I surely am. Hey, Kathleen, want to go down and get a cold drink or something to eat before I have to head for the chutes?" Aidan grinned at her and ignored Angus.

"No, thank you," Kathleen replied.

"How's about then me and you go out after the rodeo? Maybe do some dancing or a little drinking." Aidan winked. "I'd buy you a fine steak if you want, or some crawfish etouffee."

Kathleen rested a hand on Angus' thigh, then linked her other arm through his. "I don't drink, and I seldom dance," she told Aidan. "Besides, I'm with Angus."

His eyebrows shot high. "You mean you caught a ride with him?"

"No." Kathleen stood her ground. "I'm not a hitchhiker. I'm with Angus."

Angus's heart swelled with joy. Whatever happened down the road, for now, Kathleen let Aidan and the world know.

Aidan frowned. "You surely don't mean you're like his girlfriend. Why, he's old enough…"

"To whip your sorry butt if need be." Angus laid his right hand over Kathleen's. He didn't like the term girlfriend. It sounded almost juvenile, as if they were still in high school. Woman might come across as too possessive. "She's my lady, Aidan, so back off."

The young bronc rider spread his hands wide. "I didn't know, man. Good luck with the ride tonight and with Kathleen." He backed away, shaking his head. "I'll see you at the chutes."

Angus wanted to laugh, but he didn't. He gazed down

at Kathleen and stroked back a stray lock of her hair. "So, we're together."

"If I'm your lady, I hope to shout we are," Kathleen told him. "If it's time, you'd better go. I'll be here when you come back."

Angus stood and kissed her. "I'm counting on it, babe."

He was, and no matter what the future might hold, right now, he felt ten feet tall and every inch a man.

CHAPTER FIVE

Angus rode well, the best he had in months, maybe in years. He held his seat on the bucking bronc without being thrown. At the end of the evening, he ranked second and would be in the running to take home a prize purse if he did well on Saturday. He proved he could still compete, he bested Aidan O'Neill, and he hoped he impressed Kathleen. He headed to the stands to find her, but she met him halfway.

"You were amazing!" Kathleen threw her arms around him.

"I did alright." He caught her and held her tight. "Whenever you' ready, we can head out. Gotta come back tomorrow night."

She frowned as they began walking toward the parking area. "We have to go home?"

"Well, yeah, sugar. I didn't put the camper on the truck like I usually do. It wouldn't be big enough for two if I had." Angus slung one arm across her shoulders and hoped he didn't stink too bad. The combined smell of sweat and horse could be rank.

"What about eating a late supper?"

"Are you hungry?" Angus asked. Every other person they met tipped their hat or called out greetings.

"I'm starving." Kathleen took his left hand and held it.

"I could eat. I don't know what's open late around here, but we'll figure it out. It's two and a half or three hours home, though. We'll get in late, probably after midnight or closer to one."

She shrugged. "It doesn't matter, as long as we get some sleep before we come back."

"That's not a problem. Let's go find some eats. If nothing else is open, there's a travel plaza over on the highway." Angus tossed his bronc gear in the bed of the truck and motored to the truck stop. He navigated between the big rigs and led Kathleen into the restaurant. Despite the hour, the rich aroma of fresh coffee wafted through the space. They found a booth tucked into a rear corner and studied the menus.

"Coffee, to start," Angus told the server. "Kathleen?"

She shook her head. "I'd never sleep if I drink any now. Ice water with a lemon twist, please."

They both ordered patty melts, hamburgers served on grilled rye bread with melted Swiss cheese and sauteed onions. Angus had fried mushrooms with his, and Kathleen chose fries.

"I like this better than steak." She wiped her fingers on a napkin. "It's really good."

Angus laughed. "I'm not turning down a good steak, but I like this fine. When you're finished, let's get you home. Marisol will be wondering if I kidnapped you."

Kathleen shook her head. "I doubt it. She trusts you. Besides, I've been gone for the last four years. Mom is used to me coming and going. I bet she's asleep by now."

Although it was almost one-thirty before Angus pulled into the drive at Marisol's, the lights were on.

Marisol stuck her head through the front door and waved. "I wondered when you'd get back. I had about decided you were staying in Louisiana."

"I would have called you if we were." Kathleen entered the house with Angus a step behind. "Why are you still up?"

"I couldn't sleep." Marisol sighed. "Angus, thanks for getting her home."

He removed his hat. "No problem. I'm fixing to go home and sleep. I'm going back tomorrow to ride. Kathleen's coming along."

"Good night, Angus," Kathleen told him.

Since he was in for a penny, in for a pound, Angus planted a brief kiss on her lips. "Sleep well, sugar. I'll pick you up around one."

"I'll be ready." She flashed him a sweet smile and headed toward the bedrooms.

Marisol faced him and beamed. "I'll be darned. So, that's how it is. I wondered."

Angus figured he might be blushing. "I know you probably think I'm too old for her, and you might be right…"

"She could do worse. I don't think anything of the sort, Angus Beaton. Why don't you come to supper Sunday evening? I'm gonna fry chicken."

His weekend loomed busy. Tomorrow, another bronc to bust, which involved a trip to Louisiana and back. If he could, Angus planned to rise in time for church on Sunday and now supper. "Sure. I'll be here."

He woke stiff and more than a little sore on Saturday morning. A hot shower, some over-the-counter pain relievers, and the application of arnica on his bad shoulder and knee helped. So did three cups of strong, black coffee. By the time Angus picked up Kathleen, he could move without much discomfort. He hoped she wouldn't notice, but she did.

"Where are you hurting?" Kathleen scooted across the seat to take her place beside him.

"Everywhere." Angus shrugged to make light of his pain, but hitching his shoulders brought a new wave. "I cain't expect to get tossed every which way on a bronc and not suffer a little."

She placed her hand on his right knee and rubbed. "At least you'll have a few days to rest. After church and fried chicken on Sunday, I won't ask for any physical favors till Friday when my furniture arrives. By then, I should have everything else put away."

Angus exhaled. He had been afraid she'd fuss over his aches, and although he craved sympathy, he didn't want to be treated like an invalid or old man. "I can lend a hand if you need one."

Kathleen grinned. "I won't turn any help down. I'll probably go pick out bedding and some other stuff this week. If you're up to it, maybe you could hang a few pictures for me at the apartment. I'll cook if you'd like, and I'll give you some TLC. I think I can manage a decent back rub, too."

He covered her hand with his. "Yes, to all of it. Once I get through tonight, I'll be fine."

Angus would have been if he hadn't scratched after two seconds and landed hard on his right hand. Immediate pain shot through his wrist, bad enough for a sprain, although he didn't think he'd broken any bones. The medics on hand wrapped it and advised him to down some pain relievers and not to ride again for a few weeks.

"You're hurt!" Kathleen burst into the sports medicine trailer behind the chutes. "Angus, do you need to go to the hospital?" She frowned as she spoke.

"Nah. All I did is sprain my wrist. Hurts some, but it's not serious. I guess we can leave, though, whenever. I won't take home any prizes now." He held out his right hand, and she grasped it.

"Are you the girlfriend?" The medic asked.

"I am. Tell me what he needs, and I'll see he gets it." Kathleen brushed her free hand against Angus's cheek and smoothed back his hair.

"It's a sprain, not a break, but it's gonna hurt. Keep it wrapped but not too tight. Ice it every hour and have him elevate it. It's a good idea to prop it on some pillows for the next few days. Keep the pain meds coming, but if it hurts too much, get him to a doctor."

"All right. Angus, let's go home."

"I'm ready." He tried not to groan. His stomach rolled from the pain, and he prayed he wouldn't puke.

At the truck, he started to climb behind the wheel, but Kathleen shook her finger at him.

"I'll drive. Do we need to stop for meds or food or ice?"

"No. If you got something I can take, just get me a bottle of tea or ginger ale. I've got the ice bag they fixed up. Maybe it'll last till we get to the house." He winced and resisted the urge to rub his throbbing wrist.

At the next convenience store, Kathleen dashed inside and returned with soft drinks. She dug tablets from her purse and waited until he took them. "What about something to eat? They've got chicken tenders, cold sandwiches, and hot dogs inside."

"I cain't eat right now. I'm feeling sick." Angus laid his right hand over his stomach. "I just want to get home."

Three long hours later, Kathleen pulled up to his house. He'd fallen asleep on the way, but he'd muttered and groaned. With his eyes closed, he appeared younger and somehow vulnerable. Her teenage crush surged back but with something stronger. *I really care about him. It's not because I've known him forever or because he was Bart's buddy but for who and what he is.* "Wake up, we're here."

Angus roused and blinked. "Where? Oh, yeah, okay. What time is it?"

"Eleven-thirty." Kathleen pulled his keys from the ignition. "How's the wrist?"

"Hurts." So did his head, but Angus didn't mention the headache. Once inside, he flopped into his recliner. He reached to pull off his boots, then realized the task would be difficult with one hand. Angus tried to tug on the right one but moaned.

"Let me help." Kathleen knelt and removed his boots.

"Get settled. I'll fix a fresh ice pack and bring you some meds."

Angus lacked the energy to protest, so he let her play nurse. Within fifteen minutes, she had his injured wrist propped on pillows with an ice bag resting on his arm. He'd taken several ibuprofen tablets and sipped on a cold glass of tea. With the chair reclined, he thought he might fall asleep eventually.

Kathleen tucked another pillow behind his head. "Angus, you really ought to eat something. I can scramble you a couple eggs or open a can of soup if you have any. I don't know what else you've got."

"Eggs is fine, maybe with toast."

He dozed while she prepared the food, then woke to devour the simple fare. "Thanks, honey. You'd better head home before Marisol sends out a search party."

"She won't." Kathleen laughed and sat down on the couch. "I called her and told her what happened. Besides, I'm staying. You could use some help tonight, maybe tomorrow. I doubt we'll make church, but we should get over to Mom's in time for fried chicken."

"Kathleen, I don't know if that's a good idea or not." Angus wanted her to stay, but he didn't want to talk. Odds anyone would know she spent the night beneath his roof were slim, but the truth had a funny way of being revealed. "I reckon I can manage."

She shook her head. "Angus, you couldn't even get your boots off without help. Your landline phone is wired to the kitchen wall, and I'm not sure if you can manage your cell with one hand. Mom agreed it would be best. Besides, how would I get home? Mom won't drive at night, and I don't want to take your truck. You'd be here without wheels."

Angus realized she was correct. "I'd manage, though."

"I'm sure you would, but there's no reason you should." Kathleen removed the dish from his hands. "Angus, I would have helped you anytime you asked. So would Bart and Mom. You're a stubborn man."

If she'd used a different tone, he might have been insulted, but she spoke with affection. "I suppose I am, darlin'. I don't know what in tarnation you see in me."

A brilliant smile lit her face. "That and a lot more. You'd better try to sleep. Do you want to move to the couch or go upstairs?"

Moving would jar his wrist and cause agony. "I'm good right here."

Angus woke early. Across the room, Kathleen snored softly on the sofa. He grinned at the image, moved his wrist, and although it hurt, he thought it wasn't as bad. Throughout the night, she had dosed him with pain relievers at intervals, kept the ice pack fresh, and tended him as if she were a nurse, not a schoolteacher. If he didn't climb out of the chair, it would be harder later, so Angus maneuvered to his feet. To minimize the pain, he folded his left arm against his chest and made it to the bathroom. With effort, he filled the coffeepot one-handed and sat at the kitchen table to wait for the brew.

"Angus!" Kathleen called his name with alarm.

"I'm in here."

She rubbed her face as she joined him. "What are you doing?"

"Waiting for coffee. I was thinking about trying to fry some bacon, but I ain't sure I can manage." His stomach had settled, and he was hungry.

"I doubt you can." Kathleen rose, poured two cups of coffee, and brought them to the table along with the sugar bowl. "I can fix breakfast. You need to take it easy."

Angus guffawed. "I don't do easy. I kind of thought since I'm already awake, I'd like to go to church after all. Do you want to come with me?"

Her eyes widened. "I don't have clean clothes, or I would. Why in the world do you want to attend services? Doesn't your wrist still hurt?"

"It smarts, yeah, but I'm thankful. I could've got hurt a lot worse. I might've busted my head or broke a bone, or ended up in the hospital. I'd like to give God the glory." Angus seldom spoke about his deep faith, but he did now. If he and Kathleen were in a relationship, he couldn't hold anything back. "I'll run you home so you can put on a dress or something."

She pursed her lips and sighed. "If you're sure, I'll help you put on a clean shirt. I'll make you a sling, and we'll go. I guess we can grab breakfast in town. What about after church?"

"If Marisol doesn't mind, I figured we'd head over there. You can fuss over me there as easy as you can here." Angus swigged some coffee. "Right now, we've got time to get around."

It took longer than expected, but Angus and Kathleen weren't late for the service. He managed to change from jeans into Western-cut slacks, and she assisted him with his shirt. She fashioned a sling for him, and once adjusted, it did relieve some of the pain. She also rewrapped his wrist. By the time Kathleen drove them over to her mom's and changed, they had to settle for biscuits at a fast-food restaurant. They slid into a pew beside Marisol as the first hymn began. Angus sang the tune from memory and listened as the pastor shared his message about joy.

"Weeping may linger through the night of our lives," Pastor Johnson intoned. "We all have dark days and darker nights. But the promise of our Lord to us all is joy comes in the morning. God didn't mean for his people to be sad or unhappy."

The sermon struck Angus's heart. After losing his buddy, he had wondered. He questioned if it was right for him to seek happiness with Kathleen or at all. The words from Psalm Thirty removed his doubt. After the service, a dozen people asked Angus if he'd been hurt at a rodeo. Two questioned if he sat beside Kathleen by chance or if there was a reason.

"I always thought you'd make a pair," Miss Virginia Perry, a spinster who still mourned the sweetheart she'd lost during World War II, told him.

"I appreciate that, Miss Virgie." Angus glanced to see if Kathleen had heard, but she stood with a group of young women, laughing and talking. "I hope we will."

"Ain't you more than a little old for her?" Bert Travers stated. The man had to ninety if he were a day. "Why isn't she still in high school?"

"Hush your mouth," Sharon Travers, Bert's wife, chided. "That girl's graduated from college, and she'll be teaching school this year. I guess you've forgotten there's fifteen years between you and me."

Angus couldn't decide if he wanted to be mad or move past the remarks. "I'm leaving that up to the Lord, Bert," he said.

After a long moment, the old gentleman set his jaw. "Best way to do it, son. I wish you well."

At Marisol's, Angus settled into a comfortable armchair. Kathleen stood behind him and combed his hair with her fingers. "I'm glad we went to church."

"Yeah? Me, too." Angus couldn't contain his curiosity about her friends. "I guess your gal pals were happy to see you."

"Definitely. We're planning a girls' night out next Saturday."

"Sounds fun." Angus would rather spend the time with her, but he didn't dare be possessive.

Marisol served some soup she'd made the day before and sandwiches. "I won't start the chicken for a while, but make yourself comfortable, Angus," she told him after lunch. "Watch some TV, listen to music, or sit out on the patio. It's not too hot in the shade."

Kathleen dosed him and brought a new ice bag. She sat

cross-legged on the floor at his feet while they listened to vintage country music. Angus preferred the older tunes, but he didn't object when she added some Jake Owens and Chris Stapleton into the mix.

He spent a pleasant afternoon chilling. Angus savored the shift from his usual solitary life to downtime with Marisol and Kathleen. No one expected anything from him. He made conversation when he had something to say, but when he didn't, the silence wasn't awkward.

The fried chicken proved to be a treat. Angus couldn't remember the last time he had pan fried chicken, crisp and seasoned perfectly. He could taste both flour and cornmeal in the coating, which he liked. His mama had fried her chicken much the same way, and so had his grandmother. He ate three pieces, two helpings of mashed potatoes with milk gravy, two biscuits with butter, and fried corn. Kathleen had made a peanut butter pie, and although he first vowed he didn't have room for dessert, he managed a sliver.

The trio sat outside on the north-facing patio after supper. Sated and more relaxed than he'd been since Bart died, Angus enjoyed the evening. He hated to break it up and go home, so he lingered.

"I'd best head for the house before long," he announced around nine-thirty.

Kathleen stretched out a foot and nudged his leg. "I'll drive you when you're ready."

"I can steer with one hand." Angus hadn't driven in more than twenty-four hours, and he chafed with no wheels. He'd removed the sling before the meal. "I'll manage from here to the house."

"Angus." Kathleen rolled her eyes. "I don't think…"

Marisol interrupted before they could argue. "Don't fight. I want to talk to both of you. Let's go back inside. The skeeters are starting to bite." She rubbed her arms.

"What's wrong?" Angus picked up her serious tone.

Kathleen scooted closer to him. "Mom?"

"Nothing's the matter, but things are going to change." Marisol stood. "I meant to tell y'all sooner, but then Bart died and…"

"You're scaring me, Mama." Kathleen switched to her childhood name for her mother. "I don't know if I'll like this."

Angus came to his feet. His swift movement sent pain radiating through his wrist. He gritted his teeth so he wouldn't cry out. "C'mon, Katydid."

Marisol headed into the house.

Kathleen took his right hand. "What if she's sick?"

"Nah, she looks fine." Angus worried the same way, but he downplayed his concern for Kathleen's sake. "Whatever it is, we'll deal with it together."

Marisol sat in the recliner with her feet on the floor. She held a file folder and wore her reading glasses.

Angus took a place on the couch but kept his back straight. He held Kathleen's hand. "What's the deal?"

"I've got two things to tell you." Marisol paused to draw a deep breath. She released it before she continued. "Like I said, I meant to tell both my children at the same time, but Bart's gone. Angus, you're like another son, so it's fitting you're here. I'm selling the house. Actually, it's already sold to a couple from Fort Worth. They won't take possession until October, but it's a deal."

"Mom!" Kathleen cried.

Marisol lifted a finger. "Hold on, and I'll explain. Your daddy's been gone a long time. I've loved this house and raised you kids here. It's too big for one old woman, though. Bart had been gone for years, and rightly so. He had Mindy and his own family. Kathleen, you've been away to college for the last four years. Even though you're back, you have your own place. If you didn't, this is still too much house for a pair of women. I've been lonely here, and I decided to sell several years ago. I just waited for the right time. I wanted you to have your home to come back to visit for holidays and summers while you were in school."

A few stray tears rolled down Kathleen's cheeks. "I could give up my new apartment and stay here with you."

Angus squeezed her hand. "Kathleen, that's not going to solve anything. Your mama has a right to her own life just like you do."

"That's exactly right." Marisol bobbed her head in agreement.

"Where are you gonna live?" Angus's curiosity fueled his question. "An apartment or a house in town?"

"Neither one. There's a second part to my story." She scratched her chin and linked her hands in her lap. "I'm also getting married to Dr. Anthony Mackin."

Kathleen released Angus's hand as she jumped to her feet. "What? I don't believe it!"

Shock rocked through Angus, but he recognized the truth when he heard it.

"It's true. I've been a widow for more than twenty years. I loved Bobby Birdwell with all my heart, but he died not long after Kathleen was born. Angus, you surely remember."

He swallowed hard. "I do, although I hadn't thought about it in a long time."

Bob Birdwell had been an over-the-road trucker. On a run from Texas to California, somewhere between Amarillo and Tucumcari, a violent thunderstorm delivered high winds, heavy rain, and hail. Unable to keep his rig on the road and unwilling to pull over because he would lose time with his load, Birdwell rearended another semi-truck. Both vehicles had rolled, killing the drivers and blocking I-40 for hours. Bart had been seventeen, about to start his senior year of high school. Kathleen wasn't a year old."

Marisol hesitated, brushed a tear from the corner of her left eye, and sighed.

"I don't know if you ever knew this, Angus, or you remember, Kathleen, but I came from up around Caddo Lake. My first sweetheart broke my heart when he headed off to college at the University of Alabama."

"Crimson Tide," Angus announced. "I watch a little football."

Marisol nodded. "Yes, Crimson Tide. Anthony — Tony — had a four-year sports scholarship. He graduated with a degree, then transferred to Baylor, where he went through med school. I didn't wait for him. I met Bobby on the rodeo circuit, and I fell in love with the brash cowboy. By the time Tony finished his education, I had married, and we had Bart. Tony wrote me a letter when he found out. I didn't read it for years, and when I did, I cried."

Kathleen sat down with Angus. She gazed at Marisol. "Why?"

"He told me if I wasn't his wife, he wouldn't marry. And he didn't. Around the time you went to college, Kathleen, I found Tony on social media. We messaged each other and shared some jokes. After about two years, he showed up here. At first, I hesitated, but I let him come inside. We started seeing each other. He took me out to dinner, we saw movies, and visited historic places together." Marisol twisted a loose strand of hair between her fingers. "I fell in love again. We're planning a wedding this fall, so I'll be around for a while. After we're married, I'll move up near Uncertain. Tony has a house on the lake, and it's lovely."

Kathleen leaned against Angus. "What am I supposed to do, Mom?"

"I hope you'll be happy for me and give me your blessing. I hoped Bart would have given me his. Will you, Kathleen?"

She buried her face against Angus's shoulder before she faced Marisol. "I don't know. I have to think about it, Mom. I'll try, but I can't say I will yet."

Marisol paled. "That's fair." She cleared her throat. "Angus?"

The fried chicken he'd enjoyed earlier churned in his belly. He didn't want to take sides or be involved, but he already was. "It's a shock. I think you ought to be happy if you can. Life's too short. I ain't against it, but I'd feel better if I had a chance to meet this guy."

"So would I." Kathleen reached for a tissue from the box on the end table. She blotted her eyes.

Angus rose. "I'm heading home. If you want to go shopping tomorrow, Katydid, we will. Just let me know."

"I wish you'd stay." She stood, too.

"You and your mom need some time alone." Maybe the two women could work out their emotions. "I'd be in the way. C'mere for a kiss."

"I'll walk you to the truck." Kathleen took his right arm. "Mom, I'll be right back."

"Take all the time you want." Marisol's tone was dry as autumn leaves.

At his pickup, Angus pulled Kathleen into his arms. "Honey, I know it's a lot, but we'll figure it all out. If you need to talk, call me. I don't care how late or early."

She nodded. "Okay. Angus, this changes everything about how I thought my life would be."

"Not with us." He believed it. "Kiss me."

Kathleen lifted her face and put her mouth against his. The kiss was sweet and long. Afterward, he cradled her close in his arms until he finally left with his spirits troubled and mind racing with the unexpected development.

He really didn't think Marisol's news would change

anything, but he was wrong.
    It did.

CHAPTER SIX

Long after midnight, in the small hours of the morning, Kathleen called. She roused Angus from a sound sleep, and until he became aware, his wrist hadn't hurt. He'd slept in his bed, and when he sat to answer the phone, pain shot through the joint.

"Did I wake you?" Her voice wasn't much above a whisper.

"Yeah, but it's fine. Are you okay?" Angus swung his legs over the side of the bed and turned on the lamp.

"No." Kathleen's voice broke with a sob. "I'm a mess. I shouldn't be, and I feel silly, but I can't help it."

"Aw, honey, it's a big change, and it came out of the blue." Angus remembered his childhood home just outside Weatherford, Texas. He seldom thought about the small two-story house or his parents. When he first came to live with his grandfather, it hurt so much that he taught himself not to recall. "The place where you grow up is always special."

Unbidden, an image of his mama's kitchen flashed through his mind. Angus saw the shelf above the sink where Mama grew herbs in small pots. He inhaled the remembered scent of baking bread or the spicy smell of chili simmering on the stove. *She made pancakes on that last morning.* The taste of the butter and maple syrup teased his tongue as he recalled. Angus pushed the memory aware and focused on the present.

"It's not only Mom's selling the house," Kathleen told him. She listed the recent events in a rush. "It's everything. I feel overwhelmed, Angus. I graduated and came back. It's a transition after four years of living on campus in Tyler. Bart got hurt, and then he died. Mindy and the boys moved away. Mindy's not just my sister-in-law but a good friend. Now, we won't meet up or eat out, or laugh over silly stuff. I can't take my nephews to see a movie or buy them ice cream. I start my first teaching job next week. We're in a relationship, Angus. I'm moving into my own apartment, and my mom's selling her house. And she's getting married to a man I've never met. I never even heard her talk about him until now."

Her anguish touched him. Angus wished he could somehow make it all easier to handle, but he couldn't. When she sobbed, he thought his heart would break. Most of what she listed affected him, too. "Do you want me to come get you? I can."

"I don't know. Maybe." She paused and blew her nose. "You shouldn't be driving with your wrist. Can I come over? I can be there in ten minutes."

"Sure. Are you calm enough to get behind the wheel?" Angus reached for the jeans he had discarded earlier.

"I think so. Besides, there won't be any traffic. I'll see you in a few."

As soon as she hung up, he dressed. He wished he had time for a shower and to shave, but he didn't. Kathleen needed him. Although it wasn't quite three o'clock, he put on a pot of coffee. She might not want any, but he needed the boost. Angus filled his mug and set it down on the counter as the back door flew open.

"Angus, I'm here." Kathleen didn't bother to knock. "Hold me."

He spread his arms wide and gathered her to his chest. She burrowed her head against his shoulder and cried. Angus stroked her hair and rubbed her back with his right hand. He murmured words of comfort until she quieted. "Do you want some coffee?"

"It's too early. Maybe in a bit." Kathleen kissed his cheek.

Angus delighted in her touch. "Kitchen table or front room?"

"Couch so I can curl up." She exited the kitchen and took one end of the sofa.

Angus sat at the other. "Talk to me, sugar."

Kathleen sighed. "I hardly know where to start now I'm here. I feel like someone jerked the rug from beneath my feet. The life I thought I had has collapsed like a house of cards. Angus, it's like I'm drowning, and there's no one to pull me to safety."

He knew the feeling. When his parents died, he experienced the same, although he was only twelve. "I'm here, Kathleen. I won't let you go under." He sipped his coffee. Caffeine rushed through his veins, and he wasn't sleepy at all. "And you've got God. He won't fail you."

"I want to believe that, but right now, I've got more faith in you. How can I handle all this?"

In this moment, he recalled how young she was. Kathleen had little experience dealing with the often harsh blows life could deliver. "You have to take it one day at a time," he told her. "You'll get settled in your new place, and before long, it will seem like home. Once you get it fixed up with your new furniture and stuff, it'll be cozy. It won't be like this shack, just a place to hang my hat."

"Angus!" Kathleen said. "I love your house."

He laughed. "It's not much. Most of Granny's touch is long gone. I barely remember her. She was gone before Granpa brought me here. It's a man's house, nothing more or less. No pretty curtains, green plants, potpourri, or any comforts of home. I'm used to it, though."

"You could have any of those things. It's spartan, sure, but you have a history here. I'm losing mine." Kathleen shifted position.

"No one can ever take your memories, Katydid. I thought I'd nearabout forgotten my parents' house, but talking to you earlier, I realize I haven't. My mama grew herbs on the kitchen windowsill. She had an old quilt tossed over the couch with bright colors. I think her favorites were green, rose, and yellow. I didn't forget, even after all this time, and you won't either."

"I'll miss Mom." Kathleen rubbed her forehead. "Same for Mindy, Austin, and Travis."

Angus drained his cup and set the mug aside. "It's not much more than an hour up to Gladewater and not quite two to Caddo Lake. You can visit Marisol anytime, and I bet she'll be back to see you. Drive up every weekend if it makes you feel better. I'll play chauffeur if you want. In a way, they're my family, too. I don't really have anyone else except a few cousins."

"What about your Aunt Polly?"

"She's nearly ninety years old with Alzheimer's. I go see her a few times a year, but she doesn't know who I am. Makes me sad, but it's the way it is."

Kathleen uncurled and moved beside him. "I'm sorry, Angus. I know you miss Bart, too."

Grief tightened his chest. "I do. I think of something and get ready to call him, then I remember."

She rested her hand against his back. "I can't hardly think about him at all, or I start feeling sick. I get a tummyache or something. I have a headache right now."

He wished he could offer sage advice. If he could say something to ease her aching heart, he would. Angus fell silent, but he put his good arm around Kathleen. "I reckon your head hurts because you haven't slept. Why don't you stretch out here and rest? Later, if you want, we can still go buy your comforter and stuff."

Angus thought it best if she focused on the future, not the past.

"Maybe." She yawned.

"Come lay your head." He patted his knees, and she stretched out on the couch. "We'll talk more later, I promise."

Kathleen shut her eyes. "All right. Thank you."

"No problem." He stroked her hair with his right hand.

She had almost gone to sleep when she whispered words he'd longed to hear. "I love you, Angus."

His hand stilled as his heart soared. "Honey, I love you too." Angus didn't think she heard him. Her breathing changed into the light rhythm of sleep.

They hadn't dealt with all of her issues or even begun to work through them. Angus wanted to meet Dr. Tony Mackin as much as Kathleen. He couldn't judge the man until he did or have a chance to grasp his worth. If Marisol chose him, he couldn't be bad, or so he hoped. Angus spoke to Kathleen in low whispers, words he knew she wouldn't hear but somehow hoped would bring comfort to her subconscious.

"It'll all come out in the wash." He repeated the phrase his grandfather had often used to assure a young Angus things would be all right. "You'll adjust, and I know you'll be an amazing teacher. We'll manage together, and when the time's right, I'll ask you to become my wife."

Now was too soon, and he knew it. Angus didn't want a ricochet romance or the kind of relationship born out of a knee-jerk reaction. Their love had to be for the long haul. He didn't want to wait a year or more, but he would if he must. His mind brimmed with thoughts, and his heart overflowed with emotion. Despite the coffee, Angus dozed, too. He woke after six and found Kathleen still in place. His knees were stiff, and he needed to move but hated to rouse her. He endured for another half hour before she shifted.

"Good morning, Katydid."

She lifted her head and squinted at him. "My goodness, Angus. Good morning. What time is it?"

"Almost seven." Angus winced as he moved. Pins and needles shot through the limbs he hadn't moved for hours. "If you want, let's get around and do your shopping. I'll buy breakfast on the way."

Kathleen ran her hands through her tousled hair. "Sure. I brought some clean clothes. Do you mind if I take a shower first?"

"Go ahead, then I will." He scratched his chin. Bristles were rough against his hand. "I'll do the same, and we'll hit the road."

The day began fine, without a hint of what would come. On the way, after breakfast at a local café, they talked on the way to Jacksonville. Once there, he pushed the shopping buggy as Kathleen chose a comforter with bright yellow flowers and gray blossoms on a white background. She selected gray sheets to match along with several pillows, two matching the bedspread. Kathleen found a butter-yellow ceramic lamp and a matching gray. By the time she chose towels for both the bathroom and kitchen, rugs, and some other home décor, they had two heaping full carts.

"I'll still need some kitchen things, pots, pans, silverware, and dishes." She glanced toward the shelves with those items.

His sprained wrist ached. "You can get those another day. Maybe Marisol has some stuff you can use."

Kathleen pursed her lips. "I hadn't thought about that, but she might. I'll ask her. How's your sprain?"

"It hurts, although not as bad as it did." Angus flexed it and winced.

"You should have worn the sling." Kathleen retrieved her billfold from her purse. "Let's checkout. You probably want to go home."

"I want to eat first." His stomach growled. "Take your pick, Mexican or barbecue." He loaded her purchases into the bed and secured them as Kathleen climbed into the seat.

"Mexican. Barbecue's too messy."

He chose a street taco platter with both beans and rice. Kathleen had chicken fajitas, which she shared. After the meal, they returned to Rusk. The fourteen-mile trip seemed long, but Angus was weary. As soon as they unloaded the new things at Kathleen's apartment, he planned to head home for a nap.

Angus sat at her small kitchen table, the only seat until the furniture arrived in a few days. Kathleen put her bags in the bedroom closet for now, then joined him.

"I think it'll be nice once I get everything here." She reached across the table and grasped his right hand. "Do you like it?"

"Sure. It's a good place for you to live this school year."

"What would you think about living here too?" Kathleen squeezed his hand as she spoke.

"What?" He couldn't believe her question. "Living in sin's not my style, honey. I didn't think it was yours, either. Besides, I'm not in town. I'd rather be out at my place where I can see the stars at night and don't have a neighbor next door."

"I wouldn't live in sin, either." Although he'd used the same phrase, it sounded old-fashioned when she did.

"What are you talking about?" Angus was too tired to guess.

Kathleen met his eyes and smiled. "Marry me, Angus. Let's run off and get married before school starts. You can move in here with me. On weekends, we can go out to your place if you wanted."

He shook his head. He must have heard wrong. As the moments passed, her smile vanished when he didn't reply. "Kathleen, if this is a joke, I don't think it's funny."

"I'm not kidding. We should get married. If we get the license, we could tie the knot by the end of the week." She leaned forward.

Angus drew a sharp breath and jerked his hand away. He scrubbed his face with it. *Temptation.* He wanted to marry

Kathleen more than anything, but not like this. He said a silent prayer, asking God to help him find words that wouldn't drive her away for good but might explain. "Kathleen, honey, I want us married. It's the goal but in the long term. If and when we do, I'll be the one asking, and it'll be the right time. This ain't it. You're reacting to everything that's happened. I don't doubt you love me…"

Her cheeks flamed scarlet. "You heard me last night. I didn't think you were listening."

"I'm always listening to you, honey. And I told you the same. I won't marry you this way, though. You're trying to fix everything you think is wrong. If we get hitched like this, it's likely not to last. I couldn't stand it. It would kill me dead."

Her blush faded and left her pale. "But Angus…"

"No buts." Unshed tears ached in his throat, but he schooled his tone to remain firm. "I don't run away. I face the challenges life sends with faith and old-fashioned stubbornness. Will you trust me and wait? In a few months, you'll accept all this stuff. When I do ask, honey, I want an answer for life."

Kathleen laid her head on the table and cried. "All I want is to move past all this junk. I want to be happy."

Angus's heart shattered. Her pain was his. "I am happy when we're together. There's two verses from the Bible that come to mind. The first is there's a time for everything. We'll have our time. I believe it. The other one is love never fails. It doesn't, and it won't leave us behind, Katydid. Can't we just keep on for now and let it all come out in the wash?" The phrase brought him comfort, and he hoped it would ease her anxiety.

She sniffed and lifted her face toward him. "I never have understood that silly old saying, but yes, we can."

His dark mood lightened a little. "Means everything will work out in the end. It'll come out clean. Kathleen, let's go to my house. We can watch a movie or talk or whatever you want."

"I'd like to do that. You need to take care of that wrist. If you want to stop by the store, I'll make supper. If you don't mind, I'll stay the night." She held up a hand in protest. "I'll sleep in your spare bedroom or on the couch. Mama's gone off with her beau to Dallas, and I don't want to be at home alone."

"My house is yours, sugar. Let's hit the road." Angus rose and offered Kathleen his uninjured hand. After a brief hesitation, she accepted it. They walked hand in hand to his truck.

At the supermarket, Kathleen bought more groceries than Angus expected. She bought a beef roast, a big pork loin, ground beef, shredded cheese, baking mix, bacon, eggs, deli-sliced turkey, canned soup, and a dozen other items. Angus paid for it without hesitation. "Seems like a lot of food for one night."

Kathleen wrinkled her nose. "Mama said she'll be gone all week, maybe longer."

"You're more than welcome to bunk with me as long as you want." He answered her unspoken question. "If you're staying a while, better go pack a bag."

At Marisol's, Kathleen filled a suitcase with clothing, a nightgown, and toiletries.

Once home, Angus took some ibuprofen and put on the wrist brace Kathleen insisted on buying. He'd rather wear it than the homemade sling. The device eased some of the discomfort and made movement easier. Neither were very hungry after their large lunch, so Kathleen grilled ham and cheese sandwiches.

"I can open some soup, too, if you want." She plated one each.

Angus shook his head. "I'm good. I'll take a dill pickle spear on the side and maybe a handful of cheese curls."

They ate in the living room, watching one of his all-time favorite Westerns, *Silverado*. They didn't talk much, and when they did, their comments were about the movie. When it ended, although it was early, Kathleen rose, and so did he.

"I'm going to take a shower and go to bed, Angus. Good night." She faced him and rested her left hand on his chest.

"Sleep tight, sugar." Angus kissed her lips slowly and sweetly. He let his mouth stray down to her throat and kissed Kathleen there but didn't nibble.

He sank onto the couch and listened as she climbed the stairs. Angus cocked an ear to hear as she moved about the spare bedroom that had once been his. He followed her footsteps as she entered the bathroom and heard the shower when she turned it on. He resolved not to go upstairs until she'd retired for the night. Angus would clean up then, but for now, he grabbed a cold ginger ale from the fridge and pondered.

Maybe I should have said 'yes' to her proposal. I love her, and I plan to make her my wife someday. He shook his head. As much as he wanted marriage, Angus knew he'd made the right choice. He had to be patient, which was hard. He always joked patience was the virtue he had not yet accomplished. He lay awake far into the night, thinking too hard and too much. *It is what it is.*

For the next four days, Kathleen brightened his house with her presence. She did most of the cooking, although one evening, Angus made a pot of what he called slumgullion. The dish had been of his grandfather's standby recipes and consisted of ground beef, macaroni noodles, onions, tomato sauce, and Cheddar cheese.

"I've always called this goulash," she told Angus as she stirred the pot. "At college, they served something similar in the cafeteria but used the name American Chop Suey. This smells great."

"I hope it tastes good." Angus stood behind her and inhaled. "I think I got a good scald on it."

"What goes with it?" Kathleen asked.

"Crackers from the box. I'm not a fancy cook. I can make this or chili or fry a burger, but not much else. Breakfast once in a while, and I like to grill."

"I'll make cornbread." Kathleen gathered the ingredients, most of which they bought at the market, and stirred up a pan.

Each day, they visited her apartment. Kathleen sorted through Marisol's kitchen items and, with her permission, selected a cast iron skillet, two sauce pans, a rectangular cake dish, and two pie plates. She dug out a few utensils, a slotted spoon, two spatulas, and stainless-steel tongs. In town, Angus bought her a pan set with two sizes of skillets, a Dutch oven, and another sauce pot. He also bought her a pretty set of plastic but durable dinnerware in a bright floral pattern. Kathleen picked out a knife set, three cookie sheets, and inexpensive silverware.

On Friday, the furniture arrived. Angus had asked Yancey Cartwright and Zach Cooper to help arrange it. He didn't want to risk damaging his wrist further. Both men showed up on time and used their muscles until Kathleen approved the placement.

"You ought to have asked Aidan to help," Zach said as he tried out the couch. "He's younger and likely stronger."

Angus hadn't contacted Aidan O'Neill because he didn't care for the man's interest in Kathleen. "We did fine without him. Let's head to my place, and I'll feed you."

He'd promised to grill bratwurst, burgers, and hot dogs. Kathleen had made potato salad, mixed greens, and baked brownies. Angus had a dozen ears of fresh corn, which he also tossed on the grill. After the feast, his buddies headed home.

"I need to buy groceries for my apartment, and then I can move in," Kathleen told Angus as they cleaned up after the barbecue. "I want to be settled before I report to school. I need to decorate my classroom, too."

"If you need help, I can hang posters with the best of them." Angus joked. "I'll miss you, though. It's been nice having you here."

She paused with her hands in dishwater. "I'm glad you

let me stay. I thought I'd get the groceries on Monday and fix my room on Tuesday. All staff has to report on Thursday, and the first day of school will be next Monday."

Angus paused with a dish towel in his right hand. He squared his shoulders and turned away. He didn't relish a return to his lonely life. "I guess I won't see you as often, sugar. You're gonna be busy."

Since Bart's accident and death, he'd spent most days with Kathleen. They talked on the phone on the rare days they had no plans.

"I'll always have time for you, Angus. Sometimes, I wish you'd taken me up on my offer. I understand why you didn't want to right now, but.."

He put a finger across her lips. "Don't. I ain't in a mood to argue. You know how I feel, Katydid. It's not changing. I'll be available whenever you have a free minute. Until my wrist is healed, I won't be going off to rodeo. I'm about ready to quit anyhow. I'm old for it."

Kathleen emptied the sink and wiped it clean. "You're not, Angus. Labor Day's barely a month away. We're going up to Caddo Lake to visit Mom and meet Tony."

"I'm looking forward to it." Angus would pick up Mindy and the boys in Gladewater. Kathleen would be with him, and they would spend Saturday and Sunday nights at the lake. He had already decided to rent a van for the trip. "We can go visit before then, any time."

"Mom or Mindy?"

Angus shrugged. "Either or both. I'm tired. Want to watch a movie?"

"Could we play checkers instead?" Kathleen pulled a board and checkers from one of the cupboards. "I found these the other day."

A grin spread over his face. Grandpa had taught him the

game, and they had often played to pass the time. "Sure, honey."

They spent most of Saturday at her new digs. Angus hung pictures on the wall and helped put up curtains with Kathleen's help. By evening, everything had been put away. Rugs were down, towels hung on the bathroom rods, and the shower curtain was in place. Kathleen placed bowls of potpourri around, and the rose scent filled the rooms. She cooked for the first time at the apartment with supplies she brought from Angus's house.

Thick butterfly pork chops stuffed with cornbread dressing, sliced homegrown tomatoes, and succotash made a fine meal. Angus ate every scrap she put on his plate with gusto. He hoped she would invite him often for a meal, but he preferred the food she served at his kitchen table.

On Sunday, they attended church together, then drove over to Palestine. Angus treated Kathleen to a seafood feast at a local restaurant. They savored shrimp trucked in fresh from the Gulf of Mexico and ate catfish from the nearby rivers or bayous. As they returned home, he stopped at a bakery to buy a cake for Kathleen's last evening. They ate the rich chocolate confection as they watched another movie.

They made a supermarket run Monday morning. Kathleen bought milk, eggs, cheese, and assorted condiments for her fridge. She bought some frozen entrees to stock the small freezer, chose soups and canned goods, and selected salad fixings. Kathleen chose the spices and seasonings she would need, everything from simple salt and pepper to Cajun blends and garlic powder. She stocked up on a few dry mixes.

"This will be enough. I can go to the store anytime," she remarked as they checked out.

Kathleen used her mother's crockpot to fix a roast beef with potatoes, carrots, and gravy. She served it with hot rolls and the rest of the cake Angus purchased. Although the meal tasted delicious, neither spoke much. Her mind focused on the coming week.

"Call me tomorrow." She handed Angus his cowboy hat as he prepared to head home. "I'll be at the school most of the day getting my classroom ready."

"All right. I'm heading over near Marshall to look at a horse." Angus had cleaned up the old horse trailer in the barn. "Come give me sugar."

Kathleen kissed him, her lips light on his mouth. Angus needed more, so he kissed her with slow heat. He lingered for as long as he could. He walked out to his truck and didn't look back.

Summer was almost over, and their time together had ended. A new era would begin this week, and he wasn't sure what to think. So far, their relationship had remained intact, but Angus had concerns about the future.

In his lonely house, he lay awake for hours, arms tucked beneath his head, and wondered.

He prayed his life would work out and include Kathleen. *Please, God, let it be Your will, not just mine. I want to live happily ever after.*

CHAPTER SEVEN

On the first day of school, Angus woke early. He hadn't seen Kathleen for two days, a new record since they became involved. He dressed in one of his best shirts and his good jeans for two reasons. Angus had a job interview at nine-thirty with a regional dairy distributor. Each off season, both he and Bart had often driven a delivery truck to earn extra money. If hired, he would deliver milk products around East Texas on weekdays and have weekends free. After the interview, he planned to surprise Kathleen with flowers at the school.

"Angus, tell me why you want to drive one of our trucks," Marcus Middleton asked. The manager from the company based in Tyler, Texas, leaned across his desk.

Honesty seemed best. "I'm thinking about giving up rodeo. I'm forty, and I'd like to settle down. I'm not broke, but I'd like to keep my life debt-free if I can."

Marcus nodded. "I see you have your CDL, which is good, and some experience with big rigs. I also see on your resume most of your jobs have been during the rodeo off-season. Are you looking for permanent or temporary work?"

Angus hesitated. "I'm not sure. In the long run, I want to train horses, but I could use a steady job right now."

"Your references checked out. You have the license, and we need drivers. First step, you'll need to pass a physical and background check."

"Neither should be a problem." Angus had been through both on numerous occasions.

"If the results are good, we'll hire you. If everything works out, you can start the day after Labor Day." Marcus extended a hand.

He left Tyler with an appointment for a physical in three days and hope for a job. If Angus thought he might get married, he needed some income until he could get his horse business underway.

Uncertain about how to court his lady, he realized maybe he needed to do more than hang out with her. Although he'd dated a few women over the decades, Angus hadn't had a girlfriend for longer than he could remember.

His next stop was a florist, where he chose an arrangement with six red roses and a dozen daisies. Kathleen had mentioned the flowers were a favorite. Buying flowers for a woman was unfamiliar. Angus thought the last time he'd bought someone a posy had been senior prom when he chose a carnation corsage for his date.

Although he inked a message on a card, *Thinking of you on your first day at school. You've got this, babe. Love, Angus,* Angus decided to deliver the posies himself. He pulled up to the elementary building and parked. It wasn't the same school he'd attended, but a newer version. With the flowers clutched between his large hands, Angus approached the entrance. A woman exiting the building held the door, and he stepped into the hallway. Last week, he'd spent a couple of hours helping Kathleen prepare her classroom, so he didn't stop at the office. He headed down the main corridor and took a left toward the first-grade wing.

"Stop!" A man cried as Angus approached Kathleen's room. "Sir, you shouldn't be in the building. You need to return to the office and check-in, or I'm calling the authorities."

Angus halted. "I have something for Miss Birdwell."

"It's not acceptable. We have strict rules in this building."

Angus turned to see who spoke. "I'm Angus Beaton. Who are you?"

"I'm Trevor Weissman, principal." Weismann wore navy slacks, a matching blazer, and a red tie. "You have no right to barge into the school. Is the rodeo in town?"

Angus flushed. With his hands full, he hadn't removed his hat when he entered. "No, sir. Like I said, I'm just..."

"Angus?" Kathleen stuck her head through her classroom door. "What in the world?"

He turned. "I brought you flowers for your first day of teaching."

Kathleen reached for the blossoms. "They're beautiful. Thank you."

"Miss Birdwell." Principal Weissman cleared his throat. "Your attention should be on your students, not this intruder."

"My kiddos are on morning recess with Mrs. Jenkin's class. She has playground duty." Kathleen stepped forward with the flowers in her hands. "Angus isn't an intruder."

Weissman crossed his arms over his chest. "He's uninvited. He failed to sign in at the office. If he doesn't leave immediately, I'm calling the local police department. If I do, I will press trespassing charges."

Angus spread his hands wide. "I'm going."

"Wait!" Kathleen cried and advanced into the hallway. "This is ridiculous."

"Do you know this man at all, or is he a stalker?"

Angus tensed his shoulders and wondered what Kathleen would say. Would she call him her late brother's best friend? A lifelong family connection? A neighbor?

"He's my guy." She lifted her head with such speed her hair clip shook. "I wish you would call the sheriff, Mr. Weissman. Sheriff Will Garrison is my cousin and Angus' lifelong friend."

Trevor twisted his lips. He pulled a cell phone from his pocket and dialed.

Children entered the far end of the corridor. Their chatter

echoed, and Angus, despite the situation, grinned.

"I'll call you later, sugar, unless I'm locked up in jail." He laughed as he stepped out of the way of the kids.

"You won't be. Come over for supper." Kathleen straightened her posture and took charge. "Okay, children, make a restroom break and get a drink. Then we have reading."

Angus trailed the principal back to the office, but he didn't have to wait long. A county cruiser parked in front of the main entrance, and the sheriff stepped out. He stood tall in his starched uniform and wore mirrored sunglasses. Will Garrison didn't crack a smile as he sauntered into the office.

"Howdy, Angus. What in the world is going on?" he asked.

"Beats me." Angus shrugged. "I came by to bring Kathleen some flowers, and the principal got worked up because I didn't ink my name on a sheet in the office."

"Visitors must sign in when they arrive." Weissman stood behind a counter. "I have to be aware of who's in my building at all times. And when I don't know someone, it can pose a risk for the students and staff."

Will removed his shades. "Angus, are you a risk to anyone?"

"Not that I'm aware, no."

"Were you aware of this signing-in rule?" Will leaned one lean hip against the counter.

"No, sir. I haven't been inside a school since I graduated a long time ago."

The sheriff laughed. "Not so long, two years before I did. Mr. Weissman, I can personally vouch for this man. I've known him since he was twelve or so. I'm not acquainted with you at all, but I understand it's your first year in Rusk. Because of that, I'll let this go, but in the future, don't waste my time with nonsense. Angus, if you return, you'll stop and sign, right?"

"Sure. I'll likely see you in church on Sunday." Angus donned his hat and walked out with the sheriff. He thought he heard the principal mutter something about 'good old boys' but decided he wouldn't make an issue over the remark.

At five, Angus showed up at Kathleen's apartment. She opened the door before he knocked and threw her arms around him. "I'm glad you're here. I've missed you."

"It's been two days, honey." He planted a kiss on her lips. Behind her, he saw the daisies and roses on the counter, dividing the kitchen from the living room. "Did you like the flowers?"

"I do. Thank you, Angus. I'm sorry Mr. Weissman hassled you. He had no reason."

"I didn't know, but it's okay. I hear he's new to town."

"And to Texas. He's from California." Kathleen rolled her eyes. "Come sit down. Supper's almost ready."

Angus sank onto the couch. "Good. I'm hungry." The aroma of bacon filled his nose. "What are we having?"

"Breakfast for supper, bacon, pancakes, and eggs if you want."

Over the simple meal, Angus asked about her first day as a teacher. Kathleen shared stories about the kids.

"I like it even more than I imagined," she told him. "It keeps me hustling, though. If they're not whining, they're fighting, but they're so bright."

"I'm glad." Angus thought someday she'd make a good mother, hopefully to his children.

"What did you do today?" Kathleen passed him the platter of bacon after snagging a slice.

"Got a job." He grabbed three pieces and tossed them onto his plate. "Or I do as soon as the background check clears and I pass a physical. I'll be delivering milk to stores and restaurants around East Texas."

He delivered the news and waited. Kathleen's crush had

been on a bronc rider, not a delivery driver. Angus wondered if it would make a difference. If it did, then he would wonder if she loved him or if her feelings were mere infatuation.

"I thought you were going to work with horses!" She put down her fork and stared.

Angus nodded. "I am, down the road a little. Since I'm not competing, I figured I'd make some money first. Bart and I used to drive trucks once in a while for the same reason."

"I remember. Once or twice, he let me ride along." Kathleen offered a faint smile.

"I'll do the same if it doesn't get me fired." Angus studied her face. "What's the matter, Katydid? Was it a harder day than you told me, or are you upset?"

She spread her hands wide. "Busted. My day was fine, although I didn't like the way the principal treated you. I didn't know you wanted a job, that's all. I hate to think of you being out of town all the time."

He took her left hand. "It's just Monday through Friday. I'll drive a different route each day, but each one is a hundred miles out from Tyler or less. I won't be more than a couple hours away. If you needed me, I'd come on the run. I'll leave out at dark thirty each morning, but I'll be home by four."

Her frown eased. "You'll be home every night?"

"Sure. I wouldn't take a job where I wasn't. I'm done roaming and roving. I did too much of that with rodeo. Don't be mad. If you are, I'll quit now and go to work at the discount store or something." Angus half-joked, but if driving a truck caused a problem, he would give up the job before he quit on Kathleen. So far, she seemed dependent on his presence but not dismayed at his new career.

"Don't." Kathleen. "I had the idea you would be on the road most of the time, and I'd never see you."

"You'll see me so much you'll get sick of my ugly face."

Angus finished his meal. "From what they said, I won't start until the day after Labor Day. The first week, I'll ride along with another driver. After that, I'll be on my own. I report for my physical at a clinic up in Tyler on Friday, but I'm free after that for the next couple weeks."

"I can live with that." She released a slow breath. "Angus, you're not ugly. I wish you wouldn't say so all the time."

Flattered, he laughed. "I sure ain't pretty, and I'm aware of the fact. Grandpa taught me to call things the way I see them, sugar."

Kathleen swatted his arm. "Sometimes, I'd like to shake you until your teeth rattle. I won't fight with you, but I think you're good-looking. Your face has character, Angus, like an old West cowboy."

"If you say so, Katydid. Thanks for supper. I figured I'd slap together a sandwich at home." He had an unopened pack of bologna in the fridge, some cheese, and bread if it wasn't moldy. "This was a lot tastier."

"You can park your boots under my table anytime. If you come back tomorrow, we'll have smoked sausage dogs with fried potatoes." She cleared the table.

"Count me in. On Friday night, though, I'll buy you a catfish dinner and we'll go see a movie."

Kathleen brushed a hand across his shoulders. "It's a date."

Angus spent the rest of the week working around his place. He cleaned up the corral, fixed fences, and swept out the barn. Once he began his new job, he wouldn't have time for chores. He also cleaned the house, caught up his laundry, and headed for the supermarket. Although he might eat a few meals at Kathleen's, Angus wouldn't every night. He bought canned ravioli, a few frozen dinners, some soups, lunch meat, cheese, and a giant package of hot dogs. After consideration, he bought some frozen burgers, a family pack of hamburger, milk, and cereal. He used the hamburger to make a big pot of chili and another of goulash. Angus froze portions in small containers so some nights, he could heat up a tasty meal without much effort. Since he might brown bag on the job to save money, he also bought a huge jar of peanut butter, an assortment of chips, and a case of canned ginger ale. He preferred the lighter taste to the darker colas.

On Friday, he headed into Jacksonville for his physical. He passed, although when he proved his medical history, the nurse raised her eyebrows at the number of hospitalizations Angus listed.

"Are you accident prone?" Her name tag read "Nancy".

"Nah, I did rodeo for about twenty-five years. The sport does have risks." Angus gulped when he realized he'd busted broncs for two years longer than Kathleen had existed. Little details often brought the age difference home when he least expected it.

"Understandable." Nancy grinned. "You passed the exam. I'll get the information entered in the system, and you're good to go on the physical."

Angus nodded. Once back in Rusk, he didn't stop at the school. Instead, he dozed in his recliner, then showered and dressed for his date.

They enjoyed crisp catfish, brown beans, fries, and hushpuppies at a café in Palestine, then headed for the multi-plex movie theater. As they waited in line to buy popcorn, a blonde woman approached. She carried a little girl in her arms.

"Angus Beaton? I haven't seen you in so long. I was so sorry to hear about Bart."

He tried to place her face but failed. "Thanks." He struggled to say something more and to remember why she seemed familiar. "Do you still live in Rusk?"

"Lord, no. I've been in Palestine since I got married. I

married Trevor the summer after our high school graduation. I'm Debbie, used to be Donavan, now Porter. This munchkin is Tabitha."

Trevor Porter. Angus recalled the star of the high school basketball team. The forward had dated Debbie, but so had Angus. "You look good, Deb. Your daughter looks like you."

Debbie tossed her permed curls and laughed. "Angus, this is my grandbaby. I had Tiffany young, and she got married even younger. Tabby's almost two years old, and I have a grandson too."

A shiver went from the top of Angus's head to the soles of his boots. Grandmothers were supposed to be old with gray hair. They didn't wear fashionable jeans or have curls cascading to their shoulders. "Congratulations, Debbie."

She nodded. "How old are your kids, Angus? I bet you have a houseful."

Kathleen held his left hand and squeezed.

"Not a one." He tried to sound cheerful, but the encounter rattled him. Angus wished the colorful carpet of the theater lobby would swallow him up like quicksand. "Great to see you. We gotta go. I don't want to miss our movie."

"Sure. See you around." Debbie headed for one of the theaters showing an animated film.

Angus didn't move until Kathleen prodded him. "Let's get our snacks, Angus."

He acted on autopilot and purchased the biggest tub of buttered popcorn. His mind reeled with the reality—one of his classmates was a grandparent. Debbie couldn't be any older than Angus. All of a sudden, Angus felt like he should have a cane and a hearing aid. He wondered if any of his dark brown hair might be showing some gray. Lost in thought, he paid little attention to the movie and couldn't follow the plot. He draped an arm across Kathleen's shoulders and mindlessly ate popcorn with his free hand. Normally, he ate little during a movie, but he ate more than half the bucket before he quit.

The snack seldom agreed with his stomach, and before the movie ended, his belly cramped. Angus pressed his abdomen and leaned forward, willing the ache to quit. When it didn't, he groaned. "Ohhh."

"What's wrong?" Kathleen turned to him as the credits rolled.

"Ate too much popcorn." He hated to admit it. "It'll pass."

Between a tall, cold soda and a couple of antacids from a roll Kathleen pulled from her purse, Angus felt better by the time they got back to Rusk.

"It's early. Come up for a while." Kathleen tugged his sleeve. "We can talk."

"All right, sugar."

She kicked off her shoes and settled onto the couch. "What's upsetting you, Angus? You've hardly said a word since your old classmate talked to you."

Angus sighed. "A girl I graduated with, one I dated a few times way back when, is a grandmother. Makes me feel ancient. Katydid, I'm an old man…"

"Not hardly." Her eyes burned as she interrupted him. "You wouldn't stew about it if I wasn't younger. Age doesn't matter."

He ached to believe it. "I'd like to think it doesn't."

"Believe it."

"I'm trying." Lord knew he was, with everything he could muster.

"Don't try. Do it." Kathleen's voice harshened.

"All right."

They spent a few more hours together, watching vintage shows, which Kathleen liked. Angus headed for home at midnight with a promise they would head over to Toledo Bend

State Park. He'd checked out his grandpa's ancient canoe and figured it would still float. After an afternoon on the water, they returned and sat on his back porch past dark.

On Sunday, Angus picked Kathleen up for church. He savored sitting with her five pews from the front. On the circuit, he hadn't always had time to attend services. Angus enjoyed the music and the message. So far, he hadn't attended adult Sunday School, but he noticed Kathleen didn't either. Each time he showed up, more people from his past greeted him. He made some new friends, too.

Although Kathleen had a beef roast in the crockpot, after church, Angus drove out to Marisol's house. Although the 'for sale' sign remained, another attached to the original proclaimed the place to be sold.

"I wonder who bought it." Kathleen craned her head to stare at the empty house as if she could find answers.

Angus shrugged. "No idea, but our mom knows. Didn't she say it was a couple from Fort Worth? Won't she have to be here for the closing?"

"I have no idea. I've never sold property."

"Neither have I. You might give her a call." Angus had called Marisol twice, but he knew Kathleen called her at least two times each week. "We'll see her next weekend."

Kathleen exhaled a long sigh. "I know. I'm looking forward to it. I can't wait to see Mindy and the boys. She's having a rough time."

Angus twisted his lips together. "Have you talked to her? The one time I called, her daddy said she wasn't taking calls."

"He told me the same, although I did get through to her last week. I could tell she'd been crying. I think she wishes she hadn't moved. Austin and Travis are not happy with their new schools." Kathleen scooted closer to Angus. "I wish...oh, it doesn't matter."

"It does." Angus resolved he would do what he could to help his buddy's widow and children. "We'll figure something out after we talk to them, okay?"

Kathleen rested her head against Angus's right shoulder. "Sure. Let's go to my apartment and eat."

Although he'd always preferred roast beef in the oven, Angus found Kathleen's crockpot version delicious. They lingered over the meal. He savored the rich gravy served over homemade mashed potatoes. "These taters are good."

"They're lumpy, though." Kathleen stirred her portion.

"I don't mind. Proves they're real, not instant. Thanks for a fine meal, honey." Angus blotted his mouth with a paper napkin.

"*De nada.* I'm glad you enjoyed it. There's enough left for sandwiches this evening if you want. Do you have time to stay a while?"

He wouldn't mind kicking back in his recliner for a nap, but he could do without to spend more time with Kathleen. "I do, as long as I don't wear out my welcome."

She cleared the table and stacked everything into the built-in dishwasher. Kathleen walked the few steps into the living room, and he followed. "That won't happen. I like being with you, Angus. Since Bart passed, I've spent the most time ever in your company, and I'm not complaining."

"I noticed, but why?" Angus didn't want to be a substitute for her family. Besides, she'd been away for most of four years at college. He folded his long legs and perched on the edge of the couch.

"I don't understand what you're asking." A frown tightened her lips. Kathleen curled into the armchair.

"Honey, don't get me wrong. I'd rather spend time with you than not." He chose his words with care so he didn't upset or offend. "I guess I'm asking if you like hanging out with me because it's me or because you're lonesome."

Tears filled her eyes. "I love *you*, Angus. I'm not looking for someone to fill empty space. It's you, and it's been you for a long time."

"Don't cry, Katydid." He ached to believe her sweet words. If they proved to be true in the long run, he would marry her. Angus hadn't meant to hurt her feelings, though. "Honey, I love you. I'll be honest. I've lived lonely for a long time. I watched you sashay across the hotel lobby in Fort Worth and didn't recognize you, but I thought you were the prettiest thing. At the hospital, we got close, and I was smitten. By the time Marisol had me over for dinner, I realized I love you. I ain't much of a prize, and I'm too danged old for you, but it's the truth. I'm here, and unless you run me off with a stick, I ain't going anywhere."

Kathleen gazed at him. "Do you mean that?"

"Every word." If the day came, she changed her mind or realized she didn't want an elderly man as a husband, it would break his heart. Angus could wait. If he saw her love was true and wasn't a passing fancy, there would be time for marriage. "Come here, sugar."

She flew from the chair into his open arms. "Oh, Angus."

Angus pulled her into his lap. He inhaled the sweet fragrance she wore and cradled her close. For him, having found the woman who fit him like a handmade boot, he needed her the way his body required food and water. He sought her like a flower lifts upward to the sun. He had no more words, so he kissed her, his mouth slow and steady against her lips.

He spent the afternoon holding Kathleen. They didn't speak much, but they were in harmony. Although Angus hated to leave, he went home around nine.

"Stay a little longer," Kathleen whispered. They stood near her door.

"I best not. You've got school tomorrow, teacher. I'll be up around dawn, and I have to start working on getting up even earlier. Call me after you're home, sugar."

"Come over for supper." Her hands rested on his chest.

"I'll do better than that. I'll fix something, and you can come out to the house." Angus kissed her one last time. "Good night, Kathleen."

She wrapped her arms around him, then let go.

He walked out into the hot summer night. Somewhere not too far away, honeysuckle bloomed, and he enjoyed the scent.

Tomorrow, he would see her. It signaled a new level in their relationship, one he hoped would last forever.

If he could shed his lingering doubts, he would be a happy man.

CHAPTER EIGHT

After some thought, Angus rented a van for the trip to Caddo Lake. His single-cab pickup wouldn't fit Kathleen, Mindy, and two boys. He didn't want Austin to make the trip riding Mindy's lap. Angus planned with care but packed light. He figured he wouldn't need more than a clean pair of jeans, a pair of khaki slacks for Sunday, several shirts, socks, and underwear. He tossed the clothes into a backpack with his shaving gear and toothbrush.

Once school was dismissed on Friday, Angus rode with Kathleen to Jacksonville and picked up the van. After he drove it around, acclimating to the feel of the vehicle. They chose a buffet restaurant for supper. Angus enjoyed the variety offered, but Kathleen was a far better cook. He ignored the salad bar to choose fried chicken, pot roast, meatloaf, and a piece of fried fish. Kathleen had several salads, followed with fish.

"Do you want dessert?" She leaned back after she finished her plate and patted her tummy. "I'm stuffed."

"I want a bite of carrot cake, then I'm done." Angus stacked his empty dishes and fetched his cake. "We'll head home afterward so we can get an early start."

Kathleen laughed. "It's just over an hour to Gladewater and another hour, hour and a half to Uncertain."

"I still like to leave early. There's no way to know if we'll run into weather or traffic or if Mindy will be ready to roll when we get there." Angus savored a bite of cake. "I think there's a chance for rain."

"Showers and storms. I've got an umbrella packed. I can throw in an extra for you if you want."

"I'm good. I've been wet plenty of times and always dry.

I'm just glad I won't be competing. I always hated a muddy arena worse than dust in my face." Although his wrist had healed, Angus had no urge to rodeo. He doubted he would ride again. "Let's go."

Angus rose at six, and by seven, he arrived at Kathleen's apartment. He trudged up the exterior stairs so he could carry her luggage. "Good morning, Katydid."

She lifted her face for a kiss. "Come in, Angus. I've got coffee made if you want a cup for the road."

"I ain't gonna say no." He held up his travel mug. "I'll fill this up. How many bags?"

"Two suitcases, my toiletry bag, and a canvas tote I'll keep with me." She pointed to her luggage.

"Good thing I rented a van." Angus grinned. "Are you sure you brought enough?"

Kathleen wrinkled her nose. "I'd rather have too many than need something I don't have."

Angus shook his head as he poured coffee. "What's in the tote?"

"I bought some mints and candy, wipes, towels, a couple books for the boys if they get bored, a few over-the-counter meds, and a couple bottles of iced tea. If you want, I can dig out a cooler, and we can stop for more drinks." She topped up her own mug, turned off the coffeepot, and shouldered her purse.

"I think we'll be fine. We can stop if anybody needs something. Have you had breakfast?"

She shook her head. "No, did you?"

"Nah. I thought we'd stop at a little café I know in Henderson." Angus lifted her bags. "Lock up, and we'll hit the road."

The simple restaurant offered a full breakfast menu. Angus pulled out a chair for Kathleen and sat across from her. "Coffee's good here. They serve biscuits as big as my fist."

She perused the menu. "I think I'll get pancakes. They always taste better in a restaurant than at home."

"I'm having the number two platter with scrambled eggs, bacon, hashbrowns, and a biscuit on the side with gravy. You can help me eat it." Angus turned up his cup for coffee and gave the server their order.

"I'll try. I wouldn't mind a piece of bacon. How do you know all these places to eat? Everywhere we go, you're familiar with a café."

Angus laughed. "I traveled the circuit for more than twenty years. Cowboys get hungry, honey, and it'd be weird if I didn't know the best places for some grub. You look awfully pretty today."

Kathleen glanced at her outfit. She wore forest-green jeans, a soft gray T-shirt, and a light-blue cardigan sweater. "Mama likes it if I dress nicely, so I did. I wore my boots, though."

"I noticed." Angus admired the brown Western footwear. "I seldom wear anything but boots." Athletic shoes hurt his feet, and dress styles were uncomfortable. When their food arrived, he talked her into eating two slices of bacon, a spoon or two of hashbrowns, and half the biscuit.

"Angus, I shouldn't eat all your food," she protested.

"You're not. I can't finish it without help."

Before they left the café, it began raining. The sprinkles soon became a downpour, so the remainder of the trip into Gladewater took longer. Although he'd never been there, Angus had the address for Mindy's parents' home and found it without difficulty. The narrow street was part of a neighborhood sandwiched between the highways and business loop. On one end, newer homes sprouted like new garden growth, but after a few blocks, the houses were older, dating to the 1940s and 1950s. Trees lined the street, and Angus peered through the downpour to read house numbers. "I think this is it," he said as he pulled into a dirt driveway near a bungalow-style home.

"There's Mindy." Kathleen pointed at the porch.

Mindy stood with her sons at her side and waved. Her long hair had been snipped short, and her jeans sagged on her hips. She bent and spoke to the taller of the boys. Travis dashed through the rain to the van. Angus stepped out into the downpour and opened the door. "Get in before you drown," he told the kid. "You should've waited."

"I have an umbrella." Kathleen turned toward Travis. "Let me hand you a towel."

"Hi, Aunt Kathleen. Mom said to come on to the van. She'll get her own umbrella. Here comes Austin." Travis giggled as his younger brother jogged through the rain and stopped to splash in a puddle.

Angus, already soaked, grabbed Austin and delivered him to the van's middle seat. "Kid, you should've waited for me. Kathleen, hand him a towel, would you?"

Mindy appeared, laboring with the huge suitcase, balancing a floral print umbrella over her head. "Where do you want our bag?"

"I'll tuck it in back." Angus took the bag. "Get in. If you're wet, Kathleen's got towels."

"I'm okay." Mindy crawled into the seat and settled between the boys. "Thanks for picking us up, Angus. I don't imagine we'd be going anywhere if you hadn't."

"No problem." Angus eyed Bart's widow through the rearview mirror. "I'm glad to make the trip."

He shivered as the air conditioning blasted him with chilled air. "Got any more towels, honey?"

Kathleen handed him one. "You're soaked to the skin. You ought to stop and change into dry clothes."

Angus snickered. "I'd get soaked trying. See if you can change it over to heat for a few minutes. I'm hoping we drive out of this rain before we get to Caddo Lake."

"I hope you don't get sick." Kathleen met his eyes. "Angus, at least switch shirts."

"I'll dry, and I doubt I'll get sick. I hardly ever do." When he did, he became very ill, but he didn't think it was the right moment to mention the possibility.

She rubbed her right forefinger against her left. "Shame on you if you do, but I'll take care of you."

A warmth filled his chest. "Would you?"

Kathleen rolled her eyes. "You know I would."

From the second seat, Mindy interrupted the private moment. "Did you buy a van? I wouldn't have thought you'd give up your old pickup."

"Nah, I rented it for the trip." Angus sneezed. "How's life?"

Mindy made a face. "It sucks. I don't like being a widow, the kids hate their new school, and I think my parents are praying we move. Their house isn't very big, and we're crammed." She paused and sighed. "I'm sorry. I don't mean to be a downer."

"I asked." Angus hated knowing Mindy was miserable. "Hopefully, things will improve."

She shrugged. "Someday."

Angus exchanged a glance with Kathleen. The rain slackened as they came into Longview. "Do you boys want to stop? Maybe get something to eat."

"Sure," Travis cried. "I'm hungry. We didn't have breakfast."

"I want a hot dog!" Austin bounced on the seat.

Mindy frowned. "You can both wait until we get to your grandmother's. You know I don't have extra money to buy hot dogs and stuff."

"I'll pay." Angus turned around for a second. "We'll stop at the first convenience store we spot, so keep an eye out." He pulled into the parking lot and started to exit, but Kathleen put a hand on his arm.

"I'll take the boys. I need a pit stop, anyway." She swiveled her gaze toward Mindy.

"I could use one. I'll go after you get back." Angus pulled out his billfold and handed her several twenty-dollar bills. "Buy whatever they want."

Her slender fingers grasped the money. "Sure." Kathleen nodded. "C'mon, kids."

With Angus and Mindy in the van, silence reigned. He had a dozen questions he wanted to ask but didn't. He thought if they were alone, maybe she would talk or share concerns she didn't want to air in front of the kids.

"Why aren't you competing this weekend?" Mindy asked. "There must be a dozen or more rodeos within driving distance over Labor Day."

Angus shifted in the seat so they could talk. "I've quit. Bunged up my wrist last time I rode, and besides, I'm getting old. I start a job delivering milk on Tuesday."

Her eyebrows lifted to her hairline. "You gave up rodeo? I never thought you would. I figured you'd be busting broncs until…"

"I died?" Angus frowned. "I'd rather not. I got a lot of living to do yet, and I intend to get it done."

Mindy's expression turned ugly. "Bart didn't."

"I'm sorry he didn't. It's one of the many danged reasons I'm done with rodeo." Angus huffed air between his lips and ran a hand over his hair.

"So, you're driving a milk truck?" Mindy spit the question as if it had a bad taste.

"For now, yeah. I plan to train horses, maybe be a farrier too." Angus had the blacksmith equipment. It had belonged to his grandfather. If he got up to speed with the skill, he figured he could make a fair amount shoeing horses. He might also be able to fashion some iron implements or create knives. "I don't plan to sit on my bottom and stare at the four walls, Mindy."

Her eyes narrowed. "I never said I thought you would, Angus. You make me so mad."

Shock rippled through him. "Why? I ain't done anything."

"You're alive, and Bart's not." Mindy raised her volume. "I've sat late at night and asked God why it couldn't have been you who died, not my husband. He had everything to live for, and you have nothing, no wife, no family, not even a dog. I wanted to hate you, even though I love you like a brother. So did Bart, so I can't. I don't wish you dead, Angus, but I don't understand, and I never will." Her voice cracked, and she sobbed.

"Aw, Mindy." His heart ached for her. "It was Bart's time. I don't know why. There's a time for everything…"

"Don't quote the Bible at me, Angus Beaton. I've tried to find comfort, but I can't." She wept, so Angus reached a hand to offer support. Mindy slapped his cheek and shoved his hand away. "I don't know what I'm going to do. I get stomachaches every day, no matter what I eat. I'm almost broke. I can't move out from my parents if I tried."

"What about Bart's life insurance?" Angus recalled they had both taken out policies years ago.

A harsh laugh ripped from her lips. "It paid enough for his funeral and didn't leave anything more. And even though I sold the house, we didn't have all that much equity in it, so I only got a few thousand dollars."

Angus's mouth drooped with shock. "I don't have much, but I'll help you and the boys if I can."

"I won't take your money, Angus. I'm sorry, I'm crying. I hold everything inside, and I was about to break open. I probably shouldn't have come, but the kids should spend time with Marisol. I needed to get away, too."

"You're still raw. We all are, but you can't lose hope. You'll find a job and get some security. God will provide, Mindy." Angus believed it and wanted her to accept the same truth. "Kathleen will be back with the boys any minute now. Maybe you can quit crying for Austin and Travis. They ought not to see you this way."

Mindy sniffed and wiped her eyes with the back of one hand. "It's too late. Are there any tissues in this van?"

He handed her a fistful from Kathleen's tote. "I'm going into the store so you can have a few minutes. Mindy, if there's anything I can do to help, just ask."

She nodded. "That's the problem, though. There isn't. Angus?"

His fingers paused as he unhooked the seat belt. "What?"

"Are you and Kathleen…" She groped for the right words.

"Yeah, we're together." Angus waited for any backlash.

Mindy gave a tiny laugh. "I could tell. It was the way she looks at you, and you look right back. I'm glad. Bart wanted you to find someone. He never quit trying to match you up with a gal. I guess he never thought about Kathleen, though."

"I reckon he might punch me in the nose, dating his baby sister." Angus often wondered.

"I doubt that. I think he'd give you his blessing." Mindy dried her eyes and took deep breaths. "Will you bring me a lemonade or something?"

"Sure. I won't be long." Angus exited the van with speed. He found dealing with emotional outbursts awkward. He entered the store and searched for Kathleen. She sat at a small table near the back with the two boys, so he joined them. Austin and Travis were eating chicken tenders.

"Breakfast?" Angus asked.

Kathleen nodded. "I thought this would be better than hot dogs. Where's Mindy?"

"She's in the van." Angus glanced at the boys. "If you're finished, go wash your hands." Once they headed to the restrooms within sight, he continued. "She had a meltdown. Maybe you could go see about her while I buy the kids a donut or something."

"Is she okay?" Kathleen frowned.

Angus shrugged. "Yeah, just upset. I'm not so good with crying. I'll be out soon as I use the bathroom myself and see if the kids want something else."

Ten minutes later, he paid for some cookies and two bottles of chocolate milk. He also picked up the lemonade Mindy requested.

"Are you our uncle?" Travis asked as they walked out of the store.

Not yet, but maybe one of these days. "Your daddy was my best friend, so almost."

"Can we call you Uncle Angus?" Travis slipped a hand into Angus's big paw.

They'd never called him anything but Angus. The question tugged his heartstrings. "If you want, and your mama don't mind, yeah. How come, though?"

"We don't have a daddy now. It seems like we ought to at least have an uncle." Travis tightened his grip.

"Makes sense." Tears balled in Angus's throat, but he kept his tone even. "Let's hit the road. With any luck, we'll be at your grandma's new place in an hour."

He'd fished at Caddo Lake many times. Until his parents passed away, Angus had lived at Mooringsport, Louisiana. His dad had taken him to fish near Uncertain, and sometimes his grandpa joined them. As an adult, Angus had visited the surreal area where bald cypress trees towered off dark waters. Spanish moss dangled from the trees like old men's beards. Angus found Marisol's new address easily enough and parked. The two-story house backed up to Big Cypress Bayou, which fed into the lake.

Dr. Anthony Mackin obviously had serious money. Angus had half-expected a simple fishing shack.

"Nice place," he commented.

Kathleen nodded. "Bigger than I expected, but it's good. There should be plenty of room. There's Mom!"

Marisol appeared on the porch and waved. "Come on in!"

The boys burst from the van and ran to their grandmother. Mindy followed at a slower pace.

Kathleen unbuckled. "Let's go see Mom."

Angus nodded. Once they were out of the van, he stretched out a hand, and Kathleen took it. They approached the porch. "Hello, Marisol."

"Thanks for bringing my bunch and for coming." She hugged everyone, laughing. "Tony will be out in a moment."

"I'll fetch the suitcases." Angus brushed a kiss across Kathleen's lips. Might as well let her family see they were together. If a wedding was in the future, he figured they shouldn't be too surprised.

Marisol smiled. "It's about time."

A tall, grey-haired man came from the house. He wore a goatee and glasses reminiscent of the 1960s.

"Greetings, all. I'm Tony Mackin. Marisol has talked about everyone so much I almost feel as if I already know you."

"Dr. Anthony Mackin," Marisol added, emphasizing the word *doctor*.

Angus toted the luggage into the house. The downstairs featured an open floorplan with a large living room to the left and into a dining area to the right, with a huge kitchen in the rear. A bedroom opened off the far-left side of the dining area, and a narrow set of steps led upward. "Where do you want these?"

"Everyone's upstairs. The boys and Mindy are on the sleeping porch, Kathleen will sleep in the room on the right, and Angus can have the back bedroom. It's small, though."

"It'll be big enough." He appreciated the space but longed to get outside.

"We'll have brunch on the back veranda. Come down when you're ready." Marisol headed into the kitchen.

The spacious upstairs featured a bathroom as well as the porch and bedrooms.

A feast filled the kitchen counters. Sweet rolls, coffee cake, bacon, sausage, a meat and cheese platter, three different types of bread, pasta salad, a green salad, and a tub of chicken salad were available. "There's coffee, iced tea, and orange juice. "Marisol pointed to the closest counter. "There's a variety of sodas in the cooler outside. Fix a plate and head outside."

A traditional picnic table, two wrought iron tables with matching chairs, and two chaise lounges provided seating. Angus took a seat at one of the smaller tables and gawked. The deck overlooked the water. A winding path led down to a covered boathouse with an open area above. To one side, a floating fishing dock rocked with the slight current. Besides it, a boat ramp waited for launch. As much as Angus loved the piney woods of East Texas, he realized he liked this place too.

"This place looks like something from prehistoric times." Kathleen took the seat across from him. "I almost expect to see a dinosaur rear its head or something. I didn't know the bayou would be so beautiful."

"Wait until I take you out on the water." Angus glimpsed a pirogue on the bank. "It's even prettier from that view."

"Tony said we could all go fishing." Marisol pulled a chair from the other table and joined them. "I thought tomorrow. He can take one of the bigger boats so we can all go together."

"I'd like that." Angus bowed his head for a blessing. Kathleen took his hand. No one else bothered. "I hoped to borrow the pirogue and take Katydid for a ride this evening."

"Sure. Do you know how to pole one, though?" Marisol

frowned.

Angus did. "My grandma was a little Cajun lady who spoke Bayou French. We used to go over to Bayou Teche, and one of my great-uncles taught me. I doubt I've lost the knack. I've used one a few times in recent years, too."

"You're Cajun?" Kathleen's eyes widened. "I didn't know that."

"Only a little," Angus laughed. "It's where the brown eyes came from."

"You're a man of mystery, Angus Beaton. I like it, though." Kathleen leaned across the table for a kiss.

In the moment their lips locked, he forgot about everything else, the bayou, her family, and his age.

CHAPTER NINE

They fished and feasted for the rest of the long weekend. On Sunday, they trekked to a small church tucked away near Karnack. Angus enjoyed every minute, but the best were the times he took Kathleen through the bayou in the pirogue. The otherworldly scenery fueled his imagination, and he wished they could come here often. Maybe they would. They also learned Marisol had married Tony in a simple civil ceremony in Shreveport. The wedding had taken place right after Marisol moved.

"We couldn't just live together," Marisol explained. "I hope none of you mind missing the wedding."

"Of course not," Kathleen cried. "I'm happy for you, Mom."

The couple fit, like pencil and paper. Angus would have liked to have been present, but he accepted the marriage. He thought Bart would have, too.

On Saturday night, Tony fried fish he'd caught on the lake, and on Sunday, after church, Marisol warmed up a rich gumbo she'd made and frozen earlier. In case the boys didn't care for the spicy dish, she served the hot dogs Austin had craved as an alternative. On Sunday, Angus and Tony grilled burgers for an early lunch.

Angus relaxed more than he had since Bart died. Kathleen's family welcomed him and approved of their relationship, and no one mentioned the age gap. He spent time talking with Tony, and although the man was a physician, they connected. In his youth, Dr. Anthony had ridden bulls, but had given up rodeo when he began medical school.

After breakfast on Labor Day, Mindy took the boys for a

stroll along the lake. Angus and Kathleen watched from the deck. Travis and Austin had peppered their conversation with "Uncle Angus," throwing in the phrase as often as possible. Mindy seemed more together than she had on the trip over to Uncertain, but Angus worried. Her anger directed toward him still rankled, although she seemed to regain her friendly, teasing attitude he'd known for years.

"Why don't you come up and have supper with us next Friday?" Mindy asked on her return. She wore a wide smile as she parked in a chair. "My parents are going to visit my sister's family in Oklahoma."

A shiver crawled up his spine. His intuition warned the invitation might not be as simple as it sounded. "I don't know. I'll be working by then, finishing up my first week on the milk truck. I figure I'll be ready to head for home as soon as my shift's over." He would also have plans with Kathleen.

"You could spend the night." Mindy winked.

His stomach clenched hard. "You said you were crowded, Mindy. I doubt there's space."

"I could make room, Angus, for you. You should know that."

Beside him, Kathleen tapped his hand with two fingers and shook her head. *Don't,* she mouthed.

Angus had no intention to accept. "Mindy, it's a nice thought, but no, I can't. I've got plans, and it wouldn't be right. Bart's not been gone very long, and you're more like a sister than anything else. I might come up and get the boys someday, take them on an outing, or to a ball game or something."

Mindy's pleasant expression vanished. "*She's* like your sister more than I am, but apparently, that doesn't bother you a bit."

He didn't like the way this conversation was headed. "Kathleen's always been Bart's little sister, not mine. It's different now."

"He wouldn't like this, not one bit." Mindy spit the words. Her tone was as bitter as sour grapes.

"Yesterday, you said he'd give me his blessing." Angus kept his tone mild, but he was about to explode.

Kathleen stood. "Hey, Austin, Travis, let's go find your stuff. We'll leave before long."

Angus rose. He wasn't about to stay on the deck alone with Mindy. "I'll be right behind you, honey."

"I thought about it and changed my mind." Mindy's voice rose like the droning of a busy fly. "Bart wouldn't approve. You're almost twice her age! That's too old, Angus. You need a woman closer to your age, someone more mature and settled."

She hit his weak spot, his one area of doubt, but he did his best to ignore her statement. "That's enough, Mindy."

Tony came through the back door onto the deck. "Angus, Marisol wanted to talk to you for a minute, and I've got some dealings with Mindy."

Thank God. "Sure. I'll head inside."

Marisol greeted him with a scowl. "Angus Beaton, you need to stay away from Mindy."

He held both hands up in surrender. "Fine with me. I sure haven't been encouraging her."

"She wants you to come have supper and spend the night." Kathleen joined them and linked an arm through his.

"You heard me turn her down." Angus pulled her closer to plant a kiss on her lips.

"I did, but it's worse than you think." Kathleen gazed at Marisol.

"How's that?" Angus asked.

"What did she tell you in the van while I had the boys in the store?"

"Oh, Lord." He sank into a kitchen chair. "She told me

she's mad at me. Didn't much like it when I told her about the new job. Mindy said she was broke, tired of living with her folks, and she's sick every day. Then she asked if I was with Kathleen. She said Bart would be happy, but today, she said he wouldn't be. Told me I'm too old for you, honey, and dangled her invitation."

Kathleen sighed. "She told Mom and Tony you're interested in her, Angus. I didn't believe it for a minute, but that's her story. According to Mindy, you want to take Bart's place and marry her in a few months."

Angus jumped to his feet. "That's nonsense. I never said any such thing!"

"Take it easy." Marisol forced a tiny smile. "I'm aware. She also told us you planned this trip to bring her and the boys over, but Kathleen pushed you to include her. Mindy's delusional. She's not handling losing Bart well. I'm worried about Travis and Austin, too. Tony and I will take her home so she can't spin any new stories. He's also giving her a check to help out. Don't go visit or have anything to do with her. I hope she gets over this wild notion, but you wouldn't want her to cause trouble."

If Marisol's expression hadn't been so serious, Angus would have laughed. He couldn't imagine anything Mindy could do to cause problems. He wanted to cut the woman some slack, but he respected Marisol's opinion. If she thought there might be an issue, there was. He didn't want anything to affect what he had with Kathleen or what they might build together in the future. "You know I never said any of those things, don't you, Katydid?"

Kathleen stood behind his chair and rested her hands on his shoulders. "Of course I don't. I know you better than that, and so does Mindy if she really thinks about it. I've got our bags ready if you want to head home now."

Angus glanced at Marisol, who nodded. "I think it's best if you do."

He blew air between his lips. "Then let's hit the road. I gotta return this van anyway. Thanks for inviting me, Marisol. I had a great time."

"I want you to come back, both you and Kathleen. I'm sorry Mindy stirred things up. We'll do our best to settle her." Marisol hugged him. "We'll be in Rusk in two weeks to finish selling the house. The Wheelers are coming from Fort Worth to take possession of the property. Maybe we can eat out or do something."

"Plan on coming out to my place. I'll make chili or grill burgers." Angus kissed Marisol's cheek.

"Sure. Be careful going home."

They headed out on Highway 79 before noon. Angus wished the van didn't have captain's chairs because he wanted Kathleen beside him. A console separated the seats, and he would have offered his hand, but traffic was heavy with the holiday weekend. They stopped midway for a burger and shake in one of the small towns en route. In Jacksonville, Angus left the van and deposited the keys in the provided drop box. He climbed into his familiar pickup for the trip home.

"Want to come over for a bit?" Kathleen asked when they reached Rusk. "It's not quite three."

Angus would like to. His shoulders ached, and so did his wrist. A headache pounded inside his skull. If he could stretch out on her sofa or kick back in the recliner, he'd be a happy man. If she wanted to fuss over him a little, he wouldn't mind the attention. "I wish I could. I gotta go to the store for sandwich fixings for my lunches this week. I need to get to bed early so I can get up early tomorrow morning."

Kathleen rested her left hand on his thigh. "What time?"

He groaned. "The trucks leave at six o'clock sharp, so drivers have to report at five. I'll have to get up at three-thirty or four in the morning to make it on time. Tomorrow won't be as bad. I'll do orientation in the office starting at seven. The rest of the week, I'll ride with another driver."

He parked in front of her apartment building, the third within the complex. Kathleen scooted across the seat to retrieve her purse and canvas tote. "I don't even set my alarm until six thirty. I really should go grocery shopping, too. Can I go with you?"

"Sure, honey. I'd like the company. I'll get your suitcases." Angus stretched his back as he climbed out. He toted the bags upstairs. "Where do you want them?"

"Bedroom. Thank you." Kathleen pulled a cold root beer from the fridge. She tapped three pain reliever tablets into her hand. "Here, take these, and we'll go."

He grinned, pleased with her perception. "How'd you know I needed these?"

She tapped her forehead. "When you have a headache, your frown lines are deeper. Besides, you've been squinting into the sun as you drove."

Angus swallowed the meds. At the supermarket, he bought several packages of beef bologna, a large loaf of bread, a package of cheese, a jar of pickle spears, mustard, and a multi-pack of potato chips. He also bought a flat of bottled water plus a twelve-pack of ginger ale.

Kathleen bought several frozen meals, a pound of smoked turkey, a package of miniature smoked sausage links, a five-pound bag of russet potatoes, an onion, and a few other things. As they waited in the check-out line, she turned to Angus. "I have an idea."

"Okay, what?"

"You drop me off at my place. I put the groceries away and drive out to your place." Kathleen loaded her items on the belt. "I'll fix you a light supper tonight and stay for a while."

He gazed at his selections, made a mental tally of what he

had at home, and nodded. "Sure, Katydid. I'd like that. It beats having a sandwich for my supper or a can of something from the pantry."

A smile lit her face. "It's a plan."

An hour later, she scrambled eggs and made toast at Angus's. Before she began cooking, she made chocolate oatmeal no-bake cookies, which cooled on the counter.

He eyed them with interest. "Are those for dessert?"

Kathleen nodded. "Yes, and for your lunches. You need something sweet to finish your meal."

"Those are one of my favorite cookies. My mom used to make them." He sat at the table, headache gone, at ease.

"And your others are snickerdoodles, peanut butter cookies, and oatmeal raisin." Kathleen divided the eggs between a pair of plates. She plucked bread from the toaster and buttered it. "Dinner is served."

The simple meal proved perfect. They rehashed their weekend getaway. "I like Tony. I never imagined Mom getting married again, but I'm glad she did."

"They make a solid couple. I like his place on Caddo, too." Angus wouldn't trade his acres in the piney woods for anywhere else, but he liked the mystical bayou.

"It's ethereal and so beautiful. I don't think I'd want to live there, though." She finished a slice of toast.

"Neither would I, but we'll visit again." And next time, they would leave Mindy home.

"I wish we hadn't taken Mindy, although the boys loved it." Kathleen blotted her lips with a napkin. "I don't understand, but I told you she was a mess."

"You did, but that's an understatement." Angus sighed. He didn't want to talk about his buddy's crazy widow or the wild things she believed.

"Mom and Tony are planning to talk to her parents. If

Mindy's this unstable, they're thinking about getting temporary custody of the boys." Kathleen reached for the cookies and handed Angus one.

Angus released a low whistle. "Dang, that sounds serious."

Kathleen nodded. "I think it is. Let me wash the dishes, and we can hang out a little before you go to bed."

They sat together on the couch. Angus put his arm around her shoulders as they watched one episode of a favorite Western series he had on DVD. He enjoyed being close to Kathleen. When the program ended, he shut off the television and stood. "I suppose I'd better head for bed soon."

Kathleen rose. "Come for supper tomorrow after you get off work. I'll fix something, and you can tell me about your day."

"All right. I'll be there, sugar. Can I steal a kiss?" He pulled her into his arms and didn't wait for her response. He kissed her with slow precision. "Good night, Katydid. I'll see you tomorrow."

The certainty filled his heart with gladness. As long as the sun rose in the east and Angus knew he'd spend time with Kathleen, everything in his world was fine.

Although tired, Angus didn't sleep well. He lay awake, pondering his new job, his existence, and trying to figure out Mindy. He didn't fall asleep until midnight, and without the alarm, he wouldn't have awakened on time. Fueled with coffee in a stainless travel mug he'd owned for years, Angus arrived at the dairy headquarters. He joined three other new hires, all much younger, in a conference room where the human resources manager handed out paperwork. He completed his tax forms, insurance information, and provided his commercial driver's license along with other identification. Angus's CDL was current, but one of the other applicants lacked one, so he was out of a job before he began.

Angus and the remaining two other new employees spent

the morning reviewing the company handbook. They watched a short video and completed a quiz to prove they had paid attention. Angus was the only driver, so after a lunch break, which he spent in his truck, he accepted his uniforms. He stashed them in his vehicle and participated in a tour of the facility. After it ended, he met the route supervisor, who explained where Angus's assigned route would be.

"Since you're familiar with East Texas, I've put you on a loop which will include Henderson, Marshall, Kilgore, Longview, and Jefferson." Pete Dvorak sat across from Angus at a battered metal desk in a tiny office near the loading bays. "The rest of the week, though, you'll be with Bill Parker. He drives a route which includes north to Tyler and west to Athens, plus a lotta little towns in between. You should be ready to head out on your own on Monday. Do you think that'll work?"

"You bet." Angus leaned forward. He figured he could do the job without any trouble. Delivering milk and dairy products couldn't be much different than when he brought bread or restocked candy and cigarettes at convenience stores.

When the drivers returned, he met Bill Parker. The man appeared to be around the same age, and he greeted Angus like an old friend. "Welcome aboard," he cried. "I hear you're riding shotgun with me the rest of the week. I'll be glad to show you the ropes and for the company. One downside of this job, it can be lonely on the road."

"I imagine so." Angus recalled the long hours speeding down the highway with nothing but the radio. He'd done it as a driver and for years, traveling from one rodeo to the next.

"Do you live here in Jacksonville?" Bill sat on the edge of one of the loading docks. "I live just outside town with my wife and four kids."

"I'm down at Rusk." Angus took a seat beside Bill. "I've lived there since junior high."

"My brother bought a place down there, out near the Neches River. Where'd you live before?" Bill jangled his key ring as he pulled it from a pocket.

"Mooringsport, over in Louisiana." Angus changed the subject. He didn't like talking about his early life because it reminded him of losing his parents. "I've been a commercial driver before, but I used to ride rodeo."

Bill slapped his leg and laughed. "That's why you look familiar! I'm a fan. In the season, I drag the family to every rodeo within sixty miles, sometimes more. I rode bulls before I got married."

"I rode a bunch of bulls in my time." Angus smiled. He liked having some common ground with Bill. "I still did until a few months ago. I've mostly busted broncs for years, though."

"Small world, ain't it? I'd best head for the house. Kids will be home from school by the time I get there, and Denise will have supper ready before long. I'll see you in the morning." Bill offered his right hand to shake.

"Count on it." Angus shook hands. "I'll be here."

Although traffic proved heavier on the way home to Rusk, Angus wanted to shout with joy. His first day went well, and he liked Bill, so riding with him would be a pleasure, not a trial. He sang along to the country gold tunes playing on the radio, chiming in with Johnny Horton, Hank Williams, and Marty Robbins. When he realized it was later than he'd expected, he called Kathleen. "Hey, Katydid."

"Angus! Where are you? I've been looking out for you."

"I'm almost to town. I'll be at your place in ten minutes, honey." Angus kept time to the music with his fingers on the steering wheel. "See you then."

At her apartment complex, he dashed up the stairs. Kathleen opened the door before he had time to knock. She looked so pretty in a pair of faded Capri jeans and a deep pink T-shirt with a cowboy on a bucking horse. Angus pulled her close and kissed her before he said a word.

She tasted sweet and smelled like blooming flowers. "Must have been a good day." Kathleen brushed his cheek with one hand in a light a caress.

"It was all right. I think I'll like the job once I settle into it. How was school?" Angus brushed a stray lock of hair from her face.

"Wonderful. My kiddos are a lot of fun. Most are good, although a couple may be problem children." Kathleen grasped his hand. "Come sit down while I finish cooking."

She'd fried potatoes with onion, one of his favorites, and added the small smoked sausages for a hearty meal. Kathleen had a platter of cornbread muffins, and she'd poured them both tall glasses of sweet, iced tea. Angus enjoyed every bite as he shared every detail of his day. While she cleaned up after the meal, Angus sank onto the couch, and although he turned on the television, he didn't pay any attention to the program.

Kathleen joined him, rubbing lotion into her hands, and when she rested her head against his shoulder, his heart brimmed with joy. Angus could imagine coming home to her each evening and thought nothing could be better. He wanted to linger, but he had to rise early.

"I gotta go," he told her. "I'll call you tomorrow."

She shook her head. "You can, but I'd be happy to fix supper again. I like having you here, Angus. It makes this place feel more like home."

He grinned. "Sure. I'm about to fall asleep, or I wouldn't go."

Kathleen walked him to the door and hugged him. "Good night, Angus. Be careful going home."

"I will. Love you, sugar." He kissed her one more time and headed to the truck.

His declaration of love wasn't new. He'd said it before and would tell her often, but it mattered. As far as Angus could see, he'd started a new chapter in his life. He hoped the next one after this would include a wife, maybe even a family if he wasn't too old to become a daddy.

Although he made it home without incident, Angus had trouble falling asleep once there. If anything would be a problem with his new job, it would be the early start. Nothing could go wrong, or so he thought—until Mindy called while he was out on the route with Bill.

CHAPTER TEN

Until the end of his shift, the day went well. Angus arrived early and helped Bill load dairy products onto the box truck. Fueled with coffee, they headed toward Tyler with stops along the way. Bill kept the conversation lively, and once they made the first delivery, Angus admired the way Bill chatted with staff at every stop and hoped he could do the same. They paused for lunch in Tyler, and although Angus had packed his sandwich, Bill insisted on buying tacos for both of them.

The day passed quickly without incident until they returned to headquarters. As soon as Angus stepped out of the box truck, Pete waved him over. "Angus, your wife called and left an urgent message."

"I'm not married." A cold feeling swept through Angus. "It must be a mistake."

Pete shook his head. "I don't think so. Said she had to talk to you right away. She told me it's about the boys. I didn't know you had kids."

"I don't." Suspicion hit. "Did this woman give a name?"

"Yeah, she did. Said it was Mindy." Pete thrust a piece of paper at him. "I wrote it all down."

If he were a cussing man, Angus would have turned the air blue. "I figured it had to be Mindy."

Pete shrugged. "So, she is your wife?"

"Not hardly. Like I said, I ain't married. She's my best friend's widow. He died a few months ago, and she's a mess, but there's nothing between us, never was."

"You'd best tell this woman not to call, then. The company doesn't encourage personal calls during working hours and besides, everybody has cell phones these days. What do I tell her if she calls again?" Pete scratched his chest.

"Explain you know she's not my wife." Angus sighed. He'd have to phone, but he didn't look forward to talking to Mindy.

As soon as he reached his truck, Angus dialed her number.

"Oh, Angus, I was beginning to think you weren't going to call me back." Mindy sobbed into the phone. "I thought maybe that man didn't even tell you."

"What's going on?" Angus turned the key so he could run the air conditioning. "My boss said my wife called. You know very well you're not my wife, Mindy."

"I could be. I'd make a good one. Bart didn't have any complaints." Her cries shifted to laughter.

"Are the boys okay?" Angus resisted an urge to punch the dash.

"Marisol and her doctor took them away." Mindy's voice rose with the harshness of a screech owl. "They took Travis and Austin over to their place on the lake."

Good deal. He released a long breath. "I'm sure they figure it's best for the kids right now."

"I want them back! I need you to go over and get them." Mindy paused. "Hurry and come get me. We can be back tonight."

Angus sighed. "Mindy, it's not gonna happen. It's not my business, and I'm not getting involved. Please don't call work again. And don't tell people you're my wife."

"I'll say whatever I want, and I'll do what I like." Her voice slurred as she spoke.

"No, ma'am, you won't." Angus refused to be harassed. An idea formed. Between her tone, her state of mind, the wild accusations, and the fantasies she spun, he suspected she might be using drugs. Her next question confirmed it.

"Angus, do you have any pain pills lying around? I need

them if you do. I've used up most of Bart's and some that my mom had from dental work. I don't care if they're old." Her tone dropped to a whisper. "Please."

"I don't." He always turned anything he'd had left into a drop box set up for that purpose. "If you've been taking Bart's old meds or your mom's, it's dangerous. It can be addictive."

Mindy giggled. "I think I'm past addiction, Angus. I need painkillers so I won't hurt. It's all that helps."

No wonder Marisol took the kids. Mindy needs help, but I can't be the one to give it to her. If I did, it will encourage her crazy notions. "I can't help with any drugs. Where's your folks?"

"Working. They won't help me either, not anymore." Mindy panted into the phone. "The pharmacy won't refill any prescriptions now because they know Bart's dead. I tried a different one, but they wouldn't do it either."

Her desperation disturbed him almost as much as her drug abuse. Angus laid his head against the steering wheel and prayed. *Why me, Lord? Why do I have to deal with this now? Help Mindy, please, because I can't.*

Angus wanted to hang up, but he was afraid to end the call. Alone, Mindy might do things he didn't want to even think about. He remained on the phone until he heard a man's voice. "Mindy, who are you talkin' to now?"

Mindy shrieked. "It's Angus, Dad. He's coming to get me any minute. We'll go get the boys back, and then he'll marry me."

Angus shuddered. "Put your daddy on the phone, Mindy, Please."

To his surprise, she did as he asked.

"If you're really gonna do what she says, get after it." A gruff voice barked into his ear.

"Sir, I'm not. I never was. It's all in her mind." Angus wanted to cry. He couldn't imagine what Bart would make of the situation.

After a long pause, the man sighed. "I was afraid of that very thing. I'm Caleb Brown, Mindy's father. I'm sorry she's tried to involve you in her crazy notions. Weren't you Bart's best friend?"

"I was. Your daughter seems to have an addiction..."

"I'm aware." Caleb interrupted him. "Bart's mom is trying to get Mindy into a rehab facility. It's all we can do."

"Thank God." Angus lifted his head. "I'll be praying for you all, for Travis and Austin too. They are with Marisol?"

"Yeah. I couldn't argue the point. Her new doctor husband said Mindy's suffering a clinical depression. He didn't know about the pills yet because we didn't. Thanks for whatever support you've given my daughter. She thinks highly of you, but it's skewed now."

Angus had no idea how to respond. "If I can help with anything, give me a call."

Brown snorted. "I won't, but I appreciate the offer."

Angus had already spent almost an hour in the parking lot. Kathleen would be wondering, but he wanted to call Marisol. He phoned Kathleen first, though. "Hey, Kathleen, it's me."

"Where are you? I thought you'd be here by now," she cried.

"I meant to be, but there's a situation with Mindy." Angus sketched out what had happened, leaving nothing out. "I'm gonna call your mom, then I'll head your way. I won't be too much longer."

"Darlin', why don't you come here first and call Mom from my place?" Kathleen's voice softened.

The endearment cinched his decision. She seldom used any, so it melted his heart. "All right, Katydid."

Angus exceeded the speed limit more than once despite the evening traffic. His earlier good mood had vanished, and weariness replaced it. Every muscle he'd used to carry product ached, and if he sat still for more than five minutes, Angus knew he'd fall asleep. Once he reached her apartment, Angus pulled his bag with casual clothes from behind the seat so he could change from the heavy uniform. He also grabbed his clean set of work clothes so they wouldn't wrinkle in the truck. He slogged up the steps, and Kathleen met him at the door.

"I like the work uniform, but you look tired." She swiped a quick kiss across his mouth. "I hate all this mess with Mindy."

"So do I." He hadn't told her Mindy had claimed to be his wife. "Let's make the call to Marisol."

Angus sat on the couch with his phone and used the speaker function. "It's Angus, and Kathleen's beside me. I'm calling because I talked to Mindy a while ago. She phoned me."

Marisol sighed. "I doubt she had anything good to say."

"Unfortunately, no. She told me you have the boys, which I think is best, but she wanted me to take her over there to get them. I said 'no'. Then, she asked if I had any prescription pain pills. She's been taking them, and she has a problem. Her folks are trying to get her into rehab."

"I know. So are we. Tony has a place ready to accept her. I hope if we can break her addiction, she'll recover and revert to the Mindy we know. She's grieving, and I understand that. It doesn't excuse her actions, but Tony says it's not uncommon. Mindy didn't expect to be a widow at this age, and she's not dealing with it very well."

"That's an understatement. Bart knew he could die in the arena. Every cowboy does, but he always said Mindy refused to listen if he tried to talk about the possibility." Angus paused and unbuttoned his uniform shirt. He scratched his chest beneath the plain T-shirt he wore beneath. "I just don't get why she's fixated on me. It makes me uncomfortable."

"I know, Angus. I think she just longs for a man to love her and one she can lean on for support. You're a strong man with a good heart," Marisol told him. "The boys are coming inside. Do you want to talk to them?"

Angus threw up his free hand. "Not right now. I'll try to call them this weekend. I'm glad you're looking out for them. How long are you keeping them?"

"Maybe permanently. It depends on Mindy. We enrolled them in school over at Karnack for now."

Young voices were audible over the line. "I need to feed them. Angus, I'll let you know what happens. Are you there, Kathleen?"

"Yes, Mom." Kathleen rolled her eyes.

"Take care, you hear? I'll call you and Angus soon. Love you." Marisol rattled off the words and then ended the call.

Angus placed his phone on the end table. "Well, I hope rehab helps. Do I have time to change into something besides my work clothes?"

Kathleen nodded. "Sure. You can take a quick shower, too, if you want."

"I'd like to wash off. Thanks, honey." Angus loved her thoughtfulness. As soon as life settled down and he wrapped his head around their age difference, he would ask her to marry him. Right now, though, he wanted her to be sure, and he wasn't certain if she was.

Her bathroom was small, and so was the shower stall. Angus liked the ease of walking into the space and blasting the water. He adjusted the water until it was as hot as he could stand and washed off the day's grime using Kathleen's sweet-scented body wash. Angus laughed, thinking he'd smell like brown sugar and shea butter instead of his signature masculine musk. He washed his short hair with her shampoo, which left it feeling cleaner than usual. Once he donned his sweatpants and fresh T-shirt, he padded in his bare feet to the kitchen.

"Do you have a bag I can put these in?" He held up his

discarded work uniform.

"Can it go in the washer?" Kathleen glanced up from the small table where a covered casserole dish rested.

"Yeah, I think so." Angus inhaled the rich aroma wafting through the kitchen. "What's for supper?"

"Butterfly pork chops with dressing. There's gravy, too." She lifted the lid. "I'll throw these in the washer before we start, and you can take them home clean."

Angus shook his head. "You don't have to mess with them. I can do them later."

"It's no trouble. Go ahead, sit down, and fix your plate. I'll pull the rolls out of the oven when I come back."

His stomach rumbled. "I'm not gonna argue." He put a chop onto his plate, then added a mound of dressing. He ladled gravy over both and waited. Kathleen retrieved the hot bread and placed it on the table along with the butter. He held out his hands, and she grasped them. "Thank you, Lord, for this fine meal, bless the hands which prepared it, and help Mindy. She's in a bad place right now, but with Your help, she'll be all right. Help Austin and Travis, too. Thank you for my new job, for Kathleen, and for everything. Amen."

"Amen," Kathleen echoed.

Angus ate his portion, but when Kathleen offered dessert, a rich chocolate pudding pie, he placed a hand over his stomach and groaned. "I'm stuffed, sugar. Save it, and I'll have a piece tomorrow."

"I can do that. Did everything taste good?" Kathleen picked up the dishes and carried them to the sink.

"Wonderful. You're a fine cook, Katydid. Thanks for inviting me." Angus leaned back and stretched.

"You might as well come back tomorrow night. It's supposed to storm, so I thought I'd fix chicken and gravy in the slow cooker." Kathleen ran dishwater and squirted soap into the sink.

Although full, he almost drooled. "I ought not get in the habit of eating here every night, but that sounds too good to pass up. I don't want you to go to any trouble, though, cooking for me."

Kathleen laughed. "I have to eat too. If I wasn't fixing supper to share, I'd probably nuke a frozen dinner or grab a salad on the way home from school."

"Thank you." He meant it, too. "I ain't ate this well in years. I might get fat, though." Angus tempered his statement with a grin.

"That's not likely. You're too skinny now." Kathleen scrubbed a dish. "Why don't you get comfortable in the living room? I won't be long."

Angus rose. "I ought to head home. Morning comes early, and I'm tired."

She narrowed her eyes and shook her head. "You can spare a few minutes."

He could. "I'm likely to fall asleep, though. Wake me if I do."

Kathleen mumbled her answer. Angus walked the short distance to the living room and flopped into the leather recliner. He sighed with comfort and kicked the footrest back. *As long as I don't close my eyes, I'll be good. I gotta get home so I can go to bed.*

Angus woke and squinted at her surroundings. Something wasn't right. Nothing appeared familiar. He turned to roll out of bed and almost toppled the chair. A soft throw lay across his lap, and he batted it aside. "I gotta go," he muttered.

"You might as well stay," Kathleen spoke out of the darkness.

He turned toward her voice. She was curled up on the couch in pajamas. "Why didn't you wake me?"

She shrugged. "You were so worn out, and you were

sleeping so well I just couldn't.

Angus groaned. "What time is it, anyway?"

"Almost four. You haven't moved hardly at all." She laughed a little.

"I gotta be at work by five." He lowered the footrest and stood. "I shouldn't have stayed, and you ought not to have let me."

"It's all right. You had a hard time, especially with Mindy's mess. Coffee's made, and I fixed you a lunch. It's not bologna because I don't have any. I made you a turkey and Swiss sandwich. I had some corn chips and I cut a sliver of the pudding pie. Your work clothes are dry." Kathleen uncurled her feet and stood. "It won't take you twenty minutes to get to Jacksonville this time of day."

Angus wanted to fuss, but she was right. He had everything he needed. "Pour me a cup, would you, while I wash my face and get dressed. Kathleen, woman, you're spoiling me."

She caught his face between her hands and kissed him. "You need a little TLC, Angus."

With boots on his feet, buttoned into his uniform, Angus savored the single cup of java. It tasted better than what he brewed anyway, although he had no idea why. Although he'd never been much of a morning person, mostly because he hadn't had a soul to talk to in years, he liked waking up to Kathleen.

At the truck, someone a few parking slots over waved and grinned. His heart sank. *They probably think I spent the night. Well, I did, but not the way that guy probably thinks.* Angus didn't want to ruin Kathleen's reputation, but he realized they had been innocent. He knew, and so did she. Most of all, God knew, so he relaxed, although he resolved not to do anything which might make Katydid look bad.

Despite his concerns, he made it work with time to spare. Bill greeted him and waved him over.

"Pete brought pastries. You want an apple fritter or a maple bar?" He pointed at the open box.

Angus chose a fritter, then helped Bill load the truck. As they worked, Bill sniffed, then laughed. "Did you get your wife's situation straightened out?"

"Yeah. Like I said, I'm not married." Angus would rather not rehash the situation.

Bill spread his hands wide. "I just wondered because you smell like lady soap and floral deodorant." He elbowed Angus and snickered.

He flushed. Yeah, he'd showered with Kathleen's body wash and used her deodorant this morning. "I took a shower at my gal's place."

"Not married, and you've got a sweetheart. Way to go, Angus. I've been tied to my ball and chain for ten years." Bill punched his shoulder with a smirk.

"Kathleen's not like that." Angus swallowed his anger because he didn't want a fight. "I've known her all her life. We go to church together. Her brother was my buddy. Don't start thinking she's some kind of…." He groped for the right word. Strumpet seemed much too old-fashioned, and the other names that came to mind were too harsh.

Bill's expression changed, and his mouth fell open. "I get you, man. You have a good woman, and that's all right. Are you gonna marry her?"

Angus's laugh rang hollow. He really didn't have an answer, but he wanted to make Kathleen his wife more than he'd wanted anything in years. "I hope so, down the road a bit. We haven't been together very long."

"If it's right, it's right." Bill wrote down how much they'd loaded and slammed the truck's rear door. "My wife, Tina, is the same. She warms a pew every Sunday morning. Most of the time, I'm right there beside her unless the fish are biting or the hunting is good. Are you a fishing man?"

"I like to wet a line sometimes, but never on Sunday." Even on the circuit, Angus always rose early enough to find a church and attend services. "Maybe we can go sometimes."

"I'd like that. Let's get cracking. We're heading into Dallas today, and we have a bunch of deliveries."

Angus flinched. The last time he traveled this road had been returning home after Bart's death. He wasn't fond of the urban traffic at the best of times, but especially not now. Dallas and Fort Worth had become one huge city sprawl. "Let's do it. I'm glad it won't be part of my route."

Bill laughed. "You don't like the cities?"

He shrugged. "I like small towns better."

By the end of the week, Angus had no doubt he could do the job. His muscles would adjust to lifting in a few days, and he would enjoy the simple interaction with people within a ninety-mile or less radius of Jacksonville. Jefferson was the farthest out, but Angus was familiar with all the roads he'd travel. Likely, he would know a few people he encountered, and he'd be home every night.

On Friday night, as he had promised, he took Kathleen out. She chose Mexican food, and they dined on beef fajitas, refried beans, and rice. After the meal, they watched movies at Angus's house until late, although he drifted to sleep more than once.

Angus roused and made popcorn after the first movie. Kathleen took over seasoning it with butter and a little salt.

"What do you want to do tomorrow?" she asked, as she crammed a handful of popcorn into her mouth. They sat on his couch.

If it was up to him, he would stay home, laze around his place, maybe go fishing. "Did you have an idea or two?"

Kathleen smiled. "I've always wanted to visit the aquarium over at Shreveport, or we could have a picnic."

"A picnic sounds good. Or we could ride the train over to Palestine and back." He liked trains, and it wouldn't involve him driving. He wouldn't mind the chance to sit in a passenger seat and relax. Angus's fatigue faded. "Okay, we'll do it. Let's see if we can book tickets." He dug out his ancient laptop, he seldom used, and once it booted, he found the Texas State Railroad Website. Options included old-time seating with open windows, a Presidential car with plush seating, a dome with fantastic views from the top of the train, and booth-style seating in first class. He would have chosen the first choice, but for Kathleen, he paid more for dome seating. "We have seats for the 11 o'clock ride on one of the dome cars. I'll pick you up around 9:30 in the morning, so we'll have plenty of time to board."

She clapped her hands. "Awesome! I've never ridden on a dome car, and I've always wanted to, Angus."

"I do my best to make your wishes come true," he quipped. Although he joked, he meant it too.

Riding the train proved to be a perfect Saturday adventure. The tracks led from the station at Rusk through woods, across fields, and farms to Palestine. Travel was slow, but Angus enjoyed every moment. Kathleen sat beside him, their hands linked. Sometimes, he had to remind himself two months had passed since Bart died, so his relationship with Kathleen was very recent. For Angus, he knew this was his true love, the one he'd sought for almost all his life, and his heart belonged to her. He ached to believe Kathleen's feelings were as deep, but he sometimes doubted. She had admitted to a long-term crush, but infatuation didn't always equal a lasting love.

If nothing's changed in six months, then I'll propose. Angus realized the timeline would fall during the Christmas season. He had time to find a ring, to consider every aspect of the future, and to be sure where Kathleen's heart rested. *I'm still too old for her, but I don't care anymore. I just want to be certain she doesn't.*

With his decision made, Angus relaxed. He savored time spent with Kathleen and let his guard down. He wanted this for the rest of his life, and unless God threw up warning signs, he would move forward.

By mid-October, both Angus and Kathleen had settled into a routine. She taught her kindergartners every day, and he made the trek to Jacksonville. Angus headed out on his route with a different destination each day. He knew the roads well, and he knew the customers at each stop by name. He liked the job well enough, but he still dreamed of working with horses at his place. Angus kept his spending low, except where Kathleen was concerned, and watched his bank account grow. He had saved as much of his rodeo winnings over the years as possible, so he had a nice nest egg.

Most evenings, he ate supper with Kathleen, usually at her apartment but sometimes at his house. On Friday night, he always planned a date, a meal out, a movie, a festival, or some other fun. They spent Saturdays together, although often it was a quiet day with one another. Angus discovered places to share on his route. He took her to Jefferson to see the Bigfoot statue at the Port Jefferson History and Nature Center. On another outing, they visited the Jefferson General Store and drank milkshakes from the old-fashioned soda fountain. They also brought home honey butter, green tomato relish, and several flavors of jelly. "My mom made relish like this, but she called hers chow-chow," Angus told Kathleen.

"If I had a recipe, maybe I could too." She snuggled close in the truck on the way back to Rusk.

Other stops had included a visit to the Jim Reeves Memorial east of Carthage, an afternoon at the Texas Country Music Hall of Fame, and a long day trip to the Sea Rim State Park. Angus made plans to visit the Louisiana State Fair in Shreveport in late October. During his deliveries, he'd found a few local places to eat serving everything from steak to tamales and German food, so they added those to their list.

On the third Saturday in October, Marisol and Dr. Tony returned for the closing on her property. They brought Travis and Austin along. While Marisol took care of the paperwork and other business, Angus and Kathleen took the boys fishing on the Neches River. "How do you like living with your grandma?" Angus asked as he tied a bobber onto Austin's line.

"Good. I like the school better than the one at Gladewater." Austin focused on his fishing rod.

"I think Mom's gonna move there too after she gets better." Travis squatted beside the tacklebox and didn't meet Angus's eyes. "Do you think she will, Uncle Angus?"

"I know she will." Angus prayed Mindy would get the help she needed. "Marisol invited us to come for Thanksgiving, so we will. I hope your Mom can join us."

"Me, too." Travis cast his line with more expertise than Angus expected. "Are you and Aunt Kathleen getting married?"

The question took Angus by surprise, and he didn't answer for a few moments. Kathleen sat too far away to hear. "I hope so, kid."

Travis grinned. "Good."

Angus would have been content and happier than he'd ever been in his life, except for two things. Kathleen's principal, Trevor Weissman, had developed a devotion toward her and he didn't like it at all. While he didn't think Katydid preferred the Californian with his tasseled shoes and navy blazers, Angus worried she might. That was one. Right before the Louisiana State Fair, they learned Mindy had walked away from the rehab center in Dallas. No one expected the development, and when days passed without the authorities finding her, Angus feared for her safety and the fallout on the family, which was now as much his as Kathleen's.

CHAPTER ELEVEN

The weather turned colder and wet during the week before Thanksgiving. Angus would have Thursday off for the holiday but had to return to work on Friday. To make up for the lost day, he would also work on Saturday, which he didn't like. Schools were dismissed from Wednesday until Monday, so Kathleen had time off. Angus planned to drive her over to Uncertain late Wednesday, stay for the holiday meal on Thursday, and then head home. He would return on Sunday and bring her back.

Rain fell from an iron-gray sky as Angus approached Longview. He peered between the wipers and decided if showers increased, he might take a break after his first delivery at the Lazy Day Convenience Store. He had just pulled into the lot when his cell phone rang. Angus almost ignored the call until he saw Kathleen's name.

"Hey, honey, what's up?" He figured she had a question about Thanksgiving.

"Angus." Kathleen's sobs echoed in his ear. "Oh, Angus."

Dread sent a chill through him. "What's wrong?"

"Where are you?" Her voice cracked as she asked.

"I just pulled into my first stop of the day over in Longview. Are you all right, Katydid?" Angus consulted his watch. At this hour, school had not yet begun.

"I'm fine, but I was afraid you weren't." She sighed. "Thank God."

Confused, Angus rubbed his face with his free hand. "Why did you think I wouldn't be?"

"Because she said you had been in a wreck and were in critical condition." Kathleen spewed the words in a fast stream.

"Who's she?" Angus couldn't imagine anyone who might pull such a cruel prank.

"Mindy."

Angus groaned. "How? She walked out of the rehab center weeks ago, and no one's heard from her." He heard a male rumble in the background before Kathleen replied.

"She called the school and asked for me. I was already here because I have bus duty this week. Trevor called me to the phone, although he wasn't pleased."

Angus digested the information. Trevor was the principal who threatened to have him arrested. He didn't like the idea the man was with Kathleen when he was a good sixty miles away. "You ought to know better than to believe her, sugar. I can't begin to understand why she'd do such a thing."

Kathleen made a nervous sound, half sob, part laugh. "She wanted to pick me up and take me to you, Angus. I couldn't understand how she would know you were hurt…"

He clenched his teeth hard. "She wouldn't. She's up to no good. Whatever you do, don't you take off with her. I'm coming back." He had a truck filled with milk and dairy products, but this ranked as an emergency. *I'll call Pete, tell him, and take this load back to headquarters. Someone else will have to deliver today.* "I'll get there as soon as I can. Will you be at school?"

"No, Trevor wants me to call a substitute teacher. He's afraid Mindy might cause trouble, and he says he can't allow it." Kathleen's voice rose and shrilled. "I'm heading to your place. That's where Mindy said she'll pick me up."

Angus clenched his left hand into a fist. "You're not meeting her, are you?"

"No, but don't we need to find her so she gets back into rehab?"

"Yeah, you're right. She signed herself into the facility before, but I think it's gonna have to be involuntary rehab this time around." Angus tried to think. His brain didn't want to compute. "Call your Mom. Let her know. What time will Mindy show up?"

"She said at noon." Kathleen's voice quavered. "Are you sure you're all right, Angus?"

"I'm good. I'll be there before then. Go home, and I'll meet you at your apartment." He had no clue how he would square it all with work, but Angus would be there.

Angus made a call to Pete, his boss, and then hurried back to Jacksonville. Pete met him at the loading docks with a scowl. "This better be worth all the trouble."

"It is." Angus handed over the keys, clipboard, and everything necessary. "I wouldn't ask if it wasn't truly an emergency."

Pete snorted. "Is it the wife you don't have again?"

"Yeah. Like I said, she's my best buddy's widow, but she's in a bad place. I gotta get to my gal before Mindy does." Angus offered his right hand to shake. After a moment, Pete shook hands. "I owe you for this."

"You bet you do. You also earned an unexcused absence on your first solo week. After ninety days, it will drop off from your attendance, but the policy is three strikes and you're out."

It was already after nine, so Angus drove at and above the speed limit back to Rusk. He parked at the apartment complex, but before he reached the sidewalk, Kathleen came running. She threw her arms around him and held him tight. "Thank God you're all right."

Angus reveled in the soft floral scent of her perfume and treasured her hug. Tears threatened to leak from his eyes when he realized how much she cared. "Sugar, I wouldn't be any other way. You okay?"

She released him but cradled his left hand in hers. "I am now."

"Tell me how this is gonna happen." Angus had to know every detail. "You're definitely not going off with Mindy."

Kathleen shook her head. "Of course not. I talked to Mom. Tony got a judge to issue an involuntary order for rehab. Once Mindy shows up, a deputy will arrive to escort her back to the facility. She may be moving elsewhere because it seems like her problems has gone past addiction. I don't know."

"I hate this has happened. I never would have thought Mindy would dive off the deep end like this." Angus shuddered at the thought. "Bart wouldn't be happy."

"No, I know he would hate this mess. Mindy just can't handle losing him. After today, I can understand a little bit."

"You wouldn't act this way if something happened to me, and it won't." Angus paused to kiss her. "We'd best head out to my place. You better drive. If Mindy sees my truck, she'll know her ruse has failed."

Kathleen pulled her keys from her purse. "Let's go. Do you have to go back to work?"

"Not today, no. Where did she tell you I was laid up in the hospital?" He folded his lanky frame into the passenger seat. Angus had more questions than he did answers.

"Wichita Falls." Kathleen fiddled with the dash controls. She turned off the radio and cleaned the windshield with the wiper. "I guess she's been there. If she'd said Dallas or Fort Worth or somewhere closer, I might have believed her. I couldn't see how you could be up there, with or without her."

Angus swallowed hard. "With her?"

Kathleen sighed. "Mindy said you ran off with her, Angus. She swore you didn't go to work today and that you picked her up last night. I couldn't see how it would be possible, even if you were willing, but I know you're not."

"I'd hope to shout. If I was supposed to be with her, why wasn't she in the wreck, too?" Angus asked. His throat was dry, and he could use a drink, but he would wait.

"She said you left the motel to get breakfast and ended up head-on with a semi-truck." Kathleen pushed back her hair with her right hand. "I didn't believe her, but I had to call you to be sure."

"I'm glad you did. What in tarnation did she think she would accomplish if she got you in her car?" Angus rested both hands against the dash. "And where did she get a car? She left the rehab place on foot."

"I don't know, but I think she meant to hurt me." Kathleen's voice dropped almost to a whisper. "She sees me as competition. From what Mindy says, she thinks if it wasn't for me, she could have you."

Angus clutched his upper abdomen. He had a case of nerve-induced indigestion. "Impossible. I never thought of her as anything but Bart's wife.

"We're here." Mindy nodded as she turned into his place. She parked beside the house. "It's eleven thirty. She could show up at any time, so you'd better get out of sight."

"I think I'd better wait here with you so she doesn't try anything." Angus didn't want Kathleen to be hurt.

She shook her head. "You might scare her off. Go inside. You can watch from the window and take something for your stomach."

He chuckled. "How'd you know it's griping me?"

"I know you, Angus. Besides, I saw you rubbing your tummy. Are you sick?" She touched his hand as she spoke.

"Just worried. Do you want my .45 for protection?" He climbed out of her small truck and headed toward the house.

"I've got pepper spray. I'll use it if I need it." Kathleen jerked the small canister from her bag. "I hear a car. Go in the house."

Angus went. Once there, he swigged some antacid straight

from the bottle. He took up a position at the front window and hoped he wasn't visible through the curtain. Angus raised the window a little so he could hear. Although he didn't recognize the old beater that rolled to a stop beside Kathleen's car, Mindy stepped out of it.

"Are you ready to go?" Mindy asked as she stalked toward Kathleen. "We need to get on the road. It's a good four hours there, and time's wasting. Last the doctor said Angus was near death. They hooked him up to life support, so let's hit the highway."

Kathleen crossed her arms. "Has he asked for me?"

Mindy laughed. "He can't talk right now. If you want to see him, though, climb into the car."

"Where did you get this one?" Kathleen eyed it with a frown.

"Boosted it in Dallas. Well, I didn't, but Scooter did. He left rehab with me." Mindy glanced toward the house. "There's no one here, right?"

"Who would be here? I need to make sure the door's locked." Kathleen stared toward the window where Angus watched and winked.

"It doesn't matter," Mindy cried. "Who cares?"

Kathleen mounted the three steps to the porch. "I do."

Mindy caught up and grabbed her left arm. "I don't. Get in the car, or I'll use this." She opened her right hand to display an open switchblade knife. "I'm not playing games, Kathleen."

"Neither am I." Kathleen jerked free and blasted Mindy with the pepper spray.

Mindy screeched and covered her face with both hands.

A cruiser rolled up to the house. Sheriff Will Garrison stepped out. "Kathleen, are you all right?"

"Yes. Thanks, cuz. I expected a deputy." Kathleen dropped the empty canister.

Will shook his head. "It's family, so I came. Where's Angus?"

Angus stepped through the front door. "Right here."

"Good to see you, man." Will deftly placed Mindy in handcuffs. "Sorry about the circumstance. Mrs. Birdwell, I have to take you back to the office. The rehab center is sending down a team to take you back."

She lowered her hands. Although her eyes streamed and her face was red, she sneered. "I'm not going."

"I'm afraid you are. Let's go."

As soon as the cruiser hit the blacktop, Angus released a slow breath. He opened his arms, and Kathleen walked into them. "It's over, sugar."

She buried her face against his shoulder and cried.

Angus ached to do the same but whispered sweet words of comfort. "Sugar, it's all right now. Mindy will get the help she needs, and we can relax. It's been a heck of a day. Do you want to get some lunch or something?"

"I want to go to Mom's." Kathleen lifted her tear-stained face. "There's no school tomorrow, and I don't want to wait. Will you take me?"

Angus calculated. The trip would take almost two hours and two more to come back to Rusk. He could be back in time to fall into bed. He'd have to make the same journey tomorrow evening if he wanted to be there for Thanksgiving, return late Thursday, and make another trek to pick up Kathleen on Sunday. He groaned as he calculated the miles, the hours, and the cost of fuel. "I can if you really want, but I'll have to come back. I work tomorrow."

She cupped his cheek with her left hand. "Must you?"

"Aw, Kathleen, I do. My boss wasn't thrilled I skipped out today." Angus gazed at the clearing he called his front yard. He would like nothing better than to drive her to Uncertain, stay through Thanksgiving, or through the weekend.

"Can you try?" She slipped her hand into his.

Angus sighed. He loved Kathleen and valued her more than the new job. If he lost it, he would just move ahead sooner with his plan to work with horses. "I guess. Let's go inside, and I'll call Pete if he's back."

He settled onto the couch with his cell while Kathleen brought him a cold bottle of ginger ale. He sipped and said a prayer before he called the company.

Pete proved to still be out on Angus's route, so the call was bumped up to the next level of management. He'd never met Janice Janko, but Angus had heard she was both fair and tough. Angus explained his circumstances and waited.

Janice paused so long Angus thought she must have hung up on him.

"Would you be back on Friday or on Monday?" she asked.

Angus tugged at his right earlobe. He must have heard wrong. "I'm sorry. What did you ask?"

She repeated the question.

"Monday would be awesome, and I'd appreciate it, but I can come back Friday morning if necessary." Angus crossed his fingers. Friday would work.

"I'll mark down that you'll return on Monday," Janice stated. "Under normal circumstances, you would miss too many days and point out, losing your job due to attendance. There is a loophole in the handbook, though, and I'll use it."

Angus lifted his eyes upward. "Thank you." He meant the words for both the Lord and Ms. Janko. "I appreciate your help."

Janice laughed. "*De nada.* I'm a rodeo fan. I've watched you ride on many occasions, your friend Bart Birdwell, too. If you weren't already involved, I'd ask if you want to have lunch with me, but I gather you have a significant other."

He grinned. "I do, but I'm flattered."

"Take care of your business and your family. I'll square things with Pete and with Bill. Happy Thanksgiving."

Kathleen cheered when Angus shared the news. "I'll tell Mom we'll be there for supper."

With a lightness of spirit he had lacked for a long time, Angus gathered a few things in a duffle bag. They switched vehicles at her apartment, and while Kathleen packed, he drove to the nearest convenience store and filled the truck's tank. He bought a few soft drinks for the trip, and they set out, heading east toward Caddo Lake.

Although they arrived a little later than anticipated, Marisol had thick ham sandwiches waiting. Travis and Austin rushed out to meet them. Angus dropped to his knees and hugged them tight. For such young boys, they had endured a lot in the past few months. Losing their daddy hit hard, and although he wasn't sure how much they knew about Mindy's situation, it had to be hard.

"Can we go fishing, Uncle Angus? Please!" Travis cried.

Angus nodded. "First thing tomorrow, sure. Right now, I want some supper and bed."

Tony laughed and offered his hand in greeting. "We dug nightcrawlers earlier, so we're ready."

The first light of dawn touched the bayous and lake with fingers of gold. The sunshine highlighted the Spanish moss, which swayed in a gentle breeze. Angus wore a denim jacket but was more than a little chilled. Tony wore a nylon padded vest beneath a coat. Both boys wore life vests as well as winter-weight outerwear. Fueled with coffee, Kathleen rose early to make. They munched on chocolate muffins she also baked. They caught more than enough bass for a good fish fry on the night before Thanksgiving.

Everyone loaded up in two vehicles to attend a Wednesday night prayer service at a small church. Tall pines towered off the simple structure. Angus belted out traditional hymns from memory with Kathleen at his side. The preacher read from Thessalonians. "Do what the Good Book tells you," he hollered. "Rejoice evermore. That means don't quit, no matter what. Pray without ceasing. Keep the prayers going upward in good times as well as bad. Give thanks in everything. It's what tomorrow's all about. It's not the turkey or the side dishes or even the candied sweet potatoes." He paused and licked his lips. "Those are my favorites. The day's not about the football games or the fancy parades. Give thanks. Now, if any of y'all brought bread to be blessed, line up, and let's get it done. Most of the ladies and some of the gentlemen have cooking to do at home."

Marisol brought three loaves of homemade bread and a deep container of cornbread muffins.

Once home, the two women made a huge pan of cornbread stuffing. Angus, drawing on his Cajun heritage, offered to put together a rice dressing.

"Is it tasty?" Tony raised his eyebrows.

"Delicious." It was also easy to prepare.

"Go for it, then." Marisol smiled. "Travis and Austin, go to bed. Aunt Kathleen will be up in a minute to pray with you."

Austin wrinkled his nose. "Can Uncle Angus come too?"

"I surely can." He had gathered the ingredients for the dish. "I'll finish when I come downstairs."

On Thursday afternoon, with the table set for six, Angus sat down to eat with the dearest people in his life. Although Tony asked the blessing, Angus said a silent prayer. The food proved delicious. Marisol's roast turkey proved tender, and her dressing turned out perfect. Angus's rice dressing was well received. The sweet potatoes, corn, bread, cornbread muffins, green bean casserole, and mashed potatoes with giblet gravy were a little different than the average table across America. Despite the feast, the mood seemed muted to Angus. Mindy's absence contributed to the overall feeling, but he missed Bart, and so did everyone else.

Bart had loved holidays, Thanksgiving most of all. He always carved the turkey, nibbled one of the drumsticks, and ate too much. Bart had laughed, made corny jokes, and played silly tricks. One year, he had put a roasted chicken in the oven once the turkey had been removed, then told the little boys the bird had shrunk. They had believed it for a few minutes.

Angus tried to make merry, but he didn't have Bart's personality. Bart had been a Fourth of July sparkler, bright and blazing. Angus was a quiet fire in the hearth that burned steadily. Despite Bart's absence, it was a good meal, and Angus thought everyone enjoyed it as much as he did.

He'd never been a football fan, but he watched with the others because Tony liked the sport.

Long after the boys were sent to bed, the adults remained. The television had been turned off, and they talked when they wished. Kathleen, after a comfortable silence, leaned forward from her seat on the couch beside Angus. "Do you think Mindy's gonna make it through rehab this time?"

Angus had wondered the same but didn't answer.

"She will." Tony folded his arms across his chest. "She doesn't have any other real options."

True, but it may not be enough.

He planned more fishing on Friday, but Marisol wanted to go Black Friday shopping in Shreveport and enlisted Angus to drive the ladies. Kathleen wanted to go, too, so he drove Tony's SUV into Louisiana. Angus navigated the streets of Shreveport, visiting every mall and shopping center. He took them over the Texas Street Bridge so they could also shop at the Pierre Bossier Mall. By early afternoon, both women had shopped to the verge of dropping, so Angus suggested lunch. After tromping behind Kathleen and Marisol, his feet ached, but he didn't complain. He toted their packages to the van.

"You know Shreveport pretty well," Marisol remarked.

Angus laughed. "Until my folks died, I lived at Mooringsport, a few miles outside town. We did most of our trading and eating out over here or in Bossier. Besides, I've rodeoed around here many times."

"Where's a good place to eat?" Kathleen reached for his hand as they climbed into the van.

"Depends on what you want. I know a diner that's been around since at least the 1950s." Angus wrapped his fingers around hers. "I'm not all that hungry. I'd be happy with leftovers or a turkey sandwich."

Kathleen giggled. "You can have either one for supper. Let's have lunch and head back to the house."

Weary to the bone and feeling every one of his forty years, Angus agreed. At the diner, he ordered breakfast, available around the clock. He enjoyed his eggs over easy with grits, bacon, and toast. Kathleen opted for pancakes, and Marisol chose a grilled chicken salad. The food revived him enough that Angus made a side trip through Mooringsport.

"I thought you might like to see the drawbridge." He pointed it out as they wound through the small town. "Now the new road goes over the lake, people can walk on the original road and across the bridge. I didn't figure we'd do that today, but maybe sometime."

"I'd like to, Angus. Where did you live?" Kathleen leaned forward in her seat to take in the sights.

"Ah, it's not much, but I'll show you." He backtracked to Oak Street. The mobile home he'd shared with his parents remained. "There's home, sweet home."

Kathleen peered at the place. "Looks like a nice place."

He sighed. It had been, although the current owners had fixed it up more than his folks had. "I've got a lot of memories there. I try not to think of my life back then very often. Coming to live with Grandpa was a good thing for me, though. Without him, I might have ended up in foster care."

She settled back into the seat and rested her hand on his. "What about your Cajun relatives?"

Angus laughed. "It could have been cool, but it was my great-grandma, Grandpa's mom, who was Cajun. By the time my folks died, the family in South Louisiana was either dead or too old to take on a boy."

Kathleen grasped his hand. "I'm glad you came to Rusk. I wouldn't know you if you hadn't."

He lifted her fingers to his lip and kissed them. "Me too. You know what the Bible says, though, both in Romans and in Isiah — all things work together for good. Coming to Grandpa's was good, and I truly believe it was God's will for me."

Her smile brightened her face like the sun peeking through storm clouds. "I'm sure it was."

If he wasn't driving, Angus would have kissed her properly, but he could wait. He said a silent prayer that having Kathleen as his wife was also God's will. If it was, he would live the rest of his years a very happy man.

CHAPTER TWELVE

On Saturday, Angus wanted to return home. He enjoyed the time spent with Marisol and Tony, the boys, and Kathleen, but he longed for his own space. Angus would rather sleep in his bed, and he'd like to attend their familiar church on Sunday. He rose early and came downstairs before Kathleen did. When she arrived, he offered her his hand. "Come talk to me a minute."

She frowned, and her forehead wrinkled. "What's the matter, Angus?"

Despite the cool day, he led her onto the deck overlooking the lake. "Nothing, sugar. I'd like to go home, though, if you're willing."

Kathleen sat in one of the chairs. "I thought we were leaving tomorrow."

"We still can." Angus took the seat beside her. "I thought if we left this morning, we can spend time with just the two of us this evening, go to church together, and enjoy Sunday before we both go back to work."

She tilted her head to the left and sighed. After a few moments, she nodded. "All right. Going home sounds like heaven to me right now. I like spending time with my family, but as pretty as this place is, it's not…"

Angus supplied the word. "Home."

"Exactly. I'll go tell Mom we'll head out after breakfast." She stood and released his hand.

Angus had made up his mind and he wanted to go now. "How about we stop on the way? It'll save your mom the trouble." Marisol didn't hurry when she cooked. She hadn't risen yet, and once she did, she might drink coffee for a half hour before she considered fixing breakfast.

Kathleen met his gaze and burst out laughing. "All right, Angus. I'll go pack, then I'll tell Mom."

Heading west toward home felt right. Kathleen beside him made him happy, and he looked forward to a day and a half to unwind. In Marshall, he drove through a fast-food restaurant to pick up a few sausage croissants, juice, and coffee. His taut muscles relaxed, and some of his fatigue vanished. "We'll roll into Rusk before lunchtime."

"If you don't mind stopping at the market, we can pick up something for supper. Mom sent enough turkey for sandwiches at lunch if you're not tired of the bird." Kathleen sat beside him with her legs sprawled into the passenger space.

Angus made a face. "I'd rather have turkey and noodles. We can buy some bologna or ham or pick up a sandwich for lunch."

Kathleen patted his leg. "Sure. I'll need to buy some broth. I can make the noodles if you can wait for them until tomorrow."

His tastebuds tingled. "You bet, honey. I couldn't tell you when I last had homemade noodles."

At the supermarket, Kathleen half-filled a shopping buggy. Angus pushed it and at the checkout, he paid. "Did you get enough?"

She giggled. "I hope so. Did you get your stuff for your lunches this week?"

Angus pointed to the packages of bologna stuffed into one of the bags. "Yeah. Do you take a lunch or grab a school tray?"

"Both. If the cafeteria is serving something decent, I grab a tray." Kathleen helped load their purchases behind the seat. "Most days, I don't have much time for lunch. I'm usually on duty, either in the lunchroom or on the playground. Let's get this stuff home."

Home. Angus savored the word. For him, wherever

Kathleen wanted to be equaled home to him. "Which place?"

Kathleen shrugged. "Either. I bought everything I need to make turkey and noodles for tomorrow, plus supper tonight. I need to wash some clothes but if you'd rather go to your house, we can. Or drop me off, and I'll come over in a while."

"The apartment's fine." Angus yawned. He planned to take a nap either place. "Want to pick up a sack of tacos on the way?"

"Sounds like a plan." Kathleen slid into the truck.

They carried the groceries in together. She placed his perishables, still in the bags, inside the fridge. They dined on tacos and a few nacho chips before Angus settled into the recliner. He hadn't broken it in yet like the one at his house, but he could get comfortable. "If I doze, don't wake me."

"I won't." Kathleen retrieved a pillow from her bedroom and tucked it behind his head. She leaned and brushed a kiss across his mouth. "You look tired, so sleep."

Angus drifted off, listening to the domestic sounds. He heard the washer fill and swish as she washed her garments. Kathleen clattered in the kitchen, but once he shut his eyes, he tuned all noise out. He slept deeply enough to dream, something which seldom happened.

Early summer brought wildflowers blooming along the roadways. Although the sun shone, temperatures had not yet risen to triple digits. Some days, it stormed, quick showers lasting long enough to settle the dust. Rodeo season was also underway. Angus stood at the edge of the chutes in an arena he didn't recognize. The stands loomed empty. No rough stock waited to be bested, and no other cowboys or cowgirls were present. Uneasiness curled up his spine. Something wasn't right.

He heard the rattler before he saw the creature. Five feet of light gray snake with bands of black was coiled less than ten feet away. As Angus watched, the tail shook hard, and the unmistakable dry rustle echoed through the empty arena. He groped for a holster on his hip, but he wasn't armed. He didn't even have a stick, so he took very slow steps backward. Angus knew if the snake advanced, he had no way to outrun or fight the thing off. The serpent uncoiled and slithered toward him. He stared at the triangular-shaped head and wondered if he could get medical help before he died if he was bitten.

The rattling became louder and echoed around him. Angus cut his eyes to the left and gasped. A larger timber rattlesnake was visible. He saw more, some coiled, others crawling with speed toward him. He wanted to scream. Even more, every muscle in his body ached to flee, but he couldn't. If he tried, he would be a dead man within moments. The first snake coiled near his left leg, and with powerful speed, it struck. Angus saw the mouth latch onto his boot and knew it would strike again. Next time, the snake would reach above the leather and hit his unprotected leg.

Angus woke and almost leaped from the chair. His heart beat too fast, and he was breathing hard as if he'd run a fifty-yard dash without stopping.

"Angus, what's wrong?" Kathleen stood before the chair with arms crossed.

"Nightmare." His mouth was dry, and he put one hand on his chest, hoping to slow his heart. The dream disturbed him. He wasn't one to take a lot of stock in premonitions, but he'd heard stories. Grandpa said his Cajun grandma had been half a witch. If Angus remembered right, dreaming of snakes meant trouble if the reptiles came toward you.

"It must have been a bad one." Kathleen twisted her lips. "You scared me to death when you hollered."

"I didn't know I did. I'm sorry, sugar. It disturbed me something awful." He rubbed his face. "Got some ginger ale or tea?"

"Both. Supper's almost ready." Kathleen offered him her hand. "Don't tell me about it until you eat something, or it'll come true. Granny always said so."

"I won't." Angus caught sight of something bright and flashing. He glanced around the room. A three-foot-tall silver Christmas tree, decked with lights and a few baubles, sat on one of the end tables before the front window. A silk garland with pine and poinsettias wound across the wall. "You decorated."

Kathleen beamed. "Yes, I did. Thanksgiving is over, so it's time. There's less than a month until Christmas."

Angus grunted. "I guess."

Over a simple supper of fried potatoes and smoked sausage, Angus shared the highlights of his nightmare. "I hate snakes, especially rattlers. I've always been afraid I'd get bitten. My grandma always said a snake in a dream means trouble on the way."

She paused with her fork raised to take a bite. "I hope not, Angus. Don't dwell on it. I imagine it's just a dream."

"I hope." He sighed and changed the subject. "I love fried taters."

Kathleen grinned. She rose and fetched a spoon, then dipped it in the pot on the stove. "Taste the noodles for me. I think they're done. I'll put them in the slow cooker for tomorrow."

Angus smacked his lips. "Sugar, those are perfect."

She returned to the table. "I thought you could take them to your house and plug it in tomorrow morning. After we eat, I can decorate for you."

He laughed. "With what?"

Kathleen cocked her head. "Surely you have some decorations and a tree."

Angus shrugged. "I think so, in the barn or maybe the basement. Might even be down in the cellar. I haven't decorated for Christmas in years, not since Grandpa died."

"Why not?" Her mouth drooped open.

He hitched his shoulders. "Christmas hasn't really been a thing for me. I haven't had anyone to spend the day with or buy presents for. I didn't have any place to go for dinner, so I usually went to church. I went up to Jacksonville a couple times to help serve a community dinner to anyone who wanted it." Angus stated the facts. He wasn't sad or mad about it. That's the way his life had been.

She blotted her lips with a paper napkin. "Mom would have had you over if she'd known, Angus. Why didn't you say something?"

"I didn't want to horn in where I didn't belong. Besides, I never thought about it." Angus scooped the last little sausage up with a forkful of potatoes. "I guess Christmas will be different this year."

Kathleen smacked his left hand. "Yes, it will, and you'll love it."

He met her gaze without blinking. "I love *you*. If you like it, I'll be happy."

She leaned across the table and caressed his cheek. "Angus, I love you so very much."

Sunday proved much too short. After attending church together, they returned to Angus's house. He caught up his laundry while Kathleen made biscuits to go with the turkey and noodles in the slow cooker. After dinner, she insisted they hunt for whatever decorations he had. Two hours later, dust-covered and tired, they hauled the two boxes they located into the living room. There were ancient strings of lights, a few boxes of fragile ornaments, a hand-knitted stocking with Angus's name across the top, a green plastic wreath missing most of the faux holly berries, faded Christmas cards from many years earlier, a pair of white Christmas pillar candles with red and green ribbons, and an old but sturdy tree stand.

"Where's the tree?" Kathleen brushed dirt from her jeans.

"I don't know there ever was one." Angus plucked a cobweb from her hair. "Grandpa never liked anything artificial.

He cut down a likely cedar tree when he wanted a Christmas tree. Grandma was the one who used the ornaments, but after she was gone and I moved in, we decorated the thing with strings of popcorn, a few dried wildflowers if we could find any, pine cones, and such. Sometimes we put a string of lights on it, sometimes not."

She glanced down at the watch on her wrist. "We could run into town and get a small tree if you want."

Angus shook his head. "I don't. If I do put one up, I'd rather cut a cedar. I might get a few decorations and definitely new lights. Those old ones look like a fire hazard. It doesn't have to be today, though, sugar. Let's watch a movie or something."

Kathleen sighed. "All right. We'll get decorations next Saturday."

December launched wet and chill. Angus returned to work and found his job had become complicated. It hadn't occurred to him the holidays would increase the variety of products he delivered or that additional stops would be added to his routes. In addition to milk, butter, and the usual dairy items, he now loaded holiday flavors of ice cream, including candy cane, gingerbread, and sugar cookie. He also had non-alcoholic eggnog in cartons and jugs. Specialty individual ice creams shaped like Christmas trees and Santa Claus were popular.

"You'll get plenty of overtime this month." Bill had taken over a route for a driver who'd quit. "Comes in handy with end of year taxes, gifts, and all that stuff."

"I'd rather have the time off, though." Angus rearranged his truck to accommodate the new items. "I like Saturdays off, and I like getting home before dark."

Bill laughed. "You won't, not in December. Our schedules will be crazy through New Year's Eve, and then things will slack. Sometimes the company even asks for volunteers to make runs on Sunday. They pay double time for it, too."

Angus's heart sank. "I won't work Sunday. I go to church and spend the day with Kathleen."

Although he still rose early, his routine changed. Angus was now lucky to arrive home by five, sometimes six. He no longer stopped at Kathleen's apartment but headed home. Sometimes, she was there, but even when she wasn't, she always left something he could warm up so he had a hot meal. He noticed she kept up his laundry without being asked and kept the place neat.

"Angus, are you sick?" Kathleen asked one evening. He rested his chin on his left hand and ate with his right. "You don't seem to have any appetite."

He forced a smile. "I'm just worn out. I wake up tired, stay weary, and go to bed exhausted. The weather's bad. It seems like all I do is drive in the rain and get wet." He stirred his portion of cottage pie and lifted a spoonful to his mouth. "It's delicious."

A worry line bisected her forehead. "You should go get some sleep as soon as you finish eating. Tomorrow night is the kindergarten program. I wanted you to come, but maybe you should sleep instead."

Angus forced himself to listen. "I'll come. What time is it?"

"Seven, in the high school auditorium. Come over to my apartment, and we'll eat a quick supper there."

He nodded. "Will do, honey. I'm sorry I'm so tired."

"Don't be. You're working too many hours and wearing yourself too thin." Kathleen rose and stood behind him. Her hands massaged his shoulders.

"Ahh. Feels good." His tight muscles eased beneath her touch. "You're gonna put me to sleep."

Kathleen offered a light laugh. "That's the idea, babe."

Although the massage relaxed him, Angus didn't go to sleep soon or rest well. He woke to the alarm, forced his body to rise, and hit the road for another long day. He shaved two deliveries from his list so he could be at Kathleen's by five-thirty. They ate ham sandwiches with canned soup, then left for the school. Angus kissed her in the corridor as she left him to meet her class and found a seat in the crowded venue. Although the total number of kindergarten students equaled less than sixty in three classes, one of which Kathleen taught, the place was packed. Angus sandwiched into a seat on the end of a row on the right front and hoped he would have a good view from the spot.

At seven, Trevor Weissman took the stage with a microphone in hand. "Good evening, parents, families, and friends. I'd like to welcome you to the showcase our youngest students have put together. No photos during the program, please, and definitely no flash. At the end, please do not rush to the stage to find your student. Teachers will have their classes available in the lobby. I'd also like to introduce and thank our three kindergarten teachers, Miss Kathleen Birdwell, Mrs. Darcy Masters, and Mrs. Susan Trejo. Our music teacher, Mr. Samuel Simpson, also deserves thanks. Without them, this show would have never made it to the stage! Let's give them a round of applause, please."

Angus rolled his eyes, but he clapped. He didn't care for the principal and cared for his interest in Kathleen even less. As the students filed onto a three-tiered riser, Kathleen stepped to the side. Weissman stood beside her. Simpson stood before the kids, leading them in the songs, and the other two teachers were across the stage.

The tunes were familiar to Angus, although he had no children and hadn't been at a school program since he was a student. The kids sang *The Wheels of the Bus*, *The ABC Song*, *Twinkle, Twinkle Little Star*, *Row, Row, Row Your Boat*, and *This Land Is Your Land*. He enjoyed the songs but struggled to stay awake despite the music. His attention wandered from the kids to Kathleen, especially when the principal leaned close to her.

Angus steamed as Weissman whispered into her ear and twice patted her shoulder. After the program ended, as applause echoed through the auditorium, Weissman took Kathleen's hand and held it. If it wouldn't cause a ruckus, Angus would have stormed the stage and snatched her.

By the time the kids had all been reunited with the parents and the lights dimmed, Angus almost wished he hadn't attended. Fatigue settled over him, and he hoped he could make the drive to his house without falling asleep at the wheel. He yawned as Kathleen approached. His mood improved when she hugged him and kissed his cheek.

"What did you think?" Her smile lit the night as they exited the high school.

"Good program. I actually knew the songs they sang." Angus put his right arm around her shoulders. "How many of the kids are in your room?"

"Twenty-one. My kiddos were the ones filling the front row and half the second tier." Kathleen leaned against him. "I'm glad it's over, though. I always worry one of the little ones might fall off the risers or something."

"Thank God no one did." Angus unlocked his truck and helped her into the passenger seat. Once he got behind the wheel, he considered mentioning Weissman but didn't. He was too tired, and he didn't want to fight. "Let me get you home."

Kathleen invited him to stay, and he almost did, but Angus returned home. He collapsed into bed, slept, and rose in the morning for another day. By Friday, he wished he'd never taken the job, but he pushed through, took Kathleen out to dinner, and slept till almost nine on Saturday. For a man who seldom slept late, that ranked as a record.

Kathleen arrived at noon. She brought a bag of tacos, nacho chips with dip, and a pan of brownies she had baked. She wore jeans, a long-sleeved blouse, and a flannel-lined jacket.

"Hey, honey." Angus took the food from her. "Are we still cutting a tree today?"

"Of course. Do you have one picked out?" She entered the kitchen and pulled out a chair.

Angus shook his head. "I ain't had the energy this week to find one. I didn't get home before dark any night, but I know where there's a stand of cedar trees. We'll start there. I hope they haven't got too tall or wide."

"Let's eat first. I'm hungry. What did you have for breakfast?" Kathleen took a pair of plates from the cupboard. She divided the tacos and put the nachos in the middle.

"Cereal." Angus grabbed a jar of salsa from the fridge and took his place at the table. He grasped her hands in his and asked a simple blessing.

The day was sunny but brisk as he led her down a narrow path into the woods behind his house. After close to a quarter mile, Angus halted beside a small stand of cedars. Several towered above his head, but two remained small. "They've grown since I came out here, but I think one of these will work."

Kathleen eyed the evergreens. "They look scraggly. Are you sure you don't want to go buy an artificial tree?"

"It's this or nothing." Angus knelt and cleared the weeds away from the trunk. "I'm not into fake anything."

He used the bow saw he'd brought and cut down the smallest of cedars. Angus estimated it stood four or five feet tall. Once down, he lifted it over his shoulder and carried it to the house. Kathleen trailed behind. "Isn't it heavy?"

"Not too bad. Drag out the stand when we get there." Outside the back door, he shook it to get rid of bugs and brushed debris from the branches. Angus wrestled the cedar into the metal tree stand and stood it upright. He shivered in his aged jean jacket as the wind gusted.

"You should be wearing your coat." Kathleen huddled

into her outerwear.

Angus snorted. "I would if I had one. I haven't had a need for a coat in years, but it's chillier this year than most." Highs had been in the fifties and low sixties, with lows flirting with the freezing mark. It might not be cold in some parts of the country, but it was much cooler than normal for East Texas. "I guess I probably should buy one."

She opened the back door so he could wrestle the tree inside. "Definitely before you catch cold."

He toted the cedar inside. "I hope I don't. I hate being sick or having a snotty nose."

Angus placed the tree in the corner beside the kitchen doorway. The aroma filled his house, and he grinned. "What do you think? It works right here. There's even an outlet behind it."

Kathleen put her hands on her hips. "Looks good. Let's run to town to get some decorations and find a winter coat for you."

"What about this stuff?" Angus dug through the boxes sitting beside the couch.

"It's fit for the trash. Keep your stocking and pitch the rest unless something has sentimental value." Kathleen pulled the oversized sock and put it aside.

"None of it does," Angus said. "I just hate to toss out stuff I might use later."

Her eyes met his. "For what?"

She had a valid point. "Okay. I'll get rid of the rest. I don't suppose you want to decorate with popcorn strings or dried flowers." Angus dumped the decorations into a trash bag.

"Do you?"

He laughed. "I don't, not really. Maybe someday, but not this year. Let's head for the discount store."

Kathleen insisted they shop for a coat first. Angus rejected the nylon puffer jackets. "They're too shiny," he complained. He liked a buffalo plaid jacket, but she didn't think it would be warm enough. They both liked a camo-patterned parka.

Angus tried it on in the aisle. "It would work. I like the darker one, not the autumn colors."

"It fits well." She ran her hand across his back and tugged at the coat.

"I want it big so I'm not hindered unloading product." He stretched out his arms and decided it wasn't too snug. "I ain't wearing the hood, though."

She flipped it over his head, and he flinched. "Why not?"

"I'm not six years old. Let's go buy decorations before I'm out of the notion."

Kathleen made the selections, which included red and silver tinsel garlands, a garland made of plastic peppermints, two strings of multi-color miniature lights, and Western-themed ornaments. She chose boots, saddles, Santa in a cowboy hat, horses, a set of red, white, and blue five-point stars, three bright red cardinals, and one box of red satin balls. Angus picked the angel topper and wanted Kathleen to pick a stocking.

"If I'm hanging one up, so are you."

"I'll bring mine from home. Let's go decorate."

Angus admitted the tree turned out pretty. They ate chicken-ala-king over biscuits, watched an old holiday special Kathleen brought, and turned out the lights. She put a Johnny Cash Christmas CD into the player, and they listened, happy, warm, and safe for the moment.

He couldn't ask for anything more.

CHAPTER THIRTEEN

The Christmas tree boosted his spirits, and the new coat kept Angus warm, but he couldn't shake his fatigue. On the last weekend before the holiday, he and Kathleen had their first disagreement. She wanted to spend Christmas with her mom and family over on Caddo Lake. Angus preferred to stay home.

"Mom's planned a huge feast, and the boys are there. Austin and Travis need our love right now. Mindy won't be out of rehab for months. They can't even go visit her!" Kathleen raised her voice as she spoke. Some of the other diners at the chain restaurant turned toward her. "I thought we could go and make a long weekend out of the holiday."

Angus stirred his garlic mashed potatoes and cut a bite of his steak. "I can't. I gotta work the day after Christmas and probably Saturday too. Sugar, I wish I could. I reckon you could, though."

Kathleen put her fork on the table. "I don't want to go without you. I'd like us to be together for Christmas."

He sighed. "I would, too. Why don't we see if everybody can come to my place? It's decorated for the first time in years." Angus also had ordered rings from an old-fashioned jeweler who made custom designs, but he wasn't sure his purchase would be ready in time for the holiday. He planned to ask the question on New Year's Eve.

"Oh, Angus." Kathleen rolled her eyes. "I doubt Mom and Tony will want to make the trip."

Neither did he. Angus lifted his left eyebrow. "Oh, yeah? We can call and ask."

She scowled at him. "I guess we can, but I'm not thrilled."

He rubbed his face. Angus had a pounding headache. He'd spent a long Saturday on the road but rallied so he could take Kathleen out. Right now, he wished he'd stayed home. Angus had thought he would enjoy the holidays this year, and there had been moments, but most of the season had been grueling. "We'll phone when we get back to your place or mine."

Kathleen rolled her eyes. "Whatever." She picked at her chicken alfredo with little interest and avoided making eye contact.

Angus ate his ribeye cooked exactly the way he liked, but he didn't enjoy it. The hostile silence didn't improve his appetite. He swallowed a bite and attempted conversation. "How did your faculty Christmas party go last night?"

For the first time since they began dating, they hadn't gone out on Friday evening. Kathleen had attended a catered banquet for school employees. Angus had missed her, especially since she hadn't called afterward.

"It was okay." She forced the words out with effort. "I'd have rather been with you, Angus."

Her remark softened his anger. "Honey, I know. What did they serve?"

"Lasagna and garlic toast. It wasn't very good. I ended up with indigestion and was up half the night with my stomach." She put her right hand over her tummy and sighed.

"Do you feel better now?" Angus offered his left hand, and she took it.

Kathleen nodded. "I'm fine. I just didn't have a good time or sleep well. I'm sorry, Angus. I'm probably taking it out on you. Trevor was obnoxious."

"The principal?"

"Yes. He sat beside me and talked non-stop. He asked me out for New Year's Eve, and I told him absolutely not, that I'm seeing you. He made some rude comments about our age difference, and I left early."

"You should have come out to the house." If she had, though, Angus would have wanted to go punch the man in the nose.

"My stomach hurt, so I went home. I figured you would be in bed."

Angus had been. He'd come home, wolfed down a burger he bought on the way, and retired for the night. Then he rose to the alarm and repeated another long day. "Let's don't fight. If your mom says no, then I'll go."

They returned to his place, and Angus made the call. He used the speakerphone function so Kathleen could hear.

Marisol agreed without any hesitation. "As long as we can all be together, I don't care where we are," she told him. "I can bring the food and cook it at your place or Kathleen's."

"I'd like it if you did. I've been working six days a week, and I'm dog tired. If you want, you and Tony can stay here. I have a spare room. I can sleep on the couch and let the boys have mine. I actually have a tree this year." He had gifts bought, too, and would pick up more.

"Thank you, Angus. If you don't mind, we will. Tony smoked a turkey, and I'm baking a huge ham. I'll bring them plus everything else for dinner. Can we come on the 24th?"

"Sure. I'll be at work, but I'll leave a key with Kathleen." Angus realized he should have already given her one and resolved to do so.

On Sunday, after church, he provided Kathleen with a key to his home. He would have taken her to a restaurant, but instead, they picked up some takeout fried chicken. After they ate, she helped him wrap the few gifts he'd bought. Angus had chosen Western shirts for the boys, a couple of age-appropriate board games, and some paper targets. He would pick up gift cards for Marisol and Tony. He hoped to pick up the rings soon, but he'd also bought a heart-shaped locket, some perfume, and a coffee mug for Kathleen. He would wrap those later.

"Targets? Are Austin and Travis old enough to shoot?" Kathleen asked as she put the packages beneath the tree.

"Yeah. I found my old BB gun and my grandpa's the other day in the closet. I thought if the weather's good, I'll teach them. Bart would have if he was still here." Angus hoped the weather would warm up for Christmas. "I'll make sure they learn safety, too."

She smiled. "I think they'll like shooting, Angus."

He worked the three days before the holiday, including Christmas Eve. The dairy handed out bonus checks and let the drivers leave by 3, so he made it home before dark. Angus found his house full of Kathleen's family. Every light burned, and when he came through the kitchen door, he heard chatter, laughter, and music. He grinned. Maybe keeping Christmas at his house wasn't a bad idea.

Kathleen met him as he hung up his coat, and he pulled her into his embrace. He caught the scent of her sweet perfume and, beneath it, the fresh smells of cleaning products. Angus kissed her and held her close. "I'm glad to be home."

"You're early." She stroked his cheek. "Mom and everyone is here. I'm making hamburgers and homemade fries for supper. If you want to go to church tonight, we can."

He considered it. Since Christmas Eve fell on Wednesday, there would be the usual midweek service. "Nah," he told her. "I'm tired, and it's gonna be a big day tomorrow. We can stay home, pop some corn, maybe watch a movie or something."

"Great minds think alike." Kathleen laughed. "I brought a couple of holiday movies I thought the boys might like. One is *The Polar Express,* and the other is *How The Grinch Stole Christmas.*"

Angus didn't think he could stand watching a green furry wreak havoc before redeeming the holiday. "Let's go with the train, sugar."

Since the boys were still small, the evening ended early. Travis and Austin shared Angus's bed. Marisol and Tony bunked in the guest room. Angus gathered up a spare blanket and pillow. "I wish you could stay, too, baby. I hate the fact you're driving back to town."

"I could be talked into staying." Kathleen revealed a small suitcase, a sleeping bag, and a pillow. "I thought I'd take the couch if you don't mind the recliner. That way, I'm here early to help Mom in the kitchen, too."

Thank you, Lord. "I like your plan." Once downstairs, he settled into the recliner wearing sweatpants and a T-shirt. He had stoked the wood stove earlier so the house would be comfortable. "Good night, Katydid."

Kathleen leaned over and kissed him. "Sleep well, Angus."

To his surprise, he did, but he woke early. He hadn't lost his fatigue, and his body ached. Angus put on a long-sleeved flannel shirt and made coffee. Kathleen rose while he was in the kitchen. She warmed the cinnamon rolls she had baked the previous day.

"I can scramble some eggs or fry bacon to go with the rolls." She sipped coffee.

Angus wrinkled his nose. "I ain't very hungry, but you can if you want."

She fixed both, but Angus ate little. The roll tasted a little sweet, and the bacon salty. As far as he could tell, the eggs had no flavor at all. He drank multiple cups of coffee as they gathered around his tree to exchange gifts.

The boys were pleased with the cowboy shirts, but they whooped with delight when they saw the targets.

"Are we gonna shoot, Uncle Angus?" Austin asked.

"You bet we are." Angus gathered up discarded wrapping paper with a trash bag.

"Open your presents, Angus." Kathleen took over his task. "I love the locket. I'll put our pictures inside."

He managed a smile. "I hoped you would. Okay, here goes." He shook one of the packages and shrugged. "I wonder what's inside."

Kathleen bought him a fine pocketknife, and he insisted on retrieving a dime. Angus handed it to her, and she frowned. "What's that for?"

"Gotta give you silver so we don't sever our relationship." He felt silly sharing, but he'd heard the adage all his life and wasn't taking chances.

The two boys gave him a new flannel shirt, Kathleen also bought him an emerald-green Western shirt with pearl snaps that would be dressy enough for church, and Marisol gifted him with his favorite cologne. Years had passed since he received any presents, and the gesture touched him.

Angus set up a target distant enough from the house to be safe. He brought out the BB guns and went over safety with the boys. Angus explained how the weapons worked. "These aren't toys. You can get hurt, so don't ever aim them at each other or anyone. A BB can damage your eye or hurt you, understand?"

Travis nodded. "We do."

Although the sun shone, a chill wind blew, stirring the dust and rustling the bare tree branches. Angus wore his new coat and still shivered, even though he actually donned the hood. By the time they finished, both boys had hit the target a few times, and Angus had demonstrated his skill.

"Come in and eat. Dinner's on the table." Kathleen emerged swaddled in a heavy jacket.

Someone had put the leaf in the old table so it had enough room for all of them. Angus took his place at the head, with Kathleen seated at his right. He reached out and grasped her hand for the blessing.

"Gracious Lord, thank you for this fine day and for your Son. Thank you for all this fine food and family to share the meal with. Bless us today and every day. In Jesus name, we pray."

Kathleen and Marisol had provided a feast. Angus filled his plate, although his appetite remained absent. He nibbed at the smoked turkey, ate a few slices of ham, managed to down some scalloped potatoes, eat some corn, and polish off two hot rolls. He turned down seconds and claimed he was too full for a slice of the cherry cheesecake Marisol provided. Everyone, including Angus, pitched in to set the kitchen to rights, and once they finished, Marisol rounded up her bunch.

"We're heading home, Angus. Thank you for a lovely Christmas. I know you work tomorrow, so we'll get out of your hair." She hugged him as they stood in the kitchen.

"You don't have to split. Stay another night." If they did, he wouldn't mind, but he craved his own bed. Right now, he wasn't feeling his best.

"We'll come back another time. Grab a nap. You look so tired." Marisol linked her arm with Tony's. "Boys, tell Uncle Angus goodbye."

"Bye," they chorused. "Thank you."

"Aw, you're welcome. I'm glad y'all came." As soon as the door closed behind them, Angus retreated into his recliner. He pulled the blanket he'd used overnight over him.

Kathleen paused as she settled onto the couch. "Angus, what's wrong? You haven't even kissed me at all today."

He met her gaze and told the truth. "I think I'm coming down with a cold, sugar, and I don't want to give it to you."

She frowned. "Maybe you're just worn out. Do you feel sick?"

Angus shrugged. "Just achy and dry-mouthed, which usually means I'm catching cold. My throat's a little scratchy, but maybe I'll feel better if I sleep a little."

Kathleen rose and stood over him. She laid her right hand across his forehead. "You're not feverish. I hope you're not getting sick."

"So do I." He knew he was, but he wouldn't admit it to her. "If you want to go home, honey, you can."

She shot him a hard look and sighed. "If you get sick, I'll take care of you. School's out until the Monday after New Year's, so I'm staying. I'll change the sheets on the beds while you're resting. You ought to be in your bed tonight."

He felt no better when he woke after a two-hour nap. If anything, he felt worse. Angus popped a few aspirin for his aching body but refused any cold medication. It never helped for long, and when it wore off, he always felt twice as terrible. Despite all the leftovers, Kathleen opened a can of chicken and rice soup for a light supper. Angus ate most of a bowl and finished a single biscuit. At her insistence, he headed upstairs to bed early, but he didn't sleep well.

Angus woke congested and groaned. He forced himself to rise, dress in his uniform, and head downstairs. Kathleen met him in the kitchen and handed him a fresh cup of coffee.

"You look terrible." She stroked his hand as she gave him the mug.

"I've felt better." Angus downed the coffee and washed down more aspirin.

"Maybe you should call in sick." She took a cinnamon roll out of the microwave. "I warmed you a little breakfast."

"I can't. I don't want to lose the job or the holiday pay for yesterday." He eyed the roll with little interest. Mucous trickled down his throat, and his stomach was uneasy. "I'll take it with me, sugar. I gotta go."

Kathleen wrapped her arms around him for a hug. "I'll be here when you come home. Be careful, Angus. Is there anything I can pick up for you? Orange juice, cold meds, or throat lozenges?"

"Juice, maybe." For a second, he almost decided to stay home but didn't.

With every hour, Angus felt worse. He fought the cold as he delivered product and shivered despite his coat. By the time he worked the two days after Christmas, he wanted to curl up and hibernate. He hadn't had a cold this severe in years. Kathleen greeted him both evenings, fed him a simple supper, and pampered him as much as he would allow. He didn't spike a fever, but he ached from head to toe. When he wasn't sneezing, he was blowing his nose, and by Sunday, he developed a harsh cough.

"I cain't go to church," he announced Sunday morning. "I'd rather stay home and try to shake this cold."

Kathleen hovered. "You look so miserable. I can go to town and get any medication you want."

He shook his head and winced when it ached more. "It doesn't help for long. I'll be okay in a few days. It's just a cold."

"It's a nasty one." She brought him a mug of coffee.

Angus wrapped his fingers around it and savored the heat. No matter how many layers he wore or if he covered up with a blanket, he remained cold. "Thanks, sugar."

She made chicken and dumplings from scratch for dinner. Angus could barely taste it, but the soft, warm food went down easily. "This is good, sugar. Thanks for making it."

"Any time. You really need to eat. The old saying is, 'feed a cold and starve a fever.' You might feel better faster if you ate more."

"I'll try."

On Monday, against Kathleen's wishes, Angus hauled himself to work. *Three days and I'm off for New Year's. If I don't feel much better, maybe I will call in a day or two.* He picked up the rings and zipped them into an inside coat pocket. He drank huge amounts of coffee, soda, and orange juice he picked up at a drive-through in every town. He ate little, despite Kathleen's advice, because nothing tasted good to him. Swallowing hurt. On New Year's Eve, he asked to leave early, and Bill agreed.

"You've been working sick. Go home, get over it."

On the way, Angus broke down and bought some cough suppressant tablets so he could rest. Kathleen wanted to send him straight to bed, but the stairs made him wheeze, so he collapsed into his recliner. She tucked blankets over him and put a pillow behind his head.

"I'm worried." She used the flat of one hand to check Angus for fever. "You should be better by now."

"A cold lasts a week or so. It ain't been one, not quite. I'll feel less sick by Friday, probably." He hacked and rubbed his chest because it hurt. "I had plans for us New Year's Eve, but I ain't gonna make it."

"We'll do something special later. Right now, you focus on feeling good again." She sank onto the floor beside the recliner and held his hand.

Angus clung to her fingers. Kathleen proved to be a lifeline. Without her, he would have burrowed into bed and stayed there. *Nobody dies of a stinking cold. I'll be fine in a couple of days.*

He rallied on New Year's Day, not because he'd improved, but because he wanted Kathleen to smile. The worry lines knitting across her forehead concerned him. Angus ate the roast pork and dressing she made for dinner as best he could. He tried to watch a Western with her but drifted to sleep until he woke coughing.

Two of his cowboy friends, Yancey Cartwright and Frenchy, came to visit, but Angus was too sick to care. Kathleen entertained them and fed them slices of pie while Angus struggled to keep up with the conversation.

Yancey shook his hand. "We're heading out. You're too sick to enjoy company, but if you need anything, give me or Davy or any of us guys a holler."

Angus grimaced as he tried to smile. "Will do."

"I ain't never seen Angus to take sick." Yancey lowered his voice as he stood at the door, hat in hand. Frenchy had already headed outside. "I wrote my number down for you, Kathleen. Call me if you need help. I mean it."

Angus eavesdropped to hear her answer.

"Thanks. I may call. He says it's just a cold, but I'm not sure."

"Even a cold can turn into bronchitis or flu or pneumonia. Happened to my brother a few years back, and he ended up in the hospital. Take care of ol' Angus, you hear?"

"I will." Kathleen shut the front door and added a log to the wood stove.

Although he had vowed he wouldn't, Angus called in for the rest of the week. Lifting product had been too hard and made him cough harder. He tried to imagine another day behind the wheel of the truck and couldn't. He wasn't sure he could sit up for hours, let alone pilot the vehicle down the road.

"I think you need to go see the doctor." Kathleen dosed him with pain relievers and cough suppressant. "Do you want me to make an appointment?"

Angus had considered it but shook his head. "No, I don't like doctors. They always find something wrong with you." Besides, he didn't mention he feared a doc might put him in the hospital. Ever since Yancey mentioned more serious illnesses, Angus worried he might have one. He'd never felt this terrible with a cold.

Exasperated, she sighed. "Probably because if you go to the doctor, you're sick."

He had a long coughing bout, and she placed her hand on his chest.

"Angus, I can feel the congestion. You're very ill. Won't you let me make an appointment?"

He shook his head. "Nah. If I decide I need to go, I'll tell you. I promise."

"Stubborn." She paced the room. "You're too stubborn, Angus."

If he had enough energy, he would have laughed.

On Saturday morning, Angus thought he might be really sick. He couldn't stop coughing, and each round wracked his body. He choked up some nasty mucous, too, and when he blew his nose, the tissues turned bright yellow and a vile green. His skin ached, and he suspected he had a fever, although he shuddered with chills. He hadn't slept much in the recliner and didn't even attempt the stairs. He got short breathed walking to the bathroom.

"Kathleen," he croaked. She slept curled up on the couch because she refused to leave him. "Hey."

She sat up. Her hair curled wild around her face. "What's the matter, Angus?"

"I think I probably ought to go to the clinic if they can get me in." Admitting it was hard, but being sick was more difficult. "I think maybe I have a fever."

Kathleen touched his head and gasped. "You're burning up, Angus. Let me get a thermometer."

"I ain't got one." He probably should have.

"I do." She headed into the kitchen and returned. "I picked one up in town the other day. Put it under your tongue and keep it there."

Angus managed not to cough, and when she pulled it out, her eyes became huge. "104 degrees, Angus. Let me get you dressed. We're going to town."

She bundled him into sweatpants, a T-shirt, and a flannel shirt, then maneuvered him into his coat. "Can you walk to the truck?"

"I hope." He wasn't sure. "Grab my billfold for the

insurance card, sugar."

Kathleen supported him as he took slow, small steps to his pickup. She boosted him into the passenger seat, then climbed behind the wheel. She dialed the urgent care clinic in town. "I'm bringing Angus Beaton. He's been sick for more than a week, and his temperature is 104."

At the clinic, Kathleen fetched a wheelchair and rolled Angus inside. The staff made him a priority with such a high fever. He grabbed her hand. "Come with me, please."

"I intend to be beside you all the way."

Angus managed, with her help, to sit on the exam table while a nurse took his vitals. As soon as the first available doctor arrived, he listened to Angus's heart and lungs. "How long has he been ill?"

"More than a week." Kathleen supplied the answer. "He wasn't running a fever until this morning."

"His lungs are congested, and I can hear the crackles. I'd say he has pneumonia, but we'll do a chest x-ray to be certain." Dr. Joe Bowen frowned as he looked down Angus's throat.

"I hope you can get one here," Angus muttered. He wasn't about to go to the hospital.

"Absolutely."

Angus lay back on the table until the results arrived. It seemed like hours. "What's the verdict?"

"Bacterial pneumonia in both lungs. You're very ill, Angus. Do you want to go to the hospital in Jacksonville or Palestine?" Dr. Bowen frowned as he pronounced the diagnosis.

"Neither. I ain't going to the hospital." His head might be muzzy, but he knew people died there. Like Bart had.

The doctor argued, Kathleen pleaded, and Angus refused. The compromise would be Kathleen would care for him. He would be on a heavy-duty antibiotics regimen, and a portable oxygen tank would be delivered.

"If he develops breathing issues, call an ambulance." Dr. Bowen fixed his gaze on Kathleen. "Get the meds filled and take him home. He should show improvement in about three days. If not, make another appointment or get him to the hospital stat. I've given him a shot for the antibiotics, and you need to dose him with something for the fever. Also, keep in mind bacterial pneumonia can be contagious, so use precautions."

Kathleen wiped tears from her cheeks. Angus tried to touch her face but failed. "Don't cry."

"Let's get out of here. We're going to my apartment. It's closer."

Angus groaned. "I'll never make it up the stairs."

"Yancey and Frenchy can help."

Before he could protest, Angus's friends met them at the complex. His buddies toted him up the stairs, and Kathleen tucked him into the king-size bed. Yancey picked up the prescriptions and the oxygen.

Once they were alone, Angus gasped for breath when he tried to lay flat. Kathleen propped him up with pillows. "Don't you dare get any sicker. I love you, Angus."

"I love you too, sugar." If he had any remaining doubts about their age difference or if they should get married, they vanished. Her tender care convinced him she had more than a passing infatuation. If she didn't. If Kathleen didn't love him, she wouldn't worry or nurse him. For the first time, he truly understood *"in sickness and in health."*

As long as he didn't die, Angus would ask her to be his bride as soon as he felt better.

CHAPTER FOURTEEN

For a man who claimed he never got sick, Angus couldn't have been more ill. He hadn't ever been this sick or as miserable. His numerous rodeo injuries over the years had hurt, but he didn't think he had ever been down the way he was not. His heavy cold had warped into bacterial pneumonia, and he knew he would probably feel worse before the meds made him better. Angus had an ongoing headache as well as coughing, chest pain, light-headedness, and occasional shortness of breath. He experienced a strange detachment, as if things around him happened in slow motion or underwater.

Kathleen bathed his face with a cool washcloth. "Does this help?"

He shut his eyes and nodded. "Yeah, some."

"The meds should help more. You'll take the antibiotics 4 times a day for 10 days. I'll give you the first one this evening. I'll dose you at six and twelve, both a.m. and p.m. You can take acetaminophen for the fever, and the doc also wrote you a prescription for heavy-duty cough syrup. It's as needed, but I think you should take it at night so you'll get some rest." She tilted her head to indicate the medicines on her dresser. "You need to hush and rest, Angus. You really should be in the hospital."

"No." He spat the word as if it tasted rotten. "I ain't going."

She narrowed her eyes. "If you can't breathe, you will."

Angus fell silent. Talking required effort, and he lacked the strength to make much. Still, he needed her close. "Will you be here?"

She nodded. "I'll scoot the armchair to the bedroom. I need to order some groceries online, so I'll do that. Then I'll be beside you."

Angus groaned. "I really don't feel good, sugar."

Kathleen put the washrag aside. She stroked his hair and tucked an escaped tendril behind his ear. "Your fever's still awfully high. Can you take some acetaminophen? I've got ice water to wash it down."

"Yeah." He swallowed the tablets. The cold liquid went down his sore throat with ease. Angus sipped more from the straw. "Thanks, Kathleen."

She kissed his hot forehead. "Rest. I'll be back in a few."

Over the next several days, Angus got out of bed only to use the bathroom. Although it was only a few steps from the bedroom, he needed Kathleen's support to make the trip. He continued to be miserable. Angus took his meds when Kathleen brought them, sipped water when she offered, slept often, trembled with chills, ached with fever, and coughed. His chest and belly muscles hurt from the effort, but he managed to bring up some nasty mucous. Although he didn't have any appetite and his stomach churned with nausea, Angus downed the broths Kathleen fed him. He didn't vomit, but he often felt he might.

He felt no better for the first five days despite bed rest and antibiotics. Angus had almost decided he never would when he woke early in the morning and felt a little less sick. Kathleen's chair loomed empty, but before he panicked, he glanced to see her curled up beside him on the bed. She wore a long-sleeved flannel nightgown and lay with her left hand resting on his thigh. Her loose hair curled around her face and trailed across her shoulders. Angus smiled because she looked cute, and her presence comforted him.

"Hey, sugar." His voice emerged hoarse, and he raised a hand to massage his throat. A coughing fit hit, and he hacked with so much force his chest burned.

"Angus." Kathleen roused into a sitting position. She

touched his forehead. "You're not as hot."

"I think I'm a little better. I'm hungry." He thought maybe he could eat something more substantial than broth, although he wasn't sure what.

Kathleen picked up the digital thermometer and rolled it across his forehead. "Your fever *is* less, thank God. What do you think you can manage?"

"How about a double bacon cheeseburger with onion rings?" He meant it as a joke.

She rolled her eyes. "I don't think you're ready for one just yet. Do you want to try a little bit of chicken noodle soup?"

"Yeah." Another paroxysm of coughing hit. This time, he choked up a mess of ugly mucous. Deep yellow streaked with green and a little blood stained the tissues Kathleen provided.

"I'll go heat some. Do you want anything else?"

"Instant healing."

Kathleen smiled and bent to kiss his forehead. She smoothed his hair. "If I could give it, I would."

She returned with a lap tray he'd never seen before and a small bowl of soup. She helped him sit more upright, but he couldn't manage to feed himself. When the spoon wobbled in his hand, Kathleen took it and dipped a little soup into his mouth.

The rich broth, thick with noodles, scraps of chicken, and carrots, tasted fantastic. Angus savored the flavor, but he couldn't manage more than half a bowl.

"You might as well take the antibiotic now and some ibuprofen." Kathleen handed him the tablets and put a straw to his lips. "If you're okay for a few minutes, I need to shower and get dressed."

Angus offered a slow nod. "Yeah, I'm good. I ain't going anywhere."

He wished he could clean up and figured he probably stunk. Angus lacked the energy, though, so he could wait.

Although he meant to stay awake, he drifted into a light sleep. He blinked back into awareness. Kathleen had returned to the armchair, dressed in jeans and a light cotton sweater. Her hair had been brushed and tamed into a knot on top of her head, secured with a clip.

"Hey. It's time for another round of antibiotics."

He groaned. "Aw, do I still got to take those?"

"You do for five more days, through Tuesday." Kathleen moved from the chair to the edge of the bed. "I fixed fresh ice water a few minutes ago."

Angus tried to make sense of the date. "Tuesday? What day is this? I thought I went to the doctor on Saturday."

"It's Friday. Tomorrow is a week ago I got you to the clinic." She uncapped a tube of lip balm and applied it to his fever-cracked lips.

"School must have started back by now." His head might be fuzzy, but he could still count. "Aren't you teaching?"

Kathleen shook her head. "No. I've taken a short leave of absence. I couldn't leave you when you're so sick. Trevor called a substitute teacher. She's glad to get the work."

"I hope it won't mess up your job, sugar." *I've been sicker than I realized.*

"I don't think it will." She checked his temperature and smiled. "Fever's still down for now. It hasn't broken, but it's definitely less. Do you want to eat, clean up a little, or sit in the recliner?"

Angus turned his head and tried to see if he smelled. "I probably stink, but I doubt I'm up for a shower."

"I bought some bath wipes. They would be better than nothing." She held up a package of thick adult wipes. "I'll change your T-shirt, too, if you want."

"I do. And if I can make it, I'd like to be in the living room for a little bit. Maybe I wouldn't feel like an invalid." A coughing fit interrupted his words, and he grabbed tissues to catch the mucous. "Maybe I can try some more soup after I get there."

"Take the meds, and we'll do all of the above." Kathleen smiled.

An hour later, cleaned as much as he could be without water, wearing a faded T-shirt, clean underwear which he managed to pull on himself, fresh socks, and a clean pair of sweats, Angus leaned back in the recliner. His breath came short, and his head whirled, but he made it. Kathleen had supported him with a steady arm around his waist, and he'd leaned on her as he hobbled from the bedroom to the living room. Thank God it was a small apartment. "What kind of soup?"

"I have beef vegetable, more chicken noodle, chicken and rice, sirloin burger, clam chowder, or potato."

"Beef vegetable. I don't suppose I might get a biscuit with that." Angus's empty stomach growled.

"No biscuit, but I could do some crackers." Kathleen laid a light throw over his knees. "If you're hungry, you're improving."

Angus managed a larger portion of soup with her help and ate three crackers. Kathleen fixed a tiny serving of orange sherbet, and he finished it. The cool, sweet treat eased his sore throat. Although he didn't feel quite well, he paid more attention. "You took down your tree."

"I did. Do you want to watch TV?"

He frowned. The noise and moving pictures would bother him right now. "Nah." He remembered the cedar tree at his house and made a face. "I bet the tree at my place had dried out and is a mess."

"Marisol and Dr. Tony came over and took it down. Mom worried it would be a fire hazard, and they were concerned about you." Kathleen paused. "I've been crazy worried, Angus. I'm glad you're on the mend. I love you so much."

"I love you too, honey. I'm glad you took care of me. I'll

have to thank her and Tony for dumping the tree. I guess the boys are back in school." He glanced around the room, wondering where his coat might be and hoping the ring remained in the pocket.

"They did. Mom pulled them out of school on Tuesday, and they visited Mindy at the rehab center, then took care of your tree. Austin and Travis want to see you, so I think they're coming back this weekend." Kathleen picked up the dishes and swiped his right cheek with her knuckles. "Do you need anything else? I'm going to change the sheets while you're out of bed."

"Where's my coat?" Angus raised his head to peer.

"It's hanging up on the rack by the door." Kathleen frowned. "Are you cold? I'll get a blanket. You won't be going anywhere where you need a coat for a while."

"I'm okay. I just have something in the pocket, so I wanted to make sure the coat didn't get left at the doc's or something." He sighed with relief. Angus had no idea when he'd pop the question, but it wouldn't be while he didn't feel well and was too weak to walk without assistance.

By Sunday, Angus could shuffle from bed to recliner to bathroom and back. Kathleen had a big pot of chicken and dumplings simmering on the stove, and although he hadn't watched any television, he listened to some classic country tunes. He admired the green plant sitting on a table near the window, all the more after Kathleen told him the dairy sent it along with their get well wishes.

"I figured I might be out of a job." Angus was surprised.

"You're sick, not skipping work, and they're aware. Pete Devorak said your job is waiting when you're well."

He lifted an eyebrow. "When did you talk to him?"

"When I called to tell the company, you had pneumonia in both lungs." She paused for breath. "The church delivered a fruit basket. The pastor said he'll visit when you're able. If you want an orange, apple, or banana, tell me. There's plenty."

"Maybe later. Did I imagine Yancey and Frenchy, or were they here?" He had a vague impression his buddies had been present.

"They came to visit at your house, then helped me get you into the apartment. Yancey's called a couple of times to check on you." Kathleen settled on the couch. "If you feel like company, Mom said the boys would like to come over."

Angus nodded. "Sure, I'd like to see them, your Mom and Dr. Tony, too."

Kathleen grinned. "I'm glad because they'll be here for Sunday dinner. They should arrive around one or one thirty."

"What if I'd said I wasn't up to visiting?" Angus coughed into tissues.

"I would have called Mom and told her to wait." Kathleen handed him a fresh box. "Claudia called the other day."

Angus didn't know the other sisters well. Both had been older than Bart, and he barely recalled them. Susan and Claudia had chosen careers far from Texas. "How's she doing?"

"She thinks Mom went crazy, selling the place and getting married." Kathleen laughed a little. "Claudia apologized for not coming during the holidays. She stayed in California, and Susan didn't leave Baltimore. Mom said they can come at Easter. Hopefully, we can, too."

"Maybe." No one, not even Marisol, had mentioned the older girls at Thanksgiving or Christmas. "At least they won't show up today. I ain't ready for that."

"I'm not either. Do you want to watch the live stream from church this morning?" Kathleen brought her laptop to connect to the television.

"Sure." He did miss church. "Did you make coffee?"

Kathleen turned around. "I did. Do you want a cup?"

Angus hadn't had any since falling sick, but he nodded.

"Yeah, I reckon it'll perk me up for the boys."

He drank a cup and enjoyed it. Angus lowered the recliner in advance of their visit. He didn't want to traumatize the kids by appearing ill or haggard.

Travis and Austin entered wearing troubled faces. Marisol greeted Angus and crossed the room to plant a kiss on his cheek. Tony smiled and waved the boys forward. "Go see your uncle. It's all you've talked about."

"Come on," Angus told them. "Soon as I get over this crud, we'll do some more shooting." He spread his arms wide for a hug, and they rushed him. Angus pulled them close.

"I thought you might die like Dad," Travis told him. "I'm glad you didn't."

Angus shuddered. "Me, too, buddy."

The afternoon after dining on Kathleen's tender, rich chicken and dumplings, angel biscuits, and sherbet strengthened Angus. Watching the church service provided a much-needed boost. Although he didn't sing, Angus tapped his feet in time with the hymns. Visiting with the family, which would soon become his, Angus basked in comfort. He agreed to watch an old John Wayne western with the boys, and before it ended, he asked Travis to bring his coat.

"Here you go, Uncle Angus. It's chilly if you're going outside."

"Nah, I just need something out of the inside pocket." Angus retrieved the ring box and tucked it into the smaller pocket of his sweats. "Could you hang it back up before your aunt notices?"

Kathleen returned from the kitchen where she and Marisol had been gabbing. "Travis, what are you doing with Angus's coat?"

"Hanging it up for him." Travis didn't blink or flinch as he replied.

"Angus?"

He spread his hands wide. "Don't ask, Katydid."

She narrowed her eyes and faked a frown. "I won't, but I'm curious."

"Ask him later. We need to head home. The boys have school tomorrow." Marisol announced. "Angus, take care of yourself."

"I'll try. Kathleen's doing a good job." Angus recalled they had visited Mindy. "How is Mindy?"

Marisol made a face. "Kathleen can tell you. It's a long story, but I think she'll be all right in the long run."

Angus dozed away the rest of the afternoon and ate a second round of chicken and dumplings for supper. Kathleen settled onto the floor in front of the recliner, and he asked the question.

"What about Mindy?" His stomach clenched as he feared the answer.

She drew a deep breath. "Mom said she looks terrible, but her spirits were good. She'll stay at the rehab center for at least another month, then she may be released. Mom will be responsible, and Mindy will have to continue with therapy. She acted glad to see Travis and Austin, and she wants you to come see her."

He groaned. "Why? I hoped she was over the notion she and I had something going."

Kathleen offered him a half-grin. "She says she is and owes you an apology. I thought maybe when you've recovered, we can go visit."

"I'll think about it once I'm well." Angus shut his eyes. He didn't want to think about Bart's widow.

"That's fair." Kathleen leaned against his knees. "If everything works out, Mindy will move in with Mom and Tony for a while, for the boys' sake. Eventually, Mom thinks maybe she can find a job and a place to rent over on Caddo."

Angus nodded his approval. "Good. It's far enough away but close, too."

"I need to tell you something else, too." Kathleen grasped his hand in hers.

His heart sank. Hopefully, she wasn't about to tell him they weren't compatible. "What?"

"Trevor wants me back at work a week from tomorrow. He says he'll post my job and hire a replacement if I don't." Kathleen sighed. "I don't know if I should."

"You'd better. Don't lose your first teaching job over me, sugar. By then, I'll be well enough to manage. I probably ought to go home anyway." Angus kissed her hand. "I bet I've worn out my welcome."

Her eyes flashed with fire. "Never! Stay as long as you want."

Angus grinned. "Simmer down, baby. I'll stay the rest of the week, but probably I'll go home Saturday. You can come stay with me, if you want, or come out every night. You can bunk in the spare bedroom. I ain't going back to work any time soon."

He wasn't sure if he ever would, but he needed to ponder the idea thoroughly before he said anything.

Kathleen rose and pulled him upright. "As long as I see you every single day, I can live with that."

She looped her arms around his neck and kissed his mouth for the first time since he fell ill.

He kissed her back, then stopped. "I don't want you to get sick, Kathleen."

"You're not contagious any longer, Angus. Kiss me back." She returned her lips to his mouth.

Angus couldn't deny a lady's request, so he did. The long kiss made him breathless, but it warmed his heart and eased an emptiness in his soul, well worth the effort. "I love you so much,

Katydid."

She replied with a smile.

Over the next week, Angus moved slowly, but he felt a little better each day. He lacked strength, but he graduated from soups and invalid food to heartier dishes, including meatloaf, pork chops with scalloped potatoes, and oven-fried chicken. They celebrated the end of his antibiotics early in the week, and on Friday, Kathleen returned from running errands with a bacon cheeseburger for Angus. He devoured the sandwich with gusto.

Each night, they shared the wide king-sized bed but kept it chaste. Angus, an only child, had never shared a bed with anyone, so he found the experience novel. He confessed he wasn't sure about returning to his dairy route.

"Don't," Kathleen said as she scrambled eggs for a mid-morning breakfast on Saturday. "I swear the long hours and being on the road every day contributed to you getting so sick. Can you afford to quit?"

Angus nodded. "Yeah, I have some money in the bank, and my bills aren't much. I can manage until I get my own business going. I figure I'll do some blacksmithing. I've got the forge, and there isn't much competition. I also want to train horses. I might raise some rough stock, too. I don't know."

"I know you can do all of it. I hope you're done with rodeo." Kathleen placed two plates with eggs and toast on the table.

He chuckled. "I'm probably too old, and besides, I don't want to get hurt."

They linked hands for the blessing and ate.

After breakfast, he gathered up all his belongings. His truck sat in the parking area where Kathleen parked it after she took him to the doctor. "Ride shotgun with me."

Kathleen jingled her keys. "I thought I'd follow you in my car."

"I'd rather you ride with me. I ain't drove since I got sick."
He didn't doubt his ability. He just wanted her with him. "If you
stay tonight, we can go to church tomorrow morning. I'll bring
you back to the apartment after I buy your dinner."

"Let me pack a bag. Your place probably needs cleaning.
I'll have to change the sheets, and you'd better get some groceries
on the way." Kathleen tossed her keyring into her purse. "Are
you up to the supermarket?"

"I hope to shout I am." Angus cringed at the thought, but
he'd manage.

His house smelled musty after several weeks. Dust
coated most of the surfaces, and when Angus opened the fridge,
he almost gagged. Leftovers from Christmas remained, so he
dumped those. Kathleen offered to scour the shelves, but he
refused. "I can do that."

"Then I'll do laundry and clean. If you get tired, sit and
take a break. I'll check on you in a few minutes." Kathleen pulled
him close in a hug. "If you need me, holler."

Angus wasn't quick, but he got the refrigerator in order.
He washed a few dishes that remained in the sink and swept the
floor. Winded, he retreated to his recliner as Kathleen bustled
through the house. By the time she finished, his house smelled
fresh and lemony from the products she used. A gentle winter
rain echoed on the metal roof, and Angus enjoyed the sound. He
liked the sweep of the wind through the trees. It was a welcome
change from the sound of steel-belted tires against pavement and
the unending sounds of an apartment complex. No dogs barked
or children called out. He heard no emergency sirens or the noise
of vehicles at all hours.

Kathleen warmed up some of Angus's chili from the
freezer for an easy evening meal. Afterward, Angus pulled her
onto his lap in the recliner, and they cuddled. He kissed her and
stroked her hair, happy for her company.

At bedtime, he mounted the stairs with slow, cautious steps. They parted and slept in separate bedrooms. She made muffins for a light breakfast before church, which Angus enjoyed.

They walked into the sanctuary together. People flocked to Angus, shaking his hand, offering a few hugs, and welcoming him back. He sang along with every hymn and listened to the pastor's sermon. He turned down a dozen invitations for dinner. As promised, he took Kathleen out for a catfish dinner with all the trimmings.

Angus lingered over the meal. He really didn't want to take her home, but she needed to get ready for school in the morning. No matter how much conversation they shared, he couldn't stretch things out past four, so he took her home.

He carried her small bag and climbed the steps to her apartment without any trouble.

"Come in for a little while." Kathleen unlocked the door and stepped forward.

As much as Angus longed to, he shook his head. "I best not. If I do, I won't want to go. Call me tomorrow before you head to work, sugar. Are you coming to the house afterward?"

"Yes and I will. Don't try to cook. We bought plenty of groceries. How about meatballs?" She twined her hands through his.

"Sounds good." Angus held her close and kissed her. "I'm heading out."

"Call me tonight, promise?"

He grinned. "Sure."

His house loomed empty. Angus unlocked the door, turned on the radio for some country music, and sat. If it wasn't cool, he would go tromp the woods. He considered heading to the barn to look over his smithy stuff but didn't. A dark gray sky threatened more rain, and he didn't want to relapse. Angus rambled around the house like a few dry beans in an otherwise empty glass jar before he settled into his recliner. He missed Kathleen's voice, her attention and care, and her soft fragrance. Twice, he opened his mouth to tell her something before he remembered she wasn't there.

Tomorrow, he would phone the dairy and give his notice. He would talk to Kathleen and wait for her arrival. Angus would rack his brain for a romantic spot to propose, which would be no easy task in winter.

For now, though, he dozed and dreamed of Kathleen. Before he headed to bed, he called her.

"Hey, sugar, I miss you. I love you."

CHAPTER FIFTEEN

Through the week, Angus considered and rejected a number of places for his proposal. He thought about heading over to Caddo Lake, poling a pirogue to a scenic spot, and asking Kathleen there. In late January, though, or even February, temperatures were likely to be chilly, if not cold. The Tyler Rose Garden came to mind, but this wasn't the season. Nothing would be blooming. Angus thought about a day trip down to a beach, but the same conditions applied. He could take her to an upscale restaurant, but Angus preferred privacy. He thought Kathleen did, too.

Angus used his aged laptop to research and still found nothing. Numerous bed and breakfast inns were available, but they weren't married. Sharing her apartment while he was ill was one thing, and so was Kathleen sleeping in his guest bedroom. Spending a night together in one bed wasn't on his agenda. *I can wait for the honeymoon.*

Waiting until spring or summer wasn't an option. He hoped to be married by then, if not sooner. In desperation, when he couldn't come up with anything, Angus phoned Marisol.

"Hello." Her voice flowed across the miles like warm honey over cinnamon toast. "What's up, Angus?"

"I have a problem, and I hoped you might help." Angus stretched out on the couch and rubbed his face with his free hand.

"As long as it's not a problem with Mindy, and if Kathleen is fine, I'll try."

"I want to ask Katydid to marry me. I'd like it to be a romantic place, but in the middle of winter, anywhere outdoors isn't an option." Angus cleared his throat. "I thought maybe you'd have an idea or two."

When she didn't answer immediately, he wished he hadn't called.

"Let me think about it. My first husband took me to New Orleans, and we ate at one of the oldest restaurants in the French Quarter. He asked me over shrimp etouffee." Marisol pronounced the name of the city like a native, *Nawlins*. Tony asked me on the Riverwalk in San Antonio. If I remember, Bart proposed to Mindy at a rodeo. I don't imagine any of those ideas help."

"No, not really." Angus sat and scratched his chin. "I could pop the question at school, but I doubt the principal would like it if I did. I'd rather not wait till spring or summer. Heck, I'm not patient enough to hold out until Valentine's Day."

"I don't know what to suggest." Marisol sighed. "I'll try to come up with something—hey, wait. I've got an idea. Stage a romantic evening at home."

"How? Angus tried to imagine and failed.

"Fill your living room with candles, flowers, and maybe balloons. You could hang streamers like at prom and play some love songs on the stereo." Marisol's volume increased. "Pick up a special meal and have a small cake or something. Kathleen would love it!"

She would. Angus smiled. "I could manage to do that, I think. Thank you, Marisol."

"No problem, Angus. Do you have a ring?"

He fingered his front pocket. No matter what he wore, he kept the ring close. "Yes, I do."

"Then you're set! I'm happy I came up with an idea."

So was Angus.

He quizzed Kathleen over supper. Angus had dug out an ancient candle he'd found and lit it.

"I thought I might pick up a new candle or two in town. This one's old. What's your favorite?" He did his best to sound casual.

"Vanilla and lavender, although this one is pleasant. What scent is it?"

Angus laughed. "I don't have a clue. Maybe apples?"

Recalling the roses and daisies he brought her once, he almost asked about her favorite flowers. It would be too obvious, though, so he didn't. Roses would do.

Angus decided he'd pop the question on Friday night. Although Marisol suggested he set the scene at his place, he decided against it. He had a key to Kathleen's apartment, and she had one for his house. After school was dismissed for the day, Kathleen went home or came out to his place. He would ask her to marry him at the apartment.

Since they always had a date on Friday evening, Angus rolled with it. Sometimes, he picked her up at school or her place. Kathleen also often drove to his house. "I'll meet you at your apartment after school," he told her Friday morning. "I got a few ideas about what we'll do."

"I'm okay with whatever," Kathleen replied. "It's supposed to rain. I don't mind if we stay home and watch a movie or something. Do you want me to pick up takeout on the way home?"

"Nah, I'll take care of supper. Is today a short day or not?" School dismissed early on some Fridays, but not all. Angus could never quite remember the schedule.

"It's a full day." Her sigh echoed into his ear over the phone. "We have a faculty meeting after school. I doubt I'll be home before four-thirty or five."

"Not a problem, sugar. I hope you have a great day and I'll see you this evening. Love you, honey."

"I love you, Angus."

As soon as he finished the call, Angus shined his best boots and packed a change of clothing. He headed into town to the discount retailer, the one who sold both groceries and general merchandise. Although he'd made a list, he wandered the aisles searching for ideas. With Marisol's suggestions in mind, he bought several large jar vanilla candles. Angus picked up a long-handled lighter. He rejected streamers. Dangling paper and open flame wouldn't be a good combination. Besides, he wouldn't have a clue how to hang them for decoration. Instead, he picked up two silk floral garlands. Both were six feet long. One featured white and pink roses, and the other was fashioned from peonies.

Angus didn't care for any of the fresh flower bouquets, so he decided he'd stop at a florist shop. In the grocery area, he bought a large frozen shrimp scampi entrée. After a lot of thought, he bought a bag of garlic knots, a fresh green salad, and a box of rice pilaf to serve with it. He chose a lace tablecloth, and his last purchase was an eight-inch round layer cake. Angus asked the bakery attendant to add icing red roses and two hearts to the top and to write "I love you" in crimson icing.

At the floral shop, Angus chose an arrangement of white roses with light pink centers. He also bought a dozen red roses and had them placed in a box. Balloon choices were many, but he chose three, each with an "I love you" message.

He drove slowly so he wouldn't wreck the cake or spill the flowers. Angus spent hours turning the simple living room into a romantic bower. He hung the garlands on the walls and placed the candles around the room. The decorated cake rested on the long counter, dividing the space from the kitchen. After a great deal of thought, he moved the small table and two chairs from the kitchen. Angus topped it with the lace tablecloth and set the white rose arrangement in the center. He would scatter the red roses across the couch right before Kathleen arrived and keep one to hand her as he asked the question. Balloons floated in place. He had brought a CD of his favorite country love songs, and he put it on repeat on the stereo.

The ring box was tucked deep in his front pocket. After

he munched a bologna and cheese sandwich, Angus planned the meal. He figured out when he would put the scampi into the oven. He dumped the green salad into a bowl from the cabinet and spent a long time reading the rice pilaf package directions.

Thunder boomed as Angus finished staging the scene for his proposal. At three-thirty, he showered, shaved, and put on his favorite cologne. He heated the scampi and made the pilaf. Both would remain warm in the oven until serving time, along with the garlic knots. Angus practiced kneeling and paced the room with restless energy.

What if Kathleen doesn't like all this? Maybe she'll think it's corny or stupid. His stomach knotted as the tension increased. He lit the candles at four and turned off all the lights. Outside, another round of storms approached. Angus longed to sit in the recliner but didn't. He might doze, which would ruin all his plans.

Any patience Angus had vanished. His favorite singers crooned about love, marriage, and their hearts. He watched the clock on the wall, and with each sweep of the second hand, he grew antsier.

Kathleen didn't arrive at four thirty, and he worried. At a quarter before five, he heard her unlock the door. Angus dropped to his right knee. He held the engagement ring in his right hand and a single rose in his left as the door swung open.

"Angus? Is the power out?" Kathleen entered, shaking rain from an umbrella. She halted and peered through the soft candle glow. She hung her jacket and purse on the coat rack. The open umbrella lay beneath it. "What is in the world?"

He watched as she glanced around the room, noting each detail, and waited.

"Angus?" She spoke his name like an endearment.

"Honey, I love you. I don't know why it took me so long to figure out you're the woman for me, but you've got my heart." He cleared his throat. "Kathleen Mary Birdwell, will you marry me?"

She stood still for a long moment, then clasped her hands together as if in prayer. "Do you mean it? Is it for real?"

He wasn't sure if he wanted to laugh or holler. "As real as it gets."

"Yes, I'll marry you." She giggled, but he saw a single tear trail down her face.

Angus rose. He offered her the rose, and she took it. "Hold out your left hand." He slid the ring onto the third finger, and then he kissed her hand.

Kathleen admired the ring for a few seconds. She threw her arms around Angus's neck. "It's beautiful, and I love you so much."

He held her tight and thought he might never let her go. "Sugar, I was scared silly you wouldn't say 'yes.' You've made me the happiest man in Texas."

Angus kissed her as if they had all the time in the world. He carried her to his recliner, sat down with Kathleen in his arms, and kissed her more.

"Did you cook?" Kathleen asked when they paused to catch their breath.

He laughed. "I reckon you could call it cooking. Are you hungry?" He teased her lips with his mouth.

"I had a very small lunch. What did you fix?" Her fingers caressed his face as she spoke.

"Shrimp scampi, rice pilaf, a salad, garlic rolls, and I bought a cake." Angus nuzzled her neck with his mouth.

Kathleen giggled. "I didn't think you made anything but chili, goulash, and hamburgers."

"I made the rice from a box. I heated the rest and bought the salad already made. You do like shrimp, right?"

"It's one of my favorites. I didn't think you knew."

Angus flushed. "Ah, I noticed sometimes I order steak,

you choose shrimp. Let's eat."

They dined by candlelight, listening to love songs. The flickering flame highlighted the diamonds in Kathleen's ring. Two smaller diamonds flanked the larger central stone, and the matching wedding ring boasted three. Angus adored the soft light falling on her beautiful face. *This is how it'll be for the rest of my life. It won't always be this quiet. We'll have rough times, but we'll get through them together.*

"This is delicious, Angus." Kathleen polished off a spoonful of scampi. "Better than take out."

Her praise left a warm feeling. "It ain't as good as anything you cook."

Her smile shone brighter than the multiple candles. "I think it's better."

They managed no more than a few bites of the cake since they were full, but it would keep. Angus cleaned the kitchen. "Don't get too used to it, sugar, although I'll help when you need it."

"We make a good team." Kathleen picked up a dish towel to dry the dishes he had washed.

They did.

Rain drummed a relentless rhythm against the windows. If the temperature dropped ten degrees, it would become ice. Angus shuddered at the thought of an ice storm but didn't dwell on the weather. For now, he and Kathleen were snug and dry. For now, they watched a movie. Angus longed to stay but planned to go home. He would have gone, but when the showers became freezing rain, Kathleen convinced him to stay.

"I'll worry myself sick if you leave." She touched his cheek with her left hand, and the diamonds sparkled in the soft light.

Angus would have argued and vowed he could drive in all weathers, but he didn't. Snow on the roads often caused slick spots and problems, but ice could be treacherous. If he hit a patch on the way home, he could slide off the road or wreck his truck. "I'm staying, sugar. It ought to melt by tomorrow."

By the time the sun rose on Saturday, temperatures rose above freezing. Angus crawled out of the recliner, more than a little stiff, but he wore a grin. He'd slept longer than he planned. The living room had been put to rights, so he followed the rich aroma of coffee into the kitchen. Kathleen stirred batter in a large bowl, and he kissed the back of her neck. "Good morning, Katydid."

She turned and returned the kiss. "Good morning, Angus. I thought I'd make waffles."

"Sounds tasty. Maybe after we eat, you can call your Mama and share the news." Angus planned to tell his buddies first chance he had.

"I don't want to phone." Kathleen poured the batter into the heated waffle iron. "I'd rather go tell her in person."

"We can if you want. We've got a wedding to plan." Angus poured coffee and slid into a chair at the table. "I figure you and Marisol will handle it."

Kathleen served him. "I want your input, too."

"Sure, honey, but I don't know much about weddings. I've been to a few, that's all."

They headed toward Uncertain as soon as the breakfast dishes were put away. On the way, they stopped at a discount store for cold drinks, but Kathleen bought several bridal magazines.

"I thought I might find some ideas." Kathleen browsed through one as soon as they returned to the truck. "What kind of wedding do you want, Angus?"

He smiled. "I'd like to get married at church. Everything else is up to you. I'm not much on anything fancy, and I don't know if we need ten or twelve bridesmaids, but if you want them, I won't fuss. I'd rather not wait too long. I'd like to get married and start our life together."

She giggled. "I guess you don't want an autumn or Christmas wedding."

Angus swallowed a groan. "I'd rather not wait so long, but if you want either one, you can have it. We're only getting hitched once, so I want it to be your dream wedding."

Kathleen scooted across the seat after putting the magazine away. "I'm not waiting till October or December either. What about April? Isn't your birthday on the twenty-first?"

April would be springtime. Soft blue skies and wildflowers in bloom, but there might be storms, too.

"It is, but I don't want to get hitched on my birthday. A spring wedding might be pretty. What about March?"

She frowned. "March wouldn't give us a lot of time to plan. I'll need to find a dress, pick colors and flowers, and a lot more. How about the last weekend in April? It's after Easter."

He counted the weeks. "I suppose I can wait for two months, give or take a few days."

Kathleen kissed his right cheek and rested her head against his shoulder. "It'll be worth the wait."

During the two-hour drive to Uncertain, Angus had a revelation. Being married would be similar to this journey. They would be together, and he would savor each sweet moment. Marriage wouldn't bring grand romance each day but quiet moments of togetherness. Everyday life might be ordinary, but their bond would carry them through good times and bad. She babbled about wedding options, and he half-listened, content to hear the sound of her voice in his ear. *This is how we'll spend the rest of our lives. I like it.*

At Marisol and Tony's house, Angus parked and followed as Kathleen rushed to the front door.

"I didn't expect you, but it's a wonderful surprise," Marisol cried as she opened the front door. "We're spending a laid-back day. Tony made a big pot of chili. Come inside. I'm so glad you're here."

Kathleen held up her left hand. Light caught the stones and made the diamonds shimmer. "We're getting married."

Marisol squealed. "That's awesome, and I'm very happy. Congratulations!"

Angus beamed as Marisol hugged Kathleen, then him.

In the open space, Angus settled onto a comfortable couch. The spicy aroma of cooking chili wafted from the rear of the house. Kathleen spread the bridal magazines on the coffee table. "We're talking about an April wedding."

"Who's getting married?" Tony appeared. He wore a broad smile.

"Me and Angus, of course." Kathleen displayed her ring.

"Excellent news!" Tony glanced at Angus. "While the ladies talk about brides, come out to the kitchen, Angus."

"Sure." Angus figured Kathleen could figure out the details. He'd be there on their wedding day, wearing a new Western-cut suit or even a tuxedo if his bride insisted. He would agree with everything else unless she came up with a wild plan. No destination weddings on a beach or in New York City. Angus would veto a circus theme or one based on a fairy tale or futuristic space movie. He would say no to Las Vegas, although he'd been there and competed in the national finals twice. "Chili smells pretty good. I make a pot myself once in a while."

Before they sat down to lunch, Kathleen called Angus to join her. "We're making a three-way call with my sisters. I thought you should be here."

He didn't see why, but Angus sat down on the floor in front of her. "All right, sugar. I doubt I'll have anything to add, but I'm here."

With Kathleen's cell phone on speaker mode, she dialed both her sisters. Once both Claudia and Susan were on the line, Kathleen giggled. "I called because I've got some news – I'm getting married April 27. It's the Sunday after Easter."

Claudia cheered. "Awesome. First Mom, now you. I'm going to have to catch up or be the old maid!"

Susan cleared her throat. "Speak for yourself, Sis. Who's the groom? Is it someone from college or a fellow teacher?"

"Neither." Kathleen stroked the back of Angus's hair. "It's Angus."

"Angus?" Susan repeated the name. "That's an old-fashioned name. Have we met him?"

Marisol laughed. "Of course. It's your brother Bart's best friend. You know, *Angus Beaton.*"

"Congratulations, baby sister. You always did have a crush on him." Claudia sighed. "It's romantic."

"It's not." Susan interrupted. "He's way too old for you, Kathleen. You must not be thinking straight. Why, he must be at least fifty years old. I know he was older than Bart."

Kathleen bristled. "No, he wasn't, and he's not fifty. It doesn't matter, anyway."

Susan snorted. "It will when he signs up for Social Security when you're still in your thirties."

"I won't be. I've done the math, Susan. I'll be almost fifty by then. Why do you have to try to ruin everything I do?"

"Since when? I don't!!"

Marisol intervened. "Girls, please. Don't fight."

Kathleen ignored the request. "When you stopped me from becoming a cheerleader my freshman year of high school, when you talked me out of barrel racing, and you tried to get me to change what college I would attend."

Susan squealed. "I was looking out for you, just like I am now!"

Angus couldn't bite his tongue any longer. "Kathleen's a grown woman. She can make her own choices. I'm right glad she's choosing me. It's her business and mine." He tilted his head back as she spoke.

Kathleen leaned forward and kissed him. "Thank you, babe. If you're finished fussing, I want you and Claudia to be my bridesmaids, if you will. Mom will be my matron of honor."

"I'd love to," Claudia cried. "But I don't know how I can get there to dress shop, let alone for the wedding."

"Don't you have weekends off? I want our wedding to be on Sunday." Kathleen replied. "We could probably figure out the dresses if I have your size."

"I'll try." Claudia blew air into the phone. "No, I'll insist. Susan, are you in?"

"Baltimore's a lot farther from Texas than California. I'd have to fly, and that can get expensive."

Angus spoke without hesitation. "I'll buy your plane ticket if you'll come."

Marisol offered a thumbs up. "Tony and I will do the same if necessary. Susan, please plan to come. It's your sister's wedding. We lost Bart. There are no guarantees. Life is short."

No one said anything for a few moments. "I'll *try*." Susan raised her voice. "I'll try to figure something out, and I'll call you."

Kathleen flushed. "It needs to be soon. The wedding date I want is less than three months ahead."

Claudia sighed. "I will find out on Monday. Congratulations! I'm glad it's Angus. You were a good friend for Bart. You'll be a fine husband."

Susan chimed in. "Yes, congratulations. I have to go. I'm going shopping with my best friends. I'll be in touch."

The living room remained silent for a long moment. "Well, that went well." Angus reached for Kathleen's hand and tried to temper his sarcasm.

She held his left hand tight in her right. "It could have gone better."

Marisol rolled her eyes. "Or it might have been worse. It'll all work out, even if your sisters don't make it home for the wedding."

Tony stood with arms folded in the kitchen doorway. "Let's eat."

Angus rose and hugged Kathleen. "Come on, sugar. I'm hungry." He wasn't, but he wanted to restore some normalcy.

"What if they don't come?" she asked as she walked to the table. "I really want my sisters at my wedding. Bart would have been there, no matter what."

"He'll be there in spirit, and they'll come." Angus resolved they would if he had to fly to first California, then Maryland and fetch them back himself. "If you want them, I'll make sure Susan and Claudia are there."

Kathleen's frown faded. "You might need handcuffs to do it."

He laughed at the joke. "If that's what it takes," he told her. "I will."

Angus would do anything for the woman he loved, and one of the first was to make sure her wedding was everything she dreamed it would be.

CHAPTER SIXTEEN

As winter edged into spring, Angus spent his daylight hours repairing the barn and corrals. He wanted his business venture to be active before he married. Working on his land toward his dream brought a deep satisfaction no outside job ever had. Even rodeo hadn't delivered the same pride or contentment. Angus also invested in upgrading the farrier equipment his grandfather had used and began putting out the word he would be blacksmithing as well as training horses. At Kathleen's urging, he invested in a newer computer system so he could keep up with his business. In the evenings, she helped him navigate the programs and become more proficient with technology.

After heavy consideration, Angus also decided to add a downstairs master bedroom to his house. Someday, sooner rather than later, he hoped for children, and they would need space. Right now, he figured, as babies, they could bunk in the same room with him and Kathleen. As they grew a little older, he thought one of the bedrooms upstairs could be for girls and the other for boys.

Yancey sometimes did carpentry in the off-season, so Angus invited him over. After inspecting the property, Yancey thought a bedroom could be added off the right side of the kitchen. "You can tie into the bathroom facilities from here." Yancey sat at the kitchen table and sketched out his idea. "The bedroom can be as big as you want, but I'd suggest nothing larger than around 300 feet. That would be about the size of a one-car garage but plenty of space. If you've got the bucks to buy supplies and pay me, I can get started right away."

"I've got enough." Angus still had most of his rodeo

winnings saved. The money wouldn't last forever, but if everything went according to plan, he would make a living with horses. Kathleen's teacher salary would help, too. "Do you think it can be finished before the wedding?"

Yancey scratched his head. "When is it again?"

"April 27, Sunday after Easter." Angus glanced over at the calendar.

"Nah, probably not. I might get it done by late May or early June. Once the season starts, though, I'll be on the circuit." Yancey fidgeted with the pencil he'd been using. "Will it be a big problem?"

Angus shook his head. "We can start out in my bedroom now and move when the room is finished. What do I need to hire you?"

Yancey extended his right hand. "Handshake's good enough."

As Angus made progress with his new venture, the room began to take shape. Every weekend, he and Kathleen shopped for something related to the wedding. She refused to let him go dress shopping, however, and would tell him only she'd found a pattern she liked. Lacking time to sew, Kathleen had hired a local seamstress to make her gown. They visited a local flower shop to order the flowers. She chose roses and daisies for her bouquet. Each bridesmaid and the matron of honor would carry a single long-stemmed rose. Angus and his best man, Yancey, and his cowboy groomsmen would wear rosebud boutonnieres. They tasted cakes and considered various designs before ordering a confection from a baker in Palestine. One of Kathleen's friends, her college roommate Joyce, would make the punch.

"I want a simple wedding reception." Kathleen chose a white cake with white buttercream frosting with icing roses on Saturday. "We don't need a meal since our wedding is at three p.m. on Sunday afternoon."

They lingered in the bakery and devoured a cream horn each at a small table near the front window.

"I'll want to eat more than cake afterward." Angus patted his flat belly. "I wouldn't mind a steak."

Kathleen rolled her eyes. "We can grab a bite after we change clothes and head out on the honeymoon. I wish you'd tell me where we're going."

Angus grinned. "It's a surprise." He had already booked a room at a small motel near the beach in Galveston. "You'll love it, though."

"I might if I knew where. I don't know how or what to pack for somewhere unknown." Kathleen blotted her lips with a napkin.

"I'll give you some hints closer to the wedding." Angus picked up her free hand and stifled a sneeze. "Let's go home, sugar."

She gathered their trash. "Sure. Are you feeling all right, Angus?"

Every time he coughed, sneezed, or blew his nose, Kathleen questioned him like a hound on point. Part of him liked the attention, but Angus didn't care to be coddled when he was well.

"I'm fine. Don't fret, Katydid." On the way to the street, he slung his arm across her shoulders. "I want to show you what I've done around the corrals. I'm hoping to buy a horse before long."

"I thought you were shoeing and training other people's animals." She climbed into the truck and frowned.

"I will be, but I'd like a horse of my own, woman. I haven't had one in years because I didn't need one to ride bulls or bust broncs." He started the truck and leaned over for a kiss. "It'll be a joy to ride something that's not trying to pitch me in the dirt."

At his place, Angus walked around the corral and pointed

out how he'd repaired it, and added a chute. The new bedroom also had begun to take shape. A concrete foundation had been poured, and one side had been framed. "I thought we'd use your bedroom furniture when it's finished. Until then, we'll bunk in my room if it's okay with you."

Kathleen nodded. "Sure. I'm looking forward to this big room, though. How many windows?"

"As many as you want, sugar. We could add a dining room on the other side of the house if you wanted." The idea had popped into his head one night.

She laughed. "I don't think we need one. Kitchen is fine with me. The table's large enough, and you said it has a leaf if we need to make it bigger."

The round table had belonged to his great-grandparents. "It can be twice as big as it is now. I've seen twelve people seated around it without being crammed for space." Angus tried to imagine an occasion where a dozen people gathered at his table. There could be more if all Kathleen's folks came, his six closest rodeo pals were present, or if they had kids. *I think we could fit as many as sixteen, maybe more. Heck, I could even buy an extra folding table for guests if needed someday.*

By April, the room was closer to being finished than Angus had expected. Kathleen had already moved some of her kitchen stuff to the house. She brought tablecloths, the framed photos of Angus to hang on the wall, and more. Plastic totes were stacked high in the spare bedroom. Shopping bags stuffed with everything from linens and towels to kitchenware covered the twin-sized bed.

"Aren't some people going to give gifts?" Angus surveyed the stacked items.

Kathleen scribbled in a notebook she started to keep track of what they had and what they might need. "I hope so, but that's what the wedding registry is for."

He wasn't familiar so she explained again. "I went to Wal-Mart and a couple of other stores. I listed things we'd like to get as gifts. People can look up and find out what we want."

"What could we possibly need?" Angus shook his head. "I've got this house, and you have the apartment."

"Curtains and drapes. Some kitchen appliances, a good set of dishes, maybe new flatware, and a decent set of knives." Kathleen ticked each item off on her fingers. "Drinking glasses and maybe mugs."

Angus chuckled. "I reckon it'd be easier if they just put money in a bowl or basket. Then we could get what we want."

She shrugged. "Some probably will."

Whether his threat to fetch her sisters home in handcuffs had influenced them, both Susan and Claudia would arrive on Saturday for the Sunday wedding. Angus offered to pick them up at the Dallas-Fort Worth airport, but Marisol volunteered Tony. "He won't be as busy as you will." She paused and cleared her throat. "I need to tell you something else. Mindy will be released from rehab on Good Friday. We'll pick her up, and she'll be staying with us. The boys are excited but a little wary. Right now, I'm planning to bring her with us to the wedding, but if you don't want her to come, tell me, and she can stay home."

Angus sighed. "She ought to be there. I'll talk to Kathleen, but I'd say plan on it. The boys will be our ring bearers. Will she cause trouble?"

"I doubt it. She's been calm when we visit, Angus, so I hope for the best."

He'd planned to make goulash or something with a pound of hamburger he thawed but Angus didn't. He stared and saw nothing, reflecting on the situation. If Bart hadn't died, things would be different.

When Kathleen arrived after a long day with her kindergarteners on Wednesday, he shared Marisol's news. "I'm not opposed to Mindy being there for Austin and Travis, but it's really up to you. I don't mind."

Kathleen disagreed. She slammed her teacher bag onto the kitchen counter. "I don't want her there, Angus. She might claim she's the bride and try to push me out of the way at the altar. I wouldn't put it past her to show up in a white dress, wearing a veil."

Angus bit his tongue. He didn't argue. "If you don't want her there, she won't be. I'll tell Marisol."

She folded her arms across her chest. "I can let her know. I need to call her anyway with an update on the attendants' dresses. I'll have time. Spring break starts tomorrow. No school until next Tuesday, and then I'm taking personal time until the week after the wedding."

Angus parked in a kitchen chair and nodded. "Okay." He rubbed his forehead and sighed. Scriptures about forgiveness ran through his mind, but he would rather not start a fight. If he mentioned any of them, it would.

"Did you fix supper?" Kathleen gazed around the kitchen. "Or are we going out?"

"I ain't hungry. There's sandwich stuff in the fridge unless you want to stir something together." For once, he didn't want to make the effort. "Pantry's stocked now."

In advance of their wedding, they had grocery shopped to fill the shelves of the pantry.

"I don't really want to cook. I had an awful day. Some of the kids caught the stomach bug going around, and I cleaned up puke more times than I want to count. The kiddos who weren't sick were jazzed up because they'll be out of school for several days." Kathleen settled across from him at the table. "Couldn't we go back to town for a bite?"

Angus shrugged. "I don't want to, but if you want, I reckon we can."

She extended her hands across the table and caught his. "What's the matter, Angus? Are you mad because I don't want Mindy at the wedding?"

He blew air between his lips. "I ain't angry, but I'm not happy, either. Besides, I have an awful headache."

She frowned. "Do you want her there? I can't understand why."

To Angus, the answer was simple. He hesitated as he gathered his words. "If Bart hadn't died, he'd be the one standing up with me instead of Yancey. If Bart was alive, I doubt Mindy would have went off the deep end. She's been your sister-in-law for years, and I always thought you got along with her. I don't like the things she did, and I hate the fact she ended up in rehab. But, sugar, she's still family. You don't quit on family when things aren't perfect. I agree. I don't want her in our lives all the time, but I don't want to cut her out, either. I love the boys like they're my nephews, which they soon will be."

Tears overflowed Kathleen's eyes. "I'll have her there if you want."

Angus squeezed her hands. "Bart would want it, baby."

She released her grip and put her head on the table. Kathleen wept. Angus rose to stand behind her. He rubbed her back with a slow, circular motion. "I didn't mean to make you cry, sugar."

Kathleen quivered. "You're right, though. Bart would, and I wasn't thinking about my brother. Oh, Angus, I've been so selfish. I'll call Mom and tell her Mindy is welcome. As soon as I calm down, I'll fix supper."

He stroked her hair. "Nah. If you'll drive, I'll buy you a burger or something in town."

"Oh, Angus, you don't have to do that..." She twisted around and stood.

He caught her in his arms. "Katydid, I *want* to. In a week

and a half, we'll be married. The countdown has started."

They dined on burgers at a local diner and shared a platter of fries. On Saturday, Angus went to her apartment and assisted Kathleen in packing up the last of her stuff. She kept enough to get through the next week, leaving a few clothes, a single coffee mug, and her coffee maker. She had shampoo and body wash in the shower and a few towels in the cabinet. "I'll sleep here, that's all."

The original plan had been to drive up to Uncertain to share Easter dinner with Marisol and the family. After a long phone conversation, after Kathleen agreed Mindy could attend the wedding, the event changed. After church, Angus and Kathleen would drive up to Jacksonville and share dinner at an Asian buffet restaurant.

Angus would have preferred ham at home, but he agreed. On Easter, he dressed in a long-sleeved denim shirt paired with khaki slacks. His attire matched Kathleen's new denim midi-length dress. Their party of seven claimed a long table in a quiet area of the restaurant. Everyone chose their favorites from the well-stocked offerings. Angus, who preferred simple meat and potatoes, opted for some pepper steak, a serving of fried shrimp, and some cashew chicken. Kathleen filled her plate twice.

Mindy remained quiet and said little. Angus noted she had lost weight. She toyed with the food on her plate and ate little, although before they began the meal, she offered an apology to both Angus and Kathleen.

"I got out of line, and I'm sorry," she said, eyes staring at the floor. "I know now I had some issues, and I didn't deal very well with losing my husband. Thank you for letting me join you today and attend your wedding next week."

"You're family." Kathleen clasped Mindy's hand. "Bart would want you there."

The mood remained polite and bordered on tense

throughout the meal. Austin ate a few plain chicken chunks and refused ice cream.

Kathleen frowned. "Is he okay? There's a bug going around, and a lot of my students have had it."

Marisol nodded. "Austin is okay. He might have the bug, but he's been having tummy aches lately. We took him to the doctor, and he diagnosed stress as the reason. He's had a lot to deal with this year."

"We all have." Angus sighed. "It's been a hell of a year."

Angus finished what he had on his plate and ate a small bowl of plain vanilla ice cream. Kathleen fixed a large bowl filled with both chocolate and vanilla ice cream, chocolate syrup, candy sprinkles, and whipped cream.

"Are you sure you can eat all that?" Angus eyed the dessert.

She paused. "I probably can, but everything tastes good."

When she topped everything off with one more egg roll, Angus winced. He feared a bellyache in the making.

After the meal, they lingered in the parking lot.

"We'll be down early Saturday," Marisol announced. "We booked rooms at the motel. We have the rehearsal Saturday evening, right?"

Angus nodded. "Yeah, at six. Then we're having dinner afterward. The wedding will be next Sunday afternoon, at church, with a reception in the hall."

At his house, he figured they would shuck the nicer duds and watch a movie or nap. Angus came down from changing clothes to find Kathleen curled up on the couch, clutching her stomach.

"What's the matter?" He knew what the problem must be.

"I ate too much." Kathleen groaned. "I've got an awful bellyache."

He rested his right hand against her abdomen and could

feel a harsh cramp. "I've got some over the counter medicine if you want some."

"Please. I hope it helps." Kathleen bent double and groaned.

Once she took a dose, Angus convinced her to lie down on the couch. He brought a cool washcloth and wiped her face. "Anything else I can do to help?"

"I don't know. Ohhh. I shouldn't have mixed egg rolls and ice cream." She frowned. "Angus, I'm sorry."

He placed his large hand on her lower abdomen. "For what?"

"Being sick on Easter."

Angus rubbed her belly with an easy hand. "We're about to promise to love each other in sickness and in health, sugar. You already proved the point. I reckon it's my turn."

Kathleen almost smiled. "You have such a gentle touch. That helps a little."

"Good. Hush and feel better." Angus settled into a position on the floor.

"Stay close, please." She put her left hand over his.

"I ain't going anywhere."

Her bellyache passed after a couple hours, and Kathleen slept.

Angus sat beside her for a long time, then rose with his knees creaking.

He didn't want to turn on the television and disturb her rest.

They had chosen traditional vows, but both agreed they also wanted to say something before they exchanged promises. Angus planned to base his on Proverbs Chapter 31, so he got his Bible and retreated to the kitchen table. He read the passages and made notes. Although neither wanted to share before the wedding, Angus wanted his words to make sense. He would hone them until they said exactly what he wanted to say.

Kathleen woke around nine. She found him at the kitchen table. "Whatcha doing?"

Angus closed the notebook. "Working on what I'll say at the wedding. Are you feelin' better?"

"Yeah. I'm not hungry, though." She put her hands on his shoulders from the back. "I'll fix you something if you are."

"I ate a sandwich. I don't think we ought to eat at any Asian buffets anytime soon." Angus swiveled toward her.

"Fine with me. I noticed you didn't eat much. Don't you like that kind of food?" She pulled out a chair and sat at the table across from him.

Angus shrugged. "Not really. It's okay, but I'd rather have a good old burger or steak or something. I'm not a fan of those stuff-your-gut buffets anyway. It's too easy to cram your stomach and get a bellyache."

Kathleen laughed. "Yeah, I noticed. And you were right, I was stress eating. Did you think Mindy seemed all right?"

He considered the question. "She was quiet, but yeah, I think she's turned a corner. Even though she'll be at the wedding, I don't think we should spend much time with her."

"Agreed." Kathleen stood up. "I guess you'd better take me home."

"Stay if you want. I can sleep down here, or you can have the spare room. Most of your stuff's here anyway." Angus didn't want her to leave.

She sat. "Are you sure? I don't much want to go. We have so much to do this week."

He took her hands in his. "We'll get it done together."

On Monday, they met with the local restaurant that would cater the rehearsal dinner. Neither wanted fancy, so the menu would be deli meat and cheese trays, specialty breads, a vegetable platter, salad, and assorted cookies.

Tuesday, Kathleen picked up her dress, although she refused to let Angus see it. One of her teacher friends, Milli, met her at the apartment so Kathleen could try it on. The long-sleeved sheath dress had a lace top with a satin skirt that fell to her ankles. It fit well, but as she admired her reflection, Milli found one flaw.

"Where's the veil?"

Kathleen's mouth dropped open. "I don't have one. Oh, my goodness. I didn't think."

"Don't panic." Milli grinned. "I can make one if we can get some tulle. I have a hair comb with white silk roses I could use. Or, if you'd rather, I can arrange some flowers for your hair."

"I'm wearing it down, or I was. Flowers in my hair, I guess. Let me call Mom and see what she thinks."

"Flowers, white roses if you can get some." Marisol laughed. "It's not a huge problem, Kathleen. Text me a picture so I can see your gown."

"I'm worried now I might have forgotten something else. What if I did?" Kathleen chewed a fingernail.

"We'll figure it out if you did." Marisol listed the detail.

Kathleen sighed. "Okay. I have those all on the list. I have the bridesmaids' dresses, too. Are Susan and Claudia still coming Saturday morning?"

"Yes. Tony will pick them up and head for Rusk. I'll bring the boys and Mindy over to the motel." Marisol clicked her tongue against her teeth. "We'll all be there in plenty of time for the rehearsal."

"We're decorating the church on Saturday, too." Kathleen had all the bows and streamers, candles, and cute decorations. "The flowers will be there, too."

On Wednesday, Angus picked up his Western-cut tux. He'd planned to wear a suit, but Kathleen wanted his finery to match hers. Thursday was the day Kathleen took her wedding gown and the attendants' dresses to church. She and her wedding party would dress there on Sunday. For now, the garments were tucked into a large closet in the pastor's office.

They got the marriage license at the courthouse on Friday, and to celebrate, Angus took Kathleen out for a meal in Palestine. Every detail had been planned. The pastor's twin five-year-old daughters would walk down the aisle as flower girls. Austin and Travis would follow. Milli would handle the guest book and also help at the reception. "It's our next to last day being single." Angus assisted Kathleen into his truck after they had a fine lunch of fried catfish. "We don't have any place we have to be or anything to do for the rest of today. Tell me where or what, and we'll go."

Kathleen grinned. Once Angus was behind the wheel, she scooted beside him. "Could we take a long drive? I wouldn't mind to see some wildflowers blooming."

"You bet, sugar. Let me stop for fuel, and we'll hit the road."

They meandered from up around Karnack down to Marshall and in all directions. Bluebonnets, coneflowers, wild indigo, and more blossomed in the fields. Late in the day, they visited the rose gardens at Tyler, then headed back toward Rusk. Everything had been moved from Kathleen's apartment to avoid payment of another month of rent, so she'd been staying in Angus's spare room. Once her family checked into the motel, she would join them and wake up on her wedding day there. Angus would pick her up for church. Once services ended, they would remain there until their wedding at three p.m.

Kathleen would retreat to one of the Sunday school rooms to change and become a bride. Angus had no idea how he'd pass the time but he'd manage. Yancey, Jones, Frenchy, Sammy Dickens, Zach, and Coooper would be present. Only Aidan O'Neill couldn't make the wedding, but Angus didn't mind. The young man's interest in Kathleen had been more than he cared to see.

The new room addition wasn't finished, but it was close. The floor was in place, and the framing was done. If the weather was good, the room might be finished when they returned from the honeymoon.

Tomorrow, they would head to church to decorate, and then Kathleen would leave with her folks.

Angus would endure one night alone before he gained a wife.

For a man who'd almost despaired he would ever wed, life tasted sweet. Angus had never been happier as he prepared to embark on a future with Kathleen. Too keyed up to sleep, he thanked God for his woman and for the life they would share. *Lord, don't let anything go wrong before the I-do's.*

After his prayers, he slept well.

CHAPTER SEVENTEEN

The sanctuary loomed large and silent on Saturday morning. Angus and Kathleen entered together after Pastor Johnson provided a key. He placed the boxes and bags he'd carried from the truck in the back pew.

"It's strange to think we'll attend church in the morning and be married the same afternoon." Angus gazed around the sanctuary.

Kathleen frowned. "I just realized — we can't decorate now because everything will be here during Sunday services."

"Sure, we can and will." Angus didn't see any problem. "Pastor said we could."

"I guess. People will wonder, though."

"Let me. Maybe it'll encourage more of them to come back for the wedding." Angus smiled. "I hope we have more than a few."

"I probably should have mailed out invitations." Kathleen sank into a pew. "I thought about it, but I didn't want to spend money having announcements printed and mailing them. Or wait until we got them back."

"We told everybody who matters. Your family will be here. My rodeo buddies won't miss seeing me get hitched. You invited other teachers and some of your college friends. Heck, I even asked some of my Cajun cousins."

Kathleen giggled. "And we put a notice in the church bulletin and a little piece in the newspaper."

Angus kissed her. "We should have a fair crowd. We have plenty of cake and food so it won't be a problem. Do you have all the decorations we need?"

She nodded. "Everything except the flowers. They'll be ready to pick up in a couple hours. Pastor Johnson said we can store them in the big walk-in fridge right outside the backdoor so they'll stay fresh."

"I'll fetch them when it's time."

Mille, Kathleen's college friends Sammi and Elise, Marisol, Mindy, and both sisters arrived. Their cheerful chatter first delighted, then dismayed Angus. On the eve of his wedding, he found his thoughts turning to the past. He wished he could share his joy with his family. Grandpa would share his happiness and celebrate Angus had found a woman. Although his parents were long gone, Angus liked to believe they, too, would be glad. Of all his family and friends from the past, though, Bart weighed heaviest on his mind. In a few months, the one-year anniversary of his passing would arrive, although sometimes it seemed longer. Moments remained when Angus often forgot and reached for a phone to call his buddy. At least once a day and often more, Angus wanted to share a thought, a joke, a worry, or a happy moment with Bart.

Angus headed out on several errands. In addition to picking up the flowers at the florist shop, he would grab a sack of sandwiches and soft drinks for the ladies and pick up a long-handled lighter for the candles. Austin and Travis, bored with the decoration efforts, begged to go, but Angus refused. He planned to make a stop at Bart's grave. It would be a private moment, one he didn't think the boys could appreciate. They probably wouldn't understand, and the visit might cause sadness. "I'll take you with me if I go anywhere this afternoon." He ruffled both kids' hair, kissed Kathleen, and exited the church.

His first stop was Cedar Hill Cemetery. Bart's grave remained a little sunken, but new spring grass covered the earth where he had been buried. Angus parked nearby and walked to the grave. He brought no flowers because he didn't think his best friend would appreciate the gesture. Instead, he carried a handful of pine cones from the trees at his house and a rock. The rock had one of the best-preserved seashell fossils Angus had ever seen. He and Bart had found it together along the Neches River when they were both sixteen. Angus lay both on the flat headstone above his friend.

Angus removed his cowboy hat as he knelt. "Buddy, it's my wedding day. I wish you were here to stand with me at the altar, especially since I'm marrying Kathleen. I don't know if that might surprise you or make you mad, but I hope you'd give us your blessing. I like to believe if you hadn't been hurt and died, we'd still be getting hitched. Katydid misses you, and so do I. I'll do my best to be a good husband for her, even if I am old and ugly. I love her in a way I never dreamed I could love any woman. You always wanted me to find someone, and I have. I'll honor Marisol like my mother, and I'll be the best uncle I can be to your boys. We were best friends from the day we met, and I felt like you were my brother. Now you will be even though you're gone. Mindy caused no end of trouble, but I think she's on the right path now. I'll help her if I can and pray. Your family will be mine after tomorrow, and I think you'd be fine."

He paused as a hawk spread its wings wide and wheeled through the air above the cemetery. The bird paused to release a long cry as the shadow of its flight passed overhead. Angus shivered. He wasn't one to believe in ghosts or messages from the dead, but Bart had long admired hawks. He sometimes called them his spirit totem, drawing on his small amount of Cherokee ancestry. "Should I take this as your blessing?" Angus gazed skyward. "Or am I crazy?"

The hawk wheeled back around with another cry. Angus grinned. Maybe it was a message, and maybe it wasn't, but he'd take it. He said a silent prayer for his friend before he rose. He wiped a single tear from his scarred left cheek as he returned his hat to his head. He finished his errands and arrived back at the church.

Kathleen met him in the parking lot. "You were gone a long time. I was worried."

"Just took a while, sugar." Angus didn't plan to tell her about his visit to Bart's grave. "Get your gals to come help carry all this stuff inside."

A frown creased her forehead. "Are you all right? You seem upset."

"I'm fine, sugar. It's sinking in all the way. After tomorrow, we'll be together for good. No more parting ways or driving between two places. I'm happy." He offered a small smile.

She leaned forward and kissed his mouth. "Me, too. It's a huge thing, though. Take lunch inside first. Everyone's whining that they're starving."

Angus toted the bag of sandwiches and the sack containing bottled soft drinks to the church kitchen through the back door. Marisol greeted him and took the items from his hands.

"Go peek at the church. It's pretty now, but it'll be beautiful with the flowers. I don't think we'll put those out until tomorrow so they remain fresh."

After a peek into the sanctuary, Angus grinned. "Looks nice."

Kathleen joined him. "I thought so. We're finished except for eating lunch, though."

The plan was to separate. She would go back to the hotel with her family, and Angus would head home. He wouldn't see her until church in the morning. Although he spent days without her while she taught, and he'd been gone on the road daily during his stint as a dairy driver, Angus would miss her. "We could drive over to the river or up to the rose gardens at Tyler. They'll be blooming now."

She linked her arm through his. "Angus, you know I'm

going with Mom and my sisters until tomorrow."

He did, but he didn't like the idea. "Or we could walk the footbridge for a little while."

Kathleen shook her head. "We'll have the rest of our lives to do those things. If it wasn't for church, we wouldn't see each other until the wedding."

The decision to flaunt tradition and see each other before the ceremony had been her notion, not his.

"Let's go have lunch then." Angus vowed to drag the meal out as long as possible. Except for Tony and the two boys, Angus was the sole male present.

Although he'd brought a variety of sandwiches from a local shop, Angus settled for a single roast beef and cheese. He munched a few chips and swigged down a gallon of iced tea. As the women chattered, he admired the cake and listened to how they planned to make the punch.

Marisol watched him with a frown. "Are you all right, Angus? You're so quiet."

"Just thinking." His sigh echoed through the room. "I'm fine, but I'm lonesome already."

Kathleen grasped his head. "I'll walk you out to your truck. Go home, take a long nap, and enjoy the quiet. I'll see you at church."

"Do you want me to pick you up?"

A smile stretched her lips. "No, I'm coming with the family. We have beauty shop appointments this afternoon, and I want to spend time with my sisters. I haven't seen them except for Bart's funeral in ages."

Angus put his arm across her shoulders. "Be sure you pack for the honeymoon, sugar."

"It would help if you'd tell me where we're going."

"I want it to be a surprise."

At his truck, he pulled her into his arms and kissed her.

"I'm gonna miss you."

Kathleen leaned against his chest. "We're only going to be apart until tomorrow morning. Aren't you having a bachelor party?"

"Nah, not my style. Yancey might come over for a little bit. Frenchy, Jones, and Sammy might too." Angus really wished they wouldn't. He didn't want to play cards, and he wasn't a drinker. Cooper had mentioned cigars, but Angus didn't smoke either. "Can I call you?"

She traced his lips with one finger. "No, not tonight. What's really bothering you, Angus? You're not getting cold feet, are you?"

"I'm worried you'll change your mind." Might as well speak the truth and shame the devil. He would miss her, but if she had time to think, maybe she would decide an ugly, seasoned, former rodeo rider wasn't what she wanted after all. She might run off with the danged school principal or head out to California with Claudia.

Kathleen laughed and stopped. "You're serious! Angus, I love you, and I'm not going to leave you at the altar. Don't you trust me?"

He wrapped his arms around her. "I do, darlin', more than my life. Just scares me, that's all. Granny always said girls shouldn't drive their ducks to a poor market, and I worry you might be. I ain't no prize."

"Angus Beaton!" Kathleen grasped the front of his shirt with both hands. "You are to me. Stop this nonsense, or I'll be worried sick all night."

Her fussing eased some of his fear, and he grinned. "Love me?"

"I do. Hush this crazy talk. Go take a long, long nap. Get rested because I plan to wear you out."

"Is that right?" His heart lightened. "All right, sugar. I

won't call, but if you need me or just want me, call me anytime."

"I will." She kissed his mouth and let her lips linger. "I love you, and I'll see you in the morning. If you get antsy, just remember we're getting married tomorrow."

"I ain't gonna forget. I love you, woman."

Angus tried to think of somewhere to go to pass a few of the long hours stretching ahead. He considered fishing, but he wasn't in the mood. He wasn't hungry, and he didn't need to buy anything. He drove home by the slowest route possible. When his friends showed up, he'd warm up some chili from the freezer or make bologna sandwiches. Before he could consider a nap, he cleaned the house, although it didn't need it. Kathleen didn't know, but they would spend their first honeymoon night here. By the time the wedding and reception were over, it would be late to head for Galveston. Angus didn't want to arrive too late to enjoy the beaches or after dark. To make everything ready, he changed the sheets on his bed. He dug out some of the candles he'd used for his proposal and placed a bouquet he'd picked up at the florist in the bedroom. He packed his suitcase for the beach, although he didn't own more than a single pair of denim shorts. His swim trunks were ancient, dating back to his late teens, but when he tried them on, they fit.

He settled into his recliner for a nap, but he didn't rest well. When his buddies arrived, they brought takeout barbecue, fried chicken, and all the side dishes. They feasted, and then Angus lit a bonfire on the edge of the woods. Cooper and Sammy smoked cigars, but Angus didn't. They joked, shared memories about their days in the arena, and talked about Bart. The other men missed him, too. It was close to midnight before they left. Angus poured a bucket of water over what remained of the fire, took a long shower, and scrubbed himself clean. He laid out his church clothes but slept on the couch. After fixing the bed for tomorrow night, he wasn't about to dirty it.

At four a.m., he woke and wanted to head for town but didn't. Angus made coffee he only half-drank and ate nothing. The last thing he needed on his wedding day would be a bellyache. He was one of the first to arrive at church, and he waited at the back of the sanctuary for Kathleen. Most of the congregation commented on the decorations, offered congratulations, and many promised to attend.

Angus shuffled his feet and paced until he heard her voice. Kathleen entered, pretty in a dark pink dress, her hair styled in an elaborate updo. She paused when she spotted him and rushed across the floor.

"Good morning, Angus. I missed you more than I thought I would. I almost called you forty-eleven times."

"I wish you had." He kissed her pretty lips and didn't care who saw or what they thought. They linked hands and walked to the pew together. Although he sang the hymns, Angus couldn't recall a word of the sermon. As soon as the service ended and the crowds cleared, he retreated to the room where he would change for the wedding. Yancey, who attended a different church across town, showed up around one.

Kathleen withdrew to the classroom, which had become her dressing room. "Don't freak out again. It's only a few hours now."

"I wish we'd just gone to the courthouse," Angus said the words before he thought. The wedding was all Kathleen's dream, not his, and he didn't want to offend her.

Her eyes danced, and she laughed. "It would have been easier, but this is the only wedding I ever plan to have."

Before he put on the Western cut tuxedo, the only one he'd ever worn, Yancey brought a plain cheeseburger, so he ate it. At two-thirty, Angus entered the church and sat in the front pew. He prayed for calm and that nothing would go awry. His brief sleep had been haunted with nightmares about Mindy interrupting the ceremony and declaring her undying love. Angus sucked on a peppermint to freshen his breath.

At five til three, the church was more than half full. Angus took his position to the right of the altar with Yancey at his side. His palms were slick, and he thought he was more nervous than he'd ever been on the back of a bucking bronc. The organist played soft music as the bridesmaids marched down the aisle with measure step and took their places across from him. Pastor Johnson's twin daughters walked slow steps, dressed in light blue dresses made of lace. They dropped rose petals from fancy baskets as they came. Austin and Travis, resplendent in tiny tuxes, carried the rings on a satin pillow.

When the strains of the wedding march echoed through the old church, Angus forgot about his nerves. Marisol walked beside Kathleen. His bride wore a lovely gown with long sleeves fashioned from lace and a lacy bodice. She wore her hair up, decorated with white roses. Her attached skirt was silk, and she carried a huge bouquet of roses and daisies. His heart swelled. She had never been lovelier. She winked at him when she stepped into place.

"Who gives this woman in marriage?" Pastor asked.

"I do, and her family does," Marisol spoke in a clear, loud voice, then sat beside her husband in the front pew on the left.

Angus cleared his throat as he stepped forward to take her hands in his. Although they would say their vows, both had chosen to say something first. "The Bible says the price of a good woman is more than rubies. I don't know much about rubies, but I know Kathleen is worth more than anything, diamonds, money, or gold. Bible also says a husband's heart can safely trust in his wife. I believe that, and here, in a few moments, I'm going say the vows, but we've already been living most of them. I love Kathleen, and I cherish her. We've been through some good times and some worse ones. She cared for me when I was awfully sick a few months ago, and I've taken care of her. Life can be good, and it can be rough, but as long as we're together, I think we'll manage. I'm not rich, and I hope I'm not too poor, but I plan to provide for her and have her at my side until one of us dies. If I go first, I'll be waiting at heaven's entrance for her because it won't be my heaven without Kathleen. I may be uglier than homemade sin, but I give Kathleen my name and my whole heart. I love you, sugar, always. I'll rejoice you chose me for the rest of my days and beyond."

Maybe he didn't deliver it exactly as he had practiced, but Angus said the important things. A single tear slid down Kathleen's cheek as she gazed into his eyes. "Angus Beaton, I loved you since I was a silly teenage girl, and I thought you'd never notice me. You're not ugly, and I don't want to hear that from your lips again. I think you're the finest man I've known. In Songs of Solomon, Chapter Eight, the Bible reads, "'Set me as a seal upon thine heart, as a seal upon thine arm. Love is stronger than death.'" I take you, Angus Beaton, to be my lawfully wedded husband to have and to hold from this day forward, for better, for worse, for richer, for poorer, in sickness and in health, to love and to cherish until death do us part." Her voice never wavered.

Tears ran down his face as Angus, without prompting from the preacher, repeated the same vows.

"By the power invested in me by God Almighty and the state of Texas, I pronounce you man and wife. What God has joined, let no man put asunder. I present to you, Mr. and Mrs. Angus Beaton. Angus, you may kiss your bride."

From within, Angus heard the applause, the cheers, and the delight of the crowd, but he focused only on Kathleen. He kissed her and cherished her mouth with his. Angus didn't hurry, and neither did Kathleen. When the kiss ended, her fingers stroked the scar on his left cheek. "Mark of honor," she whispered. "Handsome husband."

"My wife," Angus replied.

If they could have left then, he would have gone. He didn't care about the reception or the cake, but he would stay for Kathleen's sake. They shared food, they received gifts, and at the end, they cut the cake.

Angus fed a small bite to her, and she did the same.

There were toasts made with the punch, and some of his buddies loaded the gifts into boxes, which they placed in the back of his truck.

At six, Angus would have vowed it must be midnight. They managed to leave at seven. From the moment they became man and wife, he kissed her every chance he had. They moved in tandem, holding hands or with their arms about one another.

"Let's go home." Angus grinned once they were in his truck.

Both had changed into casual clothing. Yancey would return his tux tomorrow. Marisol would care for Kathleen's beautiful gown. "Home is where we're honeymooning?" Kathleen asked.

"Tonight, yeah. It's too late to get there. We'll leave out in the morning."

She leaned against his right shoulder. "Won't you tell me where?"

"It'll ruin the surprise."

"Please." She kissed his cheek.

A wave of happiness poured over him. "All right, sugar. We're spending a week in Galveston, right on the beach."

Her shrill of delight pleased him. "Oh, that's wonderful. I love the beach."

"I'm fond of the ocean. Right now, though, let's go home."

Anticipation made all his senses tingle. Angus sped through the evening and pulled up behind the house. The moment Kathleen stepped out of the truck, he scooped her up in his arms and carried her into the house. She giggled all the way. He set her down on both feet and kissed her with a fever.

"I'm ready for bed, woman."

"I thought you wanted a steak." Kathleen caught his face between her hands and kissed him back.

"I've got a pair of T-bones, but first, I've waited a long time to have a wife."

His bedroom held the perfume of the candles he'd lit last night for their fragrance. Angus paused to light them as Kathleen cradled the roses in her arms. With care, using gentle hands, and all the love he carried in his heart, Angus made Kathleen his wife. He reveled in her fragrance, savored the taste of her lips and the soft satin of her skin.

"'Kiss me with the kisses of your mouth,'" Kathleen whispered. "'For your love is better than wine."

The ancient words written by Solomon long ago brought them both home. Afterward, they slept until they rose, hungry, and ate steak late at night.

In the morning, he carried in the gifts, glad it hadn't rained overnight, and they loaded their suitcases.

Their room overlooked the beach at Galveston, and they spent a glorious week walking the sands early in the morning and each evening. They dined on seafood and spent each night wrapped in each other's arms.

Angus found the joy he'd long sought, and Kathleen loved him.

******

Two years later…

The yearling filly adored Angus, and the more he tried to work with her, the more she blew her lips against his face with affection. "Easy, girl. The idea is getting the halter on and walking the corral with it on."

"Trixie loves you." Kathleen appeared at the fence, their daughter Lisette in her arms.

He grinned. "Gals of all ages seem to be fond these days. What are you doing?"

"Lisette wanted to see Daddy, so I brought her out before her nap." Kathleen hoisted the eleven-month-old baby higher on her hip. "I'm always up to visit you, so here we are."

Angus tied the lead rope to one rung of the corral. "Let me see my girl."

The child reached out her arms to him, and he pulled her over the top. "I probably smell like horse and sweat," he laughed. "If I had any horse but Trixie out here, I'd let Lisette ride, but Trixie's not trained yet."

His daughter looked like Kathleen in miniature, but he'd named her for his grandmother. She was a Daddy's girl and Angus glories in that. Kathleen started to climb to the next level of the corral, and he frowned.

"Don't. You be careful, sugar." He fixed his gaze on the round bump of her abdomen where the next child grew. "Are you feeling all right?"

"Fine. I'm pregnant, not sick. You should have a jacket on, Angus."

Fall colors flamed with a few hardwoods among the pines. "It's not so cold. It's October. Better take Lisette inside, though."

Angus cuddled her close for a moment, then handed the child to Kathleen. "Night, baby girl."

When he finished with the filly, Angus came through the kitchen. "Something smells good. I'm gonna wash off the horse smell."

"It's meatloaf. Try not to wake Lisette, though."

He peeked into the new downstairs bedroom. For now, they shared it with the baby. "I'll go upstairs.

As his family gathered around the kitchen table, Angus held his child on one knee. They seldom used the high chair, although Lisette ate the same meals. Between bites, Angus fed her small spoons of mashed potato with gravy and an occasional morsel of meatloaf. Although still too young to talk, she demonstrated her delight with open mouthed grins and wordless exclamations. Lisette stroked his face, her tiny fingers rubbing his scar, and he grinned.

Maybe he remained as ugly as homemade sin, but Angus didn't think so. He recognized a loving touch, and his gals had convinced him love made him a handsome man.

"I can't believe she'll be a year old next month." He bounced Lisette on his knee. "When's this one coming?"

"Doctor said late January." Kathleen rested her right hand on her abdomen and smiled. "Three more months."

Later, when Lisette slept in her crib, Kathleen put Angus's hand on her belly. "He's kicking."

He marveled at the solid movements. "Is it a boy? Did the doctor say so?"

She shrugged. "No, but I think it is."

"If you're right, we'll name him Bart."

Kathleen grinned. "I like that, and so would my brother."

Angus smiled. He lay awake deep in the night and reflected. He had the life he once dreamed about, a woman to love, a child, and another on the way.

Forget homemade sin. I'm blessed, and I'm smart enough to know it.

The man who seldom smiled had become a man who couldn't stop grinning.

Lee Ann Sontheimer Murphy is a former newspaper editor and reporter who makes her home in the Ozarks. As a widow with three grown children, her focus is on writing romance novels that range from sweet to heat, from contemporary to historical. She has written more than twenty-five novels and novellas, along with a variety of non-fiction and freelance works. A native of St. Joseph, Missouri, where the Pony Express began and outlaw Jesse James met his end, she is a graduate of Crowder College and Missouri Southern State University. She lives in what passes for the suburbs in far southwestern Missouri, a little north of Arkansas and just east of Oklahoma.